REBEL HEART

REBEL SERIES BOOK 2

J.C. HANNIGAN

Copyright © 2016 by J.C. Hannigan

Cover Design by Chelsea Barnes (CJPB Designs)
Edited by Shawna Gavas (Behind the Writer)
Formatted by Heritage Creek Formatting

ISBN 978-0-9951934-5-1 (paperback)
ISBN 978-0-9951934-2-0 (ebook)

www.jchannigan.com

CHAPTER ONE

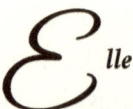 *lle*

IF THERE WAS one thing I hated, it was lineups, and the one at the grocery store had taken a *really* long time. I would never understand people who felt the need to coupon. I liked saving money as much as the next person but come on! The woman in front of me had taken up forty-five minutes of the *only* cashier's time.

My arms were loaded with groceries, and I was exhausted. I'd come off a long shift where my partner, Alex, and I were called to the scene of a six-car accident on the highway. The cause had been a young teen texting while driving. Because of that person's actions, two people were dead, and four were seriously injured.

Sometimes, I cursed my profession of choice. I loved helping people, and for every one we lost, we saved five more. But losing them...that was hard. I *knew* that we did everything we could, but I still felt the agony of having the elderly man slip away in my arms on the way to the hospital.

Days like today definitely sucked, especially when they were capped off with the Coupon Queen of Barrie.

Truthfully, I knew my irritation had very little to do with the couponing and everything to do with the day I'd had.

Muttering darkly to myself, I fished the key out of my purse and then unlocked the apartment door. I pushed it open, before kicking it shut behind me. "I'm home!" I called cheerlessly on the off chance that my roommate was back from her weekend getaway with her boyfriend. Walking into the kitchen to set down my groceries, I heard a commotion coming from the living room and glanced over quickly, only to witness the coffee table topple and a bare ass dive behind the couch.

"Oh God, ew!" I shouted, covering my eyes with my hands and spinning around so that I wouldn't have to watch my best friend and roommate's boyfriend, Brock, scramble for his clothing. "In our fucking living room, Tessa? I sit on that couch!" I wailed, horrified. Tessa exploded into a fit of giggles, and I smiled against my will.

"Sorry about that Elle. Don't worry though, we didn't get very far." Brock said sheepishly, the sound of a zipper following his sentence.

"Dude," I shivered in disgust. "You got far enough, your bare ass was on it! Now I have to steam clean the damn couch before I can go near it. Didn't you two get enough of each other this weekend?" I grumbled, bending over to pick up the groceries I'd accidentally dropped to the floor in my haste to cover my sensitive eyes. Luckily, the Mr. Noodles packets and microwavable dinners weren't any worse for wear.

"Oh come on," Tessa rolled her eyes, tugging her t-shirt back on over her head. "You've done far worse on this couch than that."

"And that's my cue to leave," Brock said. He leaned forward, his lips brushing tenderly against Tessa's lips.

The way he looked at her made my heart ache. Brock was so much like...

No, I told myself, forcing my thoughts from going there. I heard Tessa and Brock moving towards the door. I watched them out of the corner of my eye as I put away my pathetic, post-grad grocery store purchases.

"I'll see you this weekend?" Brock asked, his hand gently cupping her chin.

"Yeah, of course. I'll be there on Saturday...I'll make the arrangements for dinner. See if...everyone can be there?" Tessa trailed off.

I instantly knew who she was referring to. My shoulders stiffened as if she'd spoken his name aloud. Tessa was very careful not to utter that particular Miller's name around me, but I still knew when she was referring to him, almost instinctively.

"Okay, I'll call you later tonight, beautiful. I love you," Brock muttered. He had his arms around her, and he was kissing her tenderly, as if he was about to go off to war—not just home to Parry Sound where he lived.

Those two were so crazy in love, it made me want to both vomit and cry. Especially because Brock reminded me of someone else...someone that no matter how hard I tried, I couldn't forget.

And I was *trying*. It's not like I'd been celibate since Braden Miller took my heart and smashed it to bits. Far from it, I wasn't going to wither away and become some sad excuse for a spinster, like my mother (not that she was sad, but still). I'd had other romances since Braden, if I could even call them that. Those flings had fizzled out before they even really had a chance to grow into something more because they couldn't uphold the magic of that first love.

It was impossible to forget Braden's electric blue eyes and that arrogant smile. He'd made it extremely challenging to give myself completely to another.

It didn't help that his older brother dated my best friend, and often came over to see her.

Brock never mentioned Braden when he was around. I think he sensed that a part of me still ached for someone that had long since walked out of my life, someone that I should be over by now.

In the past four years, I'd become a fantastic actress. I even fooled myself at times.

"Okay, see you soon," Tessa grinned, slapping his ass when he went to open the door. He shook his head at her, a bemused smile on his lips. She closed the door behind him, turning and pressing her back against it with a dreamy sigh.

I swallowed hard, feeling tears prickle behind my eyelids. I stomped off to my bedroom, unbuttoning my uniform as I went.

"Elle, are you okay?" Tessa's voice followed me down the narrow hallway. I held a hand up to her, signalling her to give me a minute. I striped out of my work clothes, tossing them into my hamper, then disappeared into the bathroom. I turned on the shower, taking deep breaths to try and regain control of my emotions.

I showered quickly, refusing to allow myself the opportunity to cry. I was stronger than this, and I'd promised myself years ago that Braden Miller deserved *no more* of my tears.

But the elderly man from today...he deserved a few, as did his wife of fifty years, and the young girl who'd been too foolish to wait until she got home to text her friend.

By the time I rejoined Tessa in the kitchen, I'd collected myself. Tears no longer threatened to spill and even though there was the ever-present ache in my chest, I was able to toss on a winning smile that would fool anybody.

Anybody, it would seem, except my best friend. She crossed her arms, her eyes narrowing at me.

"What's wrong?" she asked, tilting her head, a frown marring her lips.

"Nothing," I assured her, working to keep my smile in place. "What's happening this weekend?" I asked, deflecting her question with a question of my own. Tessa didn't buy it, in fact, she outright ignored me.

"Just tell me what's up, Elle," she demanded, turning her amber eyes on me with determination. There was *no way* she'd let me get out of this conversation without a little give.

"I had a rough day at work, okay?" I sighed, my shoulders dropping a little. I padded over to the refrigerator and opened it, searching for a bottle of water. "There was an accident on the highway involving six vehicles."

"Oh, I heard about that," she frowned, concern edging her eyes. I knew she understood. Sometimes, Tessa came home in tears because she wasn't able to save an animal, and sometimes I came home like this because I'd witnessed too much death and tragedy. We'd both chosen jobs that could be hard on our hearts. Tessa leaned against the counter, chewing on her lip as she studied me. She had something to say, only she seemed to be warring with herself on whether or not she should say it.

"Just tell me," I rolled my eyes. I cracked open the lid on the water bottle and took a sip, watching my friend.

"Brock proposed!"

I gasped, choking on the water I'd been drinking. It went down the wrong pipe, and I coughed, spitting some out on the tiled floor. I wiped my mouth with the back of my hand, staring at Tessa with astonishment. She flashed her left ring finger at me, as if I needed proof of this new development. "What? When?"

I set the water down, crossing over to her and taking her hand. Brock had really outdone himself. The ring was a beautiful, princess-cut diamond, with four tiny diamonds on either side of it. It wasn't overstated; it didn't scream in your face that it was 'an engagement ring.' It was subtle, but once your eye noticed it—you realized how stunning it was, how *perfect*. It was *Tessa*.

"On the weekend!" Tessa squealed, practically bouncing on her heals. "Oh Elle, it was so amazing! We went canoeing at sunset and he did it then. I swear I almost tipped the canoe, I was so excited!"

"So...you're engaged," I summarized, still blinking with astonishment at the beautiful ring. It almost hurt my eyes. They itched and prickled, as if I wanted to cry.

"Yes! I'm getting married! Can you believe it?!"

I was torn between joining my best friend in a happy dance and sinking down to the floor and crawling into the fetal position. I took a deep breath, calming myself. There was no need to taint Tessa's happy news with a sulking face. After all, she was my best friend and I was legitimately happy for her and Brock. He treated her incredibly and he was an amazing person—sexual escapades on my couch aside.

"That's awesome," I managed, somehow keeping a genuine smile on my lips. She grabbed my hands, holding them tightly.

"Please tell me you'll be my maid of honor?" Tessa pleaded, her eyes wide and fearful, as if she thought I'd say no.

"Of course," I told her, my smile faltering at the thought of seeing him again. "I guess you haven't picked a date yet?" I asked, holding out hope that I had at least a year to adjust to the idea of having to see him again.

Tessa shuffled uncomfortably. "Well..." she trailed off, her amber eyes looking at me apologetically. "To be honest, I'd be happy eloping right now but I figured my dad would flip," she laughed awkwardly, her eyes vulnerable. "So we were thinking July."

"As in...this upcoming July?" I repeated. Tessa nodded, biting her lip nervously. "You're getting married this July?"

Already, my mind was reeling with all the things that came

with planning a wedding. It was already the middle of September. We had Stag and Does, bridal showers, bachelorette and bachelor parties to figure out, not to mention the actual wedding itself. I would be seeing an awful lot of Braden Miller, and it made me feel…sick.

"I know," she bit her lip. "It's crazy, isn't it? Maybe we should wait until after I'm done vet school…" she added doubtfully, her face falling.

Next September, Tessa was planning on moving to Guelph to attend veterinary college. She had graduated top of her veterinary technician program at Georgian College two years ago and had secured a job working at a clinic near our apartment. She loved being a technician, but her dream was to own her own clinic, and for that she'd need to take the four year veterinary program Guelph offered. She'd been saving for this day for a long time now, and we all knew how important it was to her.

"Don't be ridiculous, Tessa." I took a shaky breath, forcing a smile in place. My panic wasn't over my best friend tying the knot, because she belonged with Brock. I would have had to get used to the idea of seeing Braden again regardless, but I hadn't expected it to happen *so soon*. "Vet school is like four years long. It makes sense to get married before it starts, you'll be busy enough. Besides, who wants to be engaged for four years?"

"I know," Tessa sighed, worrying her lip. "I just…I get it, you know? How you're feeling about the whole Braden thing."

"Whoa." My eyes narrowed in anger that she'd called me out on it. "This *isn't* about Braden. I couldn't care less about him. This is me freaking out because my best friend is getting married in less than ten months and we have an entire wedding to plan."

"Sure," Tessa said, doubtfully looking at me. She didn't buy it —not that I really believed she would, but I felt better denying it. "It's just going to be a small wedding."

"Have you met your family?" I arched an eyebrow, my arms folding protectively across my chest as I smirked at her. "There's nothing *small* about them."

"Fair enough," Tessa smiled softly.

"Who else is in the wedding party?" I asked, trying to keep my face impassive as I leaned against our counter. I needed the support.

"Well, Braden is going to be Brock's best man," Tessa answered almost apologetically. "He also chose Travis, Grady, and Gordon. I'm going to ask Katie, Becky, and Krista."

Becky and Katie made sense—Becky was Brock's sister, and Katie was Tessa's sister-in-law. She was married to Tessa's oldest brother, Ben. "Krista? *Really?*" I wrinkled my nose.

Tessa bristled, annoyed at me. "Yes, really. Krista's been our friend since Kindergarten. Just because you don't talk to her any more, doesn't mean *I* have to cut her out of my life. She's a good friend to me, and she didn't betray you."

I didn't need the reminder—I knew perfectly well that it was Joanna Poole that had broken the girl code and made out with my boyfriend while we were still together. Still, Krista hadn't told me about it out of loyalty to Joanna, and that had stung almost as bad as Joanna disregarding our friendship.

"Okay, fine. You're right," I amended, sighing. The corner of my lips tugged up in a reluctant smile. Tessa never hesitated to put me in my place when I needed it, and I loved her for it.

She inhaled deeply and brushed her hair out of her eyes as she looked at me. "I know you're off this weekend…" She bit her lip again.

"You want me to come to Parry Sound with you?" I summarized, avoiding her penetrating, hopeful gaze. I saw her nodding out of the corner of my eye.

"Pretty please? Saturday night we'll be telling my family and…Brock's family at dinner, and I *need* my best friend there," Tessa pleaded, sounding unsure of herself. "Plus…you've always been my right hand man—er, woman, and what if Dad tries to talk me out of this?"

"He won't," I assured her. Bill Armstrong hadn't been a fan of Brock Miller when he first came back to town, but he'd warmed up in the last several years when he realized how deeply Tessa loved him.

"I'm his only daughter," she pointed out, arching a brow. "I think I could tell him I'm marrying the Prince of England and he'd still pitch a fit." She was right—Bill had high expectations for his only daughter.

"Fine, I'll go," I frowned. "Enough with the guilt-tripping." Tessa squealed with excitement and threw her arms around me again.

I TOSSED and turned all night, unable to get a good night's sleep. Each time I finally drifted off, I was pulled into unwanted dreams of Braden's remembered touches. I woke craving his hands on my skin.

Thoughts of Braden plagued me throughout work the next day. Tessa and Brock's wedding would undoubtedly mean I would have to face him again. He was, after all, Brock's younger brother. But I still hadn't counted on seeing him in less than a week. I had no time to prepare.

I tried to console myself. Braden's presence at the weekend dinner wasn't set in stone. There was a huge possibility that he wouldn't be there. But there was also a possibility that he *would* be there, and my treacherous heart pounded at the thought.

It was stupid, the way my heart was reacting. If the look in Braden's eyes the last time I'd seen him was any indication, whatever was between us was long dead. Seeing him again would only prove this, and it would cut my heart open all over again. I really wasn't ready for that.

My only comfort was the thought that maybe he was even more miserable than me. Maybe one look would be all it took for me to wipe the slate completely clean and finally move on.

Or maybe I'd realize that moving on would be an impossible feat for me. My mother had never moved on from my father. He'd left us, and she hadn't welcomed another man into her life since. Maybe I was destined to be like her. Maybe the Thompson girls didn't heal once their hearts were shattered.

I was in a sullen mood the entire day, a fact that didn't get past my partner, Alex.

"What's wrong?" he asked me halfway through our shift. He leaned over, fixing me with a heavy stare, concern lining his light eyes. I scowled at him.

"Nothing," I responded, trying to keep my voice nonchalant as I turned my gaze back to the front of the ambulance. We were parked just off the highway, waiting for the next call. This was one aspect of the job that I wasn't a fan of—being stuck in the ambulance with Alex Hastings in between calls.

There wasn't anything wrong with Alex, per se. He was incredibly attractive and fit. He had dark blond hair, a subtle, perpetual tan, and a dusting of facial hair over kissable lips. He also had gentle eyes and a sweet, trusting smile. He was one of those guys that truly didn't realize how hot they were, which only added to his appeal.

He was a genuinely caring guy, and he was also into me. Alex was perfect on paper, but he wasn't Braden, and the tingles I did happen to feel for him didn't come close to what I had once felt for Braden. Not that I'd even give him a chance—we worked together, and I wasn't about to make my work life awkward.

"Are you still thinking about yesterday?" Alex questioned, his brow furrowed. He leaned back in his seat, his eyes never leaving my face as he waited for me to answer. I knew he was referring to the accident on the highway.

"No, Alex," I said, sighing. "It's a long, boring story."

"We've got time," Alex pointed out, giving me a rueful smile.

I pursed my lips, contemplating. It'd be nice if I could expel some of my ugliness somewhere, and I definitely didn't want to expel it on Tessa. It wasn't her fault that the Miller brother she had chosen to fall in love with stuck around. Technically speaking, Alex was one of the only friends I'd really made out here.

I brushed a strand that had fallen loose from my tight ponytail out of my eyes while I contemplated. "My best friend just got engaged," I said on an exhale, my eyes darting to Alex's face. He looked confused by my statement.

"And?"

"And she's getting married in like ten months, and I'm going to be her maid of honor, and her fiancé just so happens to be the older brother of someone I don't particularly want to see again. Ever." I summarized.

"Ahh," he said, his lips pursing as he nodded his head with understanding. "Let me guess, he's the brother of an ex-boyfriend."

"Something like that." I sighed again.

"And you're not over him." It wasn't a question; it was a statement.

"I'm over him," I argued, a stubborn set to my jaw. "I just don't want to deal with his bullshit again."

"So don't." My partner shrugged, taking a sip of his coffee. "His bullshit isn't your problem anymore, just bring a date to the wedding and have fun."

My eyebrows shot up at Alex's suggestion, it made a lot of sense. I could focus my attention on my date and not have to worry about looking like the pathetic spinster that never moved on in front of Braden and everyone else. Braden didn't need to know that I spent more time than I cared to admit thinking about what we'd once had and missing it.

Missing him.

"Problem is finding a date," I remarked. "Barrie isn't exactly full of potential suitors."

"Ouch, that stung," Alex exclaimed, clenching a hand over his heart, a teasing smile playing on his lips. Despite his humorous front, I could tell he was a little offended.

I smiled softly at him, trying to retract the harshness of my words. "Obviously, you're the exception. Well, maybe," I added, eyeing him warily. "You may be hot, but you could have some freaky rituals that keep the girls away. Maybe you still let your mom clip your toenails or something."

"I assure you—there are no freaky rituals here, and my mom hasn't clipped my toenails since I was at least sixteen," Alex chuckled. He sent me a brief, converted look, laced with meaning. As if he realized what he was doing, he quickly pulled his eyes away from my face and looked back out the window. "I just work too much to really meet anybody."

"Same here," I said, worrying my lip.

Alex cleared his throat, his gaze flitting back to my face. "Well, I'd love to be your stand-in date for your friend's wedding, if you'd like."

I massaged my aching temple "Alex, I'm really not looking—"

"I meant as friends," he interjected quickly. "I understand that you don't want to...start anything with me. I get it, it wouldn't be wise at all. We see *way* too much of each other as it is. As hot as you are, I don't think I could handle dating someone and having to work with them. I'd never get a break," he laughed ruefully, running his hand through his short hair. His gentle hazel eyes were fixed on my face. "But I'll go as a friend, and what your ex doesn't know won't hurt him."

I stared at him and blinked. "You're a sly dog, Alex Hastings," I said, shaking my head slowly. A small smile spread across his lips. I turned my body towards his, studying him carefully as I mulled over his offer. "I don't think this is a good idea," I muttered, sighing deeply.

"Just think about it," he said, a teasing smile lifting the corner of his lips. "I'm an excellent wedding date. I can dance, I look great in a suit, and I impress the parents while making the ex-boyfriends seethe with jealousy."

I snorted with laughter; it was true, after all. I'd seen him dressed up for our work Christmas party. He did look great in a suit, and he was willing to act as a buffer and make my ex jealous.

Friday came quicker than I anticipated, probably because I was dreading it more than a root canal without freezing.

After I arrived home and showered, Tessa and I packed up my little red Camry and hit the road. For the first half of the trip, she chattered nervously about everything. Twenty minutes outside of Parry Sound though, she fell silent, her eyes focused on the scenery passing by the window. Her fingers twisted around and around in her hair, a habit she had always had when nervous.

"It's going to be fine, Tess," I told her, giving her a comforting smile.

"I know," Tessa looked at me, smiling. "I'm just nervous. I never really thought I'd ever be the type to get married so young." I bit my lip, the flood of memories washing over me at Tessa's words.

It was true: she had never been the type to daydream about weddings and babies—at least, not to my knowledge. Growing up, that'd been me. I was the hopeless romantic out of our friendship equation. I picked names out for my future babies and used to spend entirely too much time daydreaming about my wedding. When we were kids, I constantly made her play out my ridiculous ideas up in the attic of my house.

My mom had a trunk of beautiful dress clothes from her

beauty pageant days. I'd wear the white sequin gown, while Tessa would choose something else as my maid of honor. The dress swallowed me whole, but I still felt like a princess in it. I couldn't wait to get married for real.

Then I met Braden, and I fell hard for him. I could easily see my future with him. I could easily picture myself walking down the aisle, all dressed in white and joining him at the altar.

That memory stung now. In fact, I hadn't thought about weddings or babies since Braden tore my heart clean out of my chest and shredded it into pieces before my very eyes.

"I don't think he's going to be there," Tessa's voice roused me from my dark thoughts. She was looking at me sympathetically. "Brock spoke to him earlier this week and he's grad...got something to do on Monday."

I took a deep, calming breath. I wanted to tell Tessa I didn't care what Braden was up to—that I didn't care whether or not he showed up for this dinner, but it would be a blatant lie and I knew she'd see through it. Instead, I bit back my curiousness and nodded, keeping my eyes on the road and my hands gripping the steering wheel.

Tessa fell silent again, looking out the window as her own thoughts consumed her. "I can't help but wonder...am I making a mistake? Are we rushing into this? I mean, I'm only twenty-two," she said, her voice so quiet it was almost inaudible. Her gaze was still focused out the window.

"Does it feel like a mistake?" I asked softly, my eyes darting over to meet hers.

"No, it doesn't," she sighed, her head turning to face me. "I guess I'm worried about what my family will say."

"We've been over this Tess; you can't live your life to please them. You have to live your life to please *yourself.*"

"I know," Tessa said, a smile on her face. She was silent for a moment, watching me. "Thank you so much for coming with me this weekend. It means a lot to me." She added, her voice gentle.

"That's what best friends are for," I lifted my shoulder, trying to shrug away the deepness of the moment. I didn't want her to bring up *him* again. I was glad he wasn't going to be at the dinner, relieved that I could put off seeing him for a little longer, but I didn't want to get into my feelings and thoughts right now. I felt too raw. "Am I dropping you off at the farm or at Brock's?"

"Brock's, please," Tessa answered, a wicked grin on her face.

"You're a fiend," I smirked, turning down the road that led to Brock's cabin. "Holy shit...it's beautiful!" I gasped, coming to a stop in front of the elegant log house. It was the first time I'd been back to see it since he started building it. It looked less like an outback cabin, like I'd expected, and more like a cottage from a fairy-tale.

The screen door opened and Brock stepped out, his large dog at his heels.

"I'd ask for a tour, but I don't like the way he's looking at you right now," I joked, shaking my head. Brock was staring at Tessa like he wanted to do a thousand unmentionable things to her—and I'd already seen enough of Brock to last me a lifetime.

"See you tomorrow?" Tessa smirked. I smiled and nodded, then watched her walk up the pathway and into Brock's arms. My heart clenched in my chest, but I kept my smile on as I waved and slowly turned around, heading back to the highway that led into town.

CHAPTER TWO

raden

REGRET. It wasn't exactly a feeling I was accustomed to having. As the youngest child in a broken family, I'd always done whatever I wanted, whenever I wanted to, without a single fuck about the consequences.

I was eleven when my good-for-nothing father died. I still remember that time like it was yesterday. I was always so afraid when he was alive. I was a tiny kid; I could barely eat because my stomach was always twisted with nerves. Being tiny gave me the advantage of hiding. I could easily disappear inside closets and underneath beds, and my drunk-as-shit father wouldn't be able to find me.

I spent a lot of years hiding, and when he died…I became a completely different person. I felt like I could breathe for the first time ever. I developed an appetite for freedom.

My mom was always busy, always working. Before he died, after he died, that aspect of life never changed. Someone had to pay the bills, someone had to pay off the debt my father had accumulated between gambling, drinking, and spending money we didn't have on shit he didn't need—like more booze.

My older brother, Brock, was my keeper before our dad died, but afterwards, he left for Alberta to work in the mines. My older sister, Becky, was dealing with her own shit and that left me on my own. With no one around to keep me in line, I did whatever the fuck I wanted. I vandalized property, I got into fights, and I acted like a total nut job—after all, that was what everyone in town expected from me. Hell…it was all I expected from myself until she showed me that I was worth more.

Elle Thompson, with her long, flowing dark brown hair, those luminous doe-like eyes, and that creamy skin.

She was the most beautiful girl I'd ever seen, and the whole town would agree. I'd crushed on her long and hard throughout middle school. For years, I vied for her attention, acting like a complete douchebag. I did all the crap I could think of. I pulled her hair just so I could touch it, I called her names just so I could hear her voice, and I fooled around with girls in front of her, just hoping she'd turn those brown eyes my way.

When I was seventeen, I finally clued in to the fact that none of that shit was going to fly with her. Most girls liked being treated like crap by me, but Elle wasn't like most girls. That was the appeal with her. So, I asked her out. She said no, but I kept asking—and finally, she said yes.

At first, I thought I wanted her because she was hot. She was always beautiful, but puberty had graced her with curves and a rack that would drive any hormonal teenage boy mad with want. She drove me wild—God bless the person who invented the mini-skirt.

But I soon found that my desire for Elle ran deeper than flesh and bone. Her soul called to mine. She showed me how to open up, how to love and be loved. She showed me that I was worth something more than what people expected me to be.

And I thoroughly messed it up. Blame it on grief or on self-ishness, but I broke her heart, and I let her walk away from me. I told myself it was only a matter of time, Elle would see sooner or later that I was going nowhere fast, and she'd make her break. I was just ripping the Band-Aid off quickly. I told myself I was protecting my heart from the inevitable.

After she left, I spent six months drinking myself stupid until my siblings gave me the cold hard slap of reality and told me I was on the exact path to follow in Dad's footsteps. I'll never forget the look on Becky's face when she told me she couldn't have me around her son anymore, that I was too much like him.

I spent three months in rehab and then enrolled in the mechanical engineering program at Algonquin College, five hours away from home. Three years later, I graduated top of my class and returned to Parry Sound, not only because I had nowhere else to go, but because I had to fix all the damage I'd caused to those I'd loved most.

Elle was never far from my mind. She, along with my family, were the reasons I got sober and went to college. I wanted to be a better man for her, a better brother for my siblings and a better uncle for my nephew. But I took too long, and for all I knew...she'd already moved on.

It was pointless to hold out hope, and yet I did. I hungered to see her again. I thirsted for her in a way I never thirsted for a drink, and I was a goddamn alcoholic. My addiction for Elle was thicker than my addiction to booze.

Moving back home meant that eventually, I would run into Elle, and I knew I wouldn't be able to keep my distance if that happened. It was all I could think about during the five hours it took me to drive from Ottawa. I told myself that if she was truly happy without me, I'd let her go, even if it killed me. But if there was a chance she still burned for me, I was all in, and I'd never take her for granted again.

"Uncle Braden!" My nephew's voice was barely fair warning before he barrelled into me, his small arms wrapping around my legs in a furious hug. "I've missed you!"

"I missed you too, buddy," I said, affectionately rubbing the top of his head. He peered up at me with big blue eyes, a gapped grin on his face. "Dude, what happened to your teeth? Did you get knocked out?"

"No!" Aiden giggled. "I lost them! I'm seven years old now, Uncle Braden. I'm getting my big teeth!" He puffed his chest out with importance.

"Oh, that's right," I smirked. "Guess that means you'll have to start working soon."

"Working?" Aiden repeated with a frown.

"Oh yeah, once all your baby teeth fall out, you have to get a job," I replied seriously, dropping my duffle bag on the floor by the door.

"He's kidding, Aiden. You still have at least nine more years before I'll make you get a job," my older sister, Becky, said as she approached. She gave me an amused smile before wrapping her arms around me and pulling me to her. "We weren't expecting you for another week! I thought your graduation ceremony is on Monday?" she said as she pulled away to look at me.

"It is," I responded, my eyes glancing around the room. It hadn't really changed in the last four years. Things had been added to it, like the newer photos of a growing Aiden that covered the mantel. "They'll mail me my diploma."

"Didn't they ask you to speak?" Becky frowned, her forehead creasing with confusion.

"I said no," I shrugged, ruffling Aiden's hair again. The kid had shot up in height since the last time I'd seen him.

I avoided meeting my sister's eyes—I knew she wasn't happy I'd bailed out on the valedictorian speech. Both of my older siblings seemed to have no qualms speaking in public, but I did. I sounded like an idiot who couldn't string two words together.

"Well, congratulations regardless, Braden. We're so proud of you!"

"Thanks," I said, uneasy. Her excitement for me made me feel uncomfortable. I know I should have been proud—hell, I'd done it. I'd graduated top of my class in the mechanical engineering technology program I'd taken, but I couldn't help but feel a sense of dread for the future. What now? I had the degree, and I was back in the small town I'd grown up in, hoping that the mechanics garage I'd left to pursue a career would hire me back. It would be like I'd never left.

The only difference between then and now is that I was a little smarter with a degree under my belt. Along with it, a crippling amount of student debt that I had to start paying off before the interest rose.

Damned if you do, damned if you don't, I thought bitterly. I'd wanted to better myself. I'd wanted to add something more than "mechanic" to my resume. Mechanics were a dime a dozen, and I wanted to be more than that.

"Well, go get cleaned up," Becky said, her voice interrupting my thoughts. She eyed the scruffy beard I was sporting and my old, faded and torn blue jeans. "We're going out for dinner tonight."

"Still can't cook, huh?" I joked, earning a glare from my sister.

"Actually, she's gotten a little better. She still can't bake though," Aiden interjected with a toothless grin. "That's how I lost my first tooth—on a cupcake! It was harder than a rock!"

"Aiden!" Becky scolded, folding her arms across her chest as I laughed. "For the record, the dinner plans were already made. Brock asked us to meet him at the Dock in an hour."

I shook my head, still chuckling over Becky's bruised ego. "I'll tag along. Give me a few," I said, picking up my duffle bag and heading down to the basement.

I'd moved into the basement shortly after Becky brought

Aiden home from the hospital. It had been too crowded upstairs, between my mom, Becky and her new baby. Aiden cried a lot and at fifteen, I hadn't been able to handle it. Moving to the basement gave me more privacy and quiet. I could play music without disturbing Aiden, and I could sleep without his cries disturbing me.

Plus, it was really easy to sneak in and out. There was a door that led to a flight of concrete stairs, which would take me outside without ever having to walk through the kitchen. It was magical, especially when I was a teenager.

Everything was as I left it, aside from a few minor changes. The dirty clothes I'd left in discarded piles around the room were cleared away, the carpet vacuumed and my bedding looked washed and freshly made up. The room smelled cleaner, too.

I dropped my duffle bag on the floor at the end of my bed, my eyes scanning the room. They landed on the mirror above my dresser.

Six years ago, Elle had dragged my ass into the photo booth at the mall to take pictures. When we got back to my place, she slid those photos into the wood that framed my dresser mirror. I approached it, my fingers reaching out to touch it, my eyes lapping it up hungrily.

It was a set of four photo booth snaps. In the first frame, I was scowling. I hadn't wanted to go in—I'd outright protested about it, insisting that it was lame as fuck. In the second frame, Elle was kissing my cheek and I was repressing a smile, working noticeably harder to keep the scowl in place. In the third frame, she was had a carefree smile on her face and there was devotion her eyes. In that one, I was smiling too. If I remembered correctly, Elle's hand had slipped into my jeans.

In the final frame, my hand had tangled in her hair and my lips were crushed against hers, a passionate kiss forever frozen in time.

Not pictured was the quickie that followed these photos, thanks to the magic of dead small town malls and mini-skirts.

I closed my eyes, smiling at the memory, my cock stiffening in response. My hands ached to touch her again.

"Hurry up, Braden!" my sister's voice called out, cruelly interrupting my trip down memory lane.

CLEAN SHAVEN, freshly showered, and dressed in clothes that weren't worn, I was ready to crash my brother's dinner plans.

I followed Becky in my old, beat up Chevy S10 to The Dock. It was the restaurant that people went to when they wanted to celebrate something in Parry Sound. It was about as fancy as this small town got. It had beautiful exposed wood ceilings, high beams, and plenty of twinkle lights bathing the dining rooms in a soft, romantic glow.

Becky, Aiden and I walked into the restaurant. "We're supposed to meet people here at six?" Becky asked the hostess, peering around. "Oh, there they are!"

The hostess looked over her shoulder. "Oh yes, the Miller party. Please follow me," she said, leading the way to the massive table that Brock sat at. Beside him sat Tessa, his girlfriend of four years. The rest of the seats were occupied by Tessa's father and three older brothers', her oldest brother's wife and a little girl that must have been her niece.

Elle Thompson and her mother sat beside Tessa's dad. My heart skipped a beat when my eyes locked with Elle's. I swallowed hard, seeing her again—in the flesh—knocked me off kilter. I hadn't been expecting it. If anything, I'd expected to see Brock and maybe Tessa. Not Tessa's entire family, and especially not Elle.

It felt like all eyes were on me as I approached the table. Tessa's eyes widened with surprise, and even Brock looked astonished to see me. We came to a stop at the end of the table, where two empty chairs remained. Becky paused, just as caught off guard as I was, and exchanged a look with me.

"Braden! I didn't think you'd be here until next week," my brother said, standing up and walking over to give me a hug. His hands clapped against my back roughly. He stood back, leaving his hand on my shoulder while he addressed the waitress. "Can we get another chair, please?" he asked. She frowned, but nodded, disappearing to grab another seat.

"Yeah, well. My plans changed." I answered. "What's happening? Did you knock Tessa up?" I may have spoken a little too loudly, judging by the look Tessa's dad was giving both Brock and me. Brock's fingers dug painfully into my shoulder, but I didn't react. The sensation of pain drew away from the hollow ache in my chest. I grinned playfully. "Relax, I'm kidding. I know you value your Johnson too much for that."

"Sit down," Brock's jaw was clenched, a sheer sign he was already pissed at me. What are little brother's for? I dropped into the chair the waitress had brought out for me.

"What's going on?" Bill Armstrong asked, his brow creased as he looked from Brock to Tessa.

"We were sort of hoping to announce this during desert, but..." Tessa trailed off, sending me a dirty look. She seemed nervous. Brock put his arm around her shoulder, pulling her against him. She smiled up at him. "Brock proposed. We're getting married!"

At first, the table was silent while everyone absorbed this information. Then, Elle's mom, Sue, clapped with excitement and stood up. "Oh my gosh, honey, I'm so happy for you!" she exclaimed, hugging Tessa and Brock in turn.

"Are you pregnant, Tessa?" Gordon demanded, his tone threatening as he glowered at my brother. I winced, regretting my careless joke moments before.

"No, Gordon," Tessa frowned, rolling her eyes.

"Just making sure," Gordon said, cracking his knuckles. The eldest Armstrong brother, Ben, cuffed him on the back of the head.

"Stop being an idiot," he growled before turning his attention to his sister. "Congratulations! Do you guys have a date in mind?"

"Yes," Tessa smiled, glancing at Brock again. He squeezed her hand. "We're thinking this July."

"This is so exciting!" Ben's wife, Katie, exclaimed. She was grinning from ear to ear, tears forming in her eyes. The little girl sitting beside her started bouncing in her seat and clapping.

"Can I be the flower girl?" she asked hopefully, her eyes wide.

"Of course you can, Alyssa." Tessa grinned. She turned to look at Aiden. "And we were hoping you'd be the ring bearer, Aiden."

Aiden paused as he contemplated Tessa's request. "I think I could do that for you," he said solemnly, sitting up straighter in his seat.

Bill was silent, watching everyone's reactions. I didn't know if he was happy or pissed, because his thick auburn beard hid most of his face.

"Daddy?" Tessa asked, her brow creasing slightly. Elle's mom nudged him with her arm, motioning with her eyes and a slight tilt of her head to say something. Bill cleared his throat, his eyes moving from Sue's imploring face to Tessa's. Tessa was worrying her lip, waiting for him to speak.

"Why the rush, Tessa?" he finally said, leaning back in his chair as if the eight words he'd spoken had taken all of his energy and patience. "You're only twenty-two. You guys have your whole lives ahead of you."

"Well, we know that Dad," Tessa shifted uncomfortably in her seat. "But right now seems like the right time. We wanted to get married before I started vet school," Tessa answered, the happiness she'd glowed with evaporating at the disapproving tone of her father.

Bill nodded, considering her answer. "I'm glad you're not throwing away your plans to go to vet school."

"With all due respect, I'd never let her do that, sir," Brock told him, his voice carrying an edge to it that made the tension around the table spike. "Tessa's education is as important to me as it is you. I want her to follow her dreams, but I see no reason why she can't follow them with me at her side."

If my heart wasn't lodged in my throat from simply *being* in Elle's presence, I would have clapped. I was proud of my brother for standing his ground. I knew that he wanted Bill's approval, but Brock wouldn't lose any sleep over not having it.

"Bill," Sue warned, arching her eyebrows. The two of them exchanged some kind of unspoken agreement, and Bill's hard features softened as he turned to address his only daughter.

"Congratulations, sweetie," he finally said, his voice holding the affection for his only daughter. His eyes landed on Brock again, the penetrating gaze making me thankful I wasn't in my brother's shoes. "I trust you'll make my little girl happy?"

"Of course, sir," Brock promised solemnly, bringing his arm around Tessa's shoulders and drawing her closer to him.

With the tense moment between my brother and Tessa's father over, everyone started to relax a little and the waitress came back to take dinner orders. Once she'd left again, the wedding conversation resumed.

"We've sort of already talked about who we want in the wedding party..." Tessa said nervously, glancing at Elle. Elle nodded, silently encouraging her to go on with a beautiful, subtle smile on her lips. "Elle's going to be my maid of honor, and since my mom isn't around...I was hoping I could borrow Sue as the mother of the bride."

"Oh Tessa," Sue's eyes instantly welled up with tears, and she brought her hand up to her mouth as if she needed to hold in the emotion Tessa's request brought. "I'd be honored!" Elle's eyes were shining as she smiled at her mom and took Sue's free hand. She gave it a gentle squeeze.

"I was also hoping Katie and Becky would like to be bridesmaids," Tessa bit her lip, looking back and forth from her sister-in-law to my sister.

Katie nodded and smiled while Becky let out a strange little gasp, as if she was shocked. "Of course! I'd love to, thank you so much Tessa!"

"Braden, I'm hoping you'll be my best man," Brock said.

I raised my glass of coke in acceptance, nodding at him with half a smile on my lips. I still couldn't find my bloody voice, not with Elle's eyes on me. I was all too aware that it was the first time she'd willingly looked at me since I arrived. What I saw within the depths of her dark brown eyes didn't give me much hope.

She used to look at me with adoration, but now she looked at me with contempt.

"I want you to be in the wedding party, too Gordon," Brock added, glancing over to Gordon. "Along with Grady and Travis."

Something passed between the two of them, a silent conversation. Gordon's solemn face broke into a huge smile. "Of course man!"

"And Tommy," Tessa smiled at her other older brother. "Will you do us the honors of being our MC for the night?"

"Are you sure you want to give him that kind of power?" Gordon razzed, shoving Tommy, who was grinning wickedly.

"I'm sure your brother will behave responsibly and not embarrass his sister on her wedding day," Bill interjected.

Tommy's face transformed to one of utmost sincerity. "Of course Dad! I wouldn't dream of embarrassing Tessa."

The rest of the dinner passed with plenty of wedding conversation and Elle completely ignoring me again. My eyes never left her face—they refused to budge. I was staring, but I couldn't bring myself to stop. I hadn't seen her in years, and while she was never far from my mind, I hadn't realized how deeply I missed her until she was right before me.

She was every bit as captivating as she'd been in high school. Her beautiful chestnut hair hung in thick ringlets down her back. Her blouse made my mouth water. I was dying to talk to her, dying to tell her I was sorry. But she was so far away—and not just because she was sitting across the table, but because she was guarding her heart. She wouldn't listen to me even if I tried, and that stung. But what did I expect? That I'd see her again and things would go back to the way they were, before I screwed it up?

Dinner was over too soon, and I watched as Elle hugged Tessa goodbye before leaving with her mom. My fingers twitched, itching to touch her. A moment later, I stood up and chugged back the rest of my coke, wishing it'd quench the thirst I had for that girl.

"Well, congratulations you guys. I'm happy for you," I told them, speaking for the first time since my careless pregnancy comment when I first arrived. I pulled my wallet out and tossed a couple of twenties on the table before turning around and leaving.

Part of me hoped fiercely that Elle would be waiting outside in the parking lot for me, but she wasn't. I leaned against the cab of my truck, taking a moment to close my eyes in regret while I pulled my pack of smokes out of my pocket and lit one up.

Seeing her again in the flesh brought it all back—how it felt to have her, to hold her in my arms and to kiss her plump lips. If only I hadn't been so careless with her heart. I was afraid of getting hurt, I was afraid of having her leave me, so I pushed her away and I hurt her. If I had been half as smart as I was now, I would have never done that. I would have taken whatever she wanted to give me. I would have treated her like the goddamn queen she is, and if she did end up leaving...I would have accepted that, because it would have meant that it was what *she* wanted.

It would have been hard, and it would have hurt a hell of a lot...but I hated myself for causing her pain and I would do anything to go back in time and change that.

"I thought you were graduating Monday?" Brock asked, startling me. My eyes opened, watching warily as he approached me.

"I don't need to be there to graduate. They'll mail the diploma," I answered, my brow creasing with irritation. I hadn't been here for four consecutive hours yet, and my siblings were already riding me. Brock joined me, leaning up against my truck too. He looked across the parking lot, nodding slightly. "Look, I'm sorry about the knocked up comment. It was dumb." I added, feeling like a complete asshole.

"I know," my brother exhaled, sending me a serious look. "Just next time...try to watch what you say around Tessa's dad. He doesn't joke around."

"No kidding," I shivered, remembering the dark steely look Bill had given me after the words tumbled from my mouth. Bill Armstrong had *always* intimidated me, even from afar. I was going to have to be careful not to cause any turbulence between my brother and his soon-to-be father-in-law.

"So, what's your plan? Are you sticking around?"

"For a while," I answered. "I'm going to go talk to Chuck tomorrow, see if he's got a position at the garage I could take for the time being."

"You staying with Becky and Aiden?" Brock asked. I nodded in response, and he pursed his lips. "I'm glad you're home... but...the drinking?"

"Haven't touched it since I left rehab," I told him through narrowed eyes. He was thinking about the last time I'd lived with Becky and Aiden, and it pissed me off.

"Good," he sighed. "I just don't want to see you go off the

rails again. Being back in this town…it could be a trigger for you. Becky doesn't need any extra stress, and Aiden doesn't need to see you go through that again."

My jaw clenched, aggravation rising within my chest. "I won't cause any problems."

"What about Elle?" Brock asked, the question coming out of the left field and catching me completely off guard. Her name was a punch in the gut, knocking the proverbial wind out of me.

"What about her?" I demanded.

"Seeing her again can't be easy. I know you still love her… just don't try and drown those feelings, alright?"

"Thanks for the vote of confidence," I growled, pushing off the side of my truck and stomping over to the driver's side.

It pissed me off that my brother had no faith in me. It was like the last several years were for nothing. I pulled open the old door, but Brock's hand on my arm stopped me. The guy was still two times bigger than me, even after all the effort I'd put in at the college gym.

"You know I didn't mean it like that, Braden," he told me, his gray eyes deep with sincerity. "I'm going to worry about you, you're my little brother. I want to see you succeed. I don't want you to torment yourself with the past. That's the fastest way to fall right back again."

"I know," I responded, forcing myself to relax. "Don't worry about me though, I've got this."

THE NEXT MORNING, I drove into town and pulled into the almost empty parking lot of Chuck's Garage. Everything seemed the same as it had the day I left. The sign above the garage was maybe the biggest indicator that time had passed. The once-bright red paint had chipped away to a faded rust colour.

I parked my truck, letting the memories of this place wash over me like rain. Once upon time, Chuck had been the only person in town willing to take a chance on the youngest son of the town drunk. My reputation for trouble and chaos was a well told story around these parts, but he'd seen something in me.

I was fifteen years old, and I needed a job. Bad. Debt collectors were knocking on our door every single day, and Mom was only making enough to cover our basic needs. Becky had just gone through a traumatizing time, Brock was in jail and our family was still trying to pick up the pieces. I figured if I got a job, I could help minimize some of the stress.

I'd always loved working on cars with my grandpa, and I had a natural inclination to do so. Hell, I'd done most of the labor under the careful instruction of Grandpa. I could understand the mechanics of an engine, how everything worked, with far more ease than I could understand anything academic.

Chuck's seemed like the natural choice—especially after every other place in town turned me away the moment I walked in with my resume. Chuck was the only person who didn't tell me they weren't hiring the moment I walked in.

He stared at me for several long minutes after I'd stomped into the garage and told him I wanted a job. "Why should I hire you, boy?" he asked, the amusement dancing behind his tired brown eyes.

"Because I know my way around an engine. I restored a 1969 Dodge Charger with my Grandpa when I was seven." I told him confidently. Chuck's busy eyebrows rose, impressed. "I'm a hard worker, and you could use some help around the shop from the looks of it," I added. I didn't need to look in the direction of the disorganized tools and mess of parts to know this much was true.

He continued to stare at me for several long beats before sighing. "Tell you what kid," he said gruffly, scratching at his chin with grease covered hands. "If you can figure out the problem with that Caravan, and fix it yourself...I'll give you a job."

"Is that supposed to be a challenge?" I'd asked as I rolled up my sleeves.

Three hours later, I had the Caravan fixed and a job.

I shook my head, trying to clear the memories away and get on with the task at hand: seeing if Chuck would give me my job back. I slammed the truck door behind me, heading straight inside the open garage.

At first glance, it was empty except for a Subaru Forester in the bay and a mess of parts and tools all over the place. Chuck had never been the organized type. I breathed in deeply, the smell of grease and oil and metal working to ease my nerves. I'd spent a lot of time here, found a purpose here.

"You're back," Chuck's raspy voice came from behind me— the office. I turned around, my hands still in my jean pockets. He looked exhausted and older than his 55 years. His skin had a slight grey tinge to it, and he'd lost weight. Chuck's outward appearance concerned me; working too hard for too long had taken its toll on him, and guilt over my departure nagged at me. But Chuck would sooner kick my ass than talk about his health, so I pushed my concerns aside.

"Hey, Chuck," I said, the right corner of my lips lifting up. "Need any help around here?"

"You can get started on the Subaru. Transmission's shot."

CHAPTER THREE

lle

SEEING him again had drudged up everything—and I mean *everything*. The way he'd looked at me from across the table, his blue eyes practically burning with intensity—as if he wanted to devour me. My old reactions were still the same—the jump in my heart rate, the flutters in my lower abdomen. I'd wanted him to act on the desire rolling off him in waves.

I felt utterly stripped bare in his presence, like he could read every thrum of my heartbeat. And the traitorous way my body responded to his presence didn't help, it was as if it had forgotten how completely he'd devastated me. It was the most peculiar thing; even though he'd shattered my heart, it still sped up in his presence...it still *craved* him. I could so easily fall back into that old habit; into him.

Mom and I left the moment dinner was over. I couldn't put myself through sitting there any longer. My heart was twisting and my blood was on fire in my veins. I wanted to cry and scream and rage at him—and that wasn't my style. Not anymore, I refused to give him the satisfaction of seeing me hurt over him.

A lone tear trailed down my face, and I wiped it away furiously. When it all happened, when he'd broken my heart in front of an entire room full of people, I honestly hadn't thought it was over. I couldn't believe it—our love was supposed to be forever. How else could one explain the fireworks between us? But he didn't come after me. He never tried to call or even text. He just disappeared, he let me leave for college without so much as a goodbye—like I'd never mattered at all.

I believed it. I believed that I hadn't mattered to him. It was easy to, with the hostile look in his eyes when he'd nailed the coffin shut on our relationship.

But now...I didn't know what to think. Sparks still flew between us, the fire in the pit of my stomach still burned for him, and the way he looked at me made me feel...

Well, it made me feel things. It made me feel alive.

"Are you okay honey?" Mom asked, drawing me back out of my head. I turned to look at her. Her eyes were focused on the road, but she kept glancing at me with worry lining her face.

"Define okay," I sighed, turning my head to look back out the window again.

"It wasn't easy seeing him tonight, huh?"

"I don't get it," I seethed, my arms folding protectively across my chest. "Why can't I just get over him?"

"He was your first love," Mom answered, turning up our driveway. "First loves don't die quick. Hell, I don't think they ever really die. You carry the memories of it throughout your life."

"I really hope that isn't true," I sighed, opening the car door and stepping out. "Otherwise this wedding is going to really suck for me."

"Who knows." Mom grinned at me as we walked up the

front porch. "Maybe the reason why you can't let go is because your story isn't finished yet."

I scoffed at her words, because there was no way in hell I was going to go down that road a second time. I'd sooner cut my heart clean out of my chest than give it to Braden Miller again. "Or, maybe he just screwed me up for everyone else. Kind of like what Dad did to you." I said, voicing my deepest fear. Mom paused, my words hitting her where it hurt. "I didn't mean it like that Mom."

"Do you really think that, Elle?" Mom asked me, her brow furrowing. She unlocked the door, holding it open for me.

"What else am I supposed to think?" I responded with a question of my own as we walked into the house. I dropped my purse down on the bench by the door and turned to face her. "You never moved on after he left. I've never seen you date anybody, ever," I added, my eyes never leaving her face.

"I didn't have time to date when you were little," Mom answered. She turned and started for the kitchen, flicking on the light as she went. "Tea?" She asked me. I nodded and she grabbed the kettle off the stove, filling it with water from the tap. She brought it back to the stove and flicked the gas burner on.

"Okay, I get that...but I'm all grown up now. You don't have the excuse of being a full-time parent. Why don't you get out into the dating pool again?" I pulled a chair out from the kitchen table and sat down, angling my body to face her.

"Oh honey, I'm too old for that," Mom shook her head with a small smile as she leaned against the counter. "I've spent over two decades on my own. I like my life the way it is."

"You never get lonely?" I pressed, thinking about how alone I often felt. I knew I should try dating again, but it was hard.

"Everybody gets lonely from time to time," Mom shrugged. "I keep busy though, I'm not sure I'd want to rearrange my life and how I've been living it for someone else. Plus, pickings are slim in this town," she winked.

"Online dating, Mom," I told her.

She wrinkled her nose in response and shook her head.

"I'M REALLY clueless about this whole wedding thing," Tessa sighed a week later as she stared at the overwhelming pile of bridal magazines on our coffee table. "I mean, it says right here that you need at least a *year* to plan a wedding."

"That's why we're getting started right now," I told her. "The most important thing is picking the day, which you've already done, I think?" I looked at her for clarification.

"July twenty-third," she answered with a sad smile on her lips. I froze. July twenty-third was the day that Deanna Miller had died four years ago. "Brock wanted the twenty-third. He wanted to make something beautiful out of that day, because he knows it stings for his family. He also thought it would be a good way to honor her memory."

"It is a good way to honor her memory," I agreed. The words seemed to get stuck in my throat, so I cleared it and went back to my list. "Now, we're working out the details. We need to send out save the dates, especially because it's a summer wedding. People's summer schedules fill up quickly, so we'll want to pick dates for the other events too. Have you talked to Brock yet about doing a Stag and Doe?"

"He's not into that," Tessa made a face. "Besides, it says right there that getting people to crowdfund your wedding is cheap."

"True," I shrugged. "That's one less thing we have to do then." I crossed out *Stag and Doe* on our to-do list and moved on to the third item. "Bachelor/bachelorette parties, yay or nay?"

"Obviously yay," Tessa grinned. "I don't care if I have to twist

Brock's arm to get him to have a bachelor's party. You only get married once!"

I resisted the urge to make a smart comment about that—I was trying to keep my jaded, bitter feelings about relationships and love on the down low so that I wouldn't ruin Tessa's wedding bliss with my own shortcomings. The key was focusing on all the tasks on the wedding to-do list and treating it more like a party event. I was good at organizing parties; I'd thrown a lot of them in high school.

"I've reserved July ninth for the bachelorette party. The best man is going to have to figure out when to host the bachelor party, because that's his job," I said, purposely avoiding speaking Braden's name out loud. I paused to take a sip of red wine.

"Or we could do a combined one, maybe like a camping trip or something," Tessa suggested.

I nearly spat my wine out. "No combined party," I said, glowering at her. "I've planned out your bachelorette party in my mind years ago and trust me, it does *not* include the guys. We're doing a traditional night on the town in Toronto. I've already been in contact with Caroline."

"Alright, alright! I'll pass the message on," Tessa picked her cell phone up and fired out a text. I didn't bother asking her who she was sending it to, because I already knew.

"Now we have to talk about the bridal shower. How does June sound? It gives us a couple of weeks to get the invitations for that out."

"Can we skip the bridal shower?" Tessa asked softly, her eyes distant. "I mean, that's kind of a family thing right? Your mom, your grandma, and all your female relatives and close friends sit around eating fancy sandwiches and what not. Aside from my bridesmaids and your mom, there's really nobody I'd want to invite and everyone is already going to be doing enough and spending enough."

My heart squeezed at Tessa's words, and I knew she was

thinking about her mother. Tessa's mom had died when she was very young. Aside from her cousin Caroline and her father's sister, Caroline's mom, she didn't have any female relatives. Her grandparents on both sides had also passed on.

"Okay, no bridal shower," I amended, crossing it off our to-do list while now feeling guilty for nixing her combined bachelor/bachelorette party idea. "So, let's talk more about the save-the-dates. Did you want to do a cute little magnet? Or maybe a coaster?"

"Why would we do a coaster?" Tessa giggled. "Nobody uses coasters anymore. I think a magnet is more practical."

"Magnet it is." I leaned forward and picked my open laptop up, bringing up a website I'd found that we could use to make and print magnets. I fiddled with it for a bit, finding a template I thought she'd like. "How's this?" I asked, showing her the sample.

"Oh! I like that!" Tessa said eagerly, her eyes sweeping across the screen to read the script. "'Brock Miller and Tessa Armstrong are getting hitched: save the date. July 23rd, 2017'." She read with a smile on her face. "The horseshoe is cute," she added with a smile.

"Okay, I can place an order for these as soon as we narrow down your guest list."

Tessa leaned forward and grabbed a worn piece of paper she'd tucked inside one of the magazines. "Already done. Brock and I discussed it on the weekend. He said he doesn't care how many people are there, so long as I make sure his friend Grayson gets an invite too, with a plus one. We've capped it at fifty."

"Fifty?" I arched a brow, impressed. "That's really intimate."

"I know," Tessa grinned. "I don't want the whole town and their cousins invited, I just want the people I care about there."

"Makes sense," I told her. I triple checked that everything on the magnet was spelt right and that I hadn't screwed up on the date. "Your turn—check that this is right." Once I had Tessa's approval, I ordered a package of eighty magnets. I closed my laptop when I received an email with the order confirmation.

"Alright, wedding planning duties are officially adjourned for tonight," Tessa declared, topping up my glass of wine. "Now let's get to the girl talk part of the evening. Tell me...how are you feeling after seeing Braden last weekend?"

"Irritated," I admitted. "Why'd he have to go and get even *hotter*?" I grumbled, thinking about how he'd grown up.

I'd only seen him in jeans and a t-shirt, but he had definitely increased his muscle mass since the last time I had seen him. The scruff along his chiselled jaw only added to the appeal. He also had bloody tattoos! He was irresistible before, but now...I was having a hard time fighting the deep attraction I felt for him, even after everything he'd put me through. Which is exactly why I insisted on keeping our contact to a minimal.

Tessa laughed. "I saw the sparks flying between you two. Seems like the old chemistry is still hot."

"Ugh," I rolled my eyes. "Maybe *you* felt sparks—sparks of my anger. Regardless, I'm not entertaining the thought. I've moved on, remember?"

"Sure, sure," Tessa waved her hand, her wine sloshing over her lap. "Damnit," she muttered, trying to blot it away with her sleeve.

"I'm serious," I told her. "I'm moving on. I'll be bringing a date to the wedding, and it won't be Braden."

"Who will it be?" Tessa's curiosity was piqued.

"Alex," I said quickly, taking a sip of my wine. I hadn't decided until that moment, really. The name just flew out of my mouth before I could stop it.

"Alex as in sexy paramedic Alex? I thought you didn't want to jeopardize your working relationship?"

"Yeah, yeah, I know my rule," I sighed. "But he's the only sane person I've met in Barrie, and I don't mind his company. He's cute, he's obviously got a job, he's into me and I'm attracted to him, too," I told her.

It was true—I did find Alex attractive. Especially lately. I had an inch that needed to be scratched, and Alex fit the bill. All I had to do was give him a fair shot and stop comparing every single person I considered dating to Braden. Apples and oranges.

CHAPTER FOUR

raden

"I HEARD he's been in rehab."

"It's only a matter of time before he falls off the wagon again."

"Mmhmm. The apple doesn't fall far from the tree, that's for sure. I'd expect no less after being raised by a man like Brent Miller."

"It's sad really, when you think about it."

"It is, but it's still no excuse for that kind of behaviour. Remember how he broke Sue Thompson's little girl's heart? That girl could have been his redemption. She was so sweet, he never deserved her."

My heart dropped, and anger surged through my veins. I couldn't explain why I was so pissed off, it's not like they weren't saying anything inaccurate. I was dangerously like my father—I knew that, and I didn't deserve Elle Thompson when I had her—I knew that too. I wasn't even sure if I deserved her now.

Even though there was some truth to it, gossip still pissed me off. I was accustomed to it, I'd practically grown up with my every move watched, dissected, and judged. Even when I was a little kid, I'd feel their whispers and their stares. Now that I was twenty-three, I'd grown tired of playing nice and ignoring their rudeness.

I wanted to stomp over there and give those catty old ladies a piece of my mind, but I had my seven-year old nephew with me, and even though I was sick and tired of the witch hunt, I was trying to turn over a new leaf. Yelling at some old ladies in the middle of the grocery store at six o'clock at night probably wasn't going to help.

"Can we get chips, Uncle Braden?" Aiden asked, dragging my attention away from the miserable old ladies. His blue eyes were wide as he pleaded with me silently. I probably should have said no, Becky hated buying junk food for him, but I couldn't help myself.

"Yeah bud, why don't you go grab a bag?" I suggested. Aiden grinned and took off before I could tell him not to run. Smiling, I shook my head with amusement at my nephew as I followed him.

Becky had called me and asked me to pick up Aiden from his friend's house and grab some groceries on my way home from work. The nurse that was supposed to take over her patients never showed up, and Becky was stuck at the hospital until the on-call nurse could come.

The three whispering elderly ladies clammed up when they caught sight of me walking past them. "Good evening, Mrs. Anderson, Mrs. Stovin, Mrs. Reece," I flashed a smile at them that was anything but friendly. "Hope you're all doing well." My words may have been polite, but the hidden message wasn't. I practically said *fuck you* with my eyes and they knew it.

They gaped at me as I continued walking, and it gave me immense satisfaction to see the astonished looks on their faces.

Aiden had about three bags of chips in his arms when I finally caught up to him. "Put two of those bags back, bud.

There's no way we'd be able to polish them off before your mom gets home. Do you want to get caught?"

"No," Aiden pouted, peering down at the bags. "I can't make up my mind though!"

I chuckled and ruffled his dark hair. "Go for Dill Pickle. That's my favourite."

"Really?" Aiden said excitedly. "That's my favourite too!"

"Problem solved then, let's get out of here," I told him. He dropped the bag of chips into the cart I was pushing and we made our way to the checkout line.

I had just finished lifting Aiden up into the truck and was walking the cart back when someone called my name. "Braden!"

I turned around, my hand on the cart so it wouldn't take off without me, and watched as Ezra Johnson jogged over. Ezra had been my best friend growing up. I hadn't seen him in four years. In fact, the last time I saw him, he was hoisting my drunk, belligerent ass off the floor at Flanigan's.

"Give me a moment, okay Aiden?" I told my nephew, ruffling his hair. He nodded, grabbing his Gameboy and firing it up. I closed the door and turned to face my friend.

"I heard you were back in town," Ezra said, coming to a stop a few feet away from me.

"Yup...I got back last week. How are you doing?" I swallowed hard, shame settling in my gut. After I went to rehab, I took off without so much as a *see you later* to all my friends. I was never very good at goodbyes, which is why I preferred not to bother with them.

"I'm alright. How are you doing?" His light eyes held no contempt towards me, just a quiet understanding.

"Good, I'm doing good," I answered. It was almost true too—while the gossipy old ladies were annoying, it was still good to be home. I missed my life the way it was before I did everything in my power to screw it up.

I had a lot of work ahead of me: I had to repair all the relationships and friendships I'd managed to damage. I hadn't just hurt my family and Elle, and I knew that. My regrets played on a continuous loop, and I knew I had to find a way to make amends.

"That's great," Ezra managed. We assessed each other for a moment, both of us probably thinking about the last few times we'd seen each other.

"Look man, I'm really sorry about everything," I sighed, hoping my words conveyed the depth of my regret.

"I get it," he shook his head, smiling sadly. "You were grieving, you weren't yourself."

"Yeah," I inhaled, my eyes dropping to the ground. "Well, I'm sorry about that."

He was quiet for a few moments longer, studying me. "We still get together on Fridays after work for wings. You're welcome to join us."

"At Flanigan's?" I questioned, my throat going dry and itchy. I hadn't set foot in the place since my last bender.

"We could try Wild Wings," Ezra offered, shrugging. "It's up to you."

"Nah, if I can make it I'll meet you at Flanigan's," I said, waving away Ezra's concern like a bad smell. I would have to adjust to this kind of thing sooner rather than later, I just couldn't make it a habit.

"You sure?"

"Yeah man, I'm sure. See you tomorrow."

FLANIGAN'S WAS PACKED on Friday night, which was a surprise considering the tourist season was over. It seemed like everyone from high school was at the local watering hole.

I did my best to ignore the hush that seemed to fall over the crowd of people playing pool as I made my way inside. I nodded at them in recognition, my eyes quickly moving past as I scanned faces to find Ezra and Peter. They were sitting at booth, a large plate of wings and a pitcher of beer in front of them.

My mouth watered at the sight of the beer, and I hesitated for a moment. I closed my eyes, drawing in a deep breath. While it had been just under three years since my last drink, the thirst was still hard to tolerate.

"Hey," I said, nodding at Peter as I slid into the seat beside Ezra. Peter's strong jaw clenched, and tension radiated off of him. His eyes light eyes seemed darker with contempt. He did not look happy to see me. I had a feeling that Ezra hadn't mentioned I would be joining them.

"Hey Braden, glad you could make it!" Ezra grinned. Peter said nothing. He just scowled at me.

"Look Peter... I owe you an apology."

"That's the understatement of the year," he griped. I ignored him—he was right. This apologize was several years overdue.

"I don't remember what I said, but I know it was bullshit." I continued on. The lie was hard to swallow. While I didn't remember my exact words, I knew that the artillery behind them came from Peter's most guarded secret. "I'm a piece of shit and I know it."

Peter let out a reluctant smile. "Yeah, you're a narcissistic piece of shit. You should have known we would have had your back, you didn't have to drop us like that."

"I know," I said, hoping my words conveyed the depth of my remorse. I'd had an awful lot of time to think about my mistakes, and how I treated Peter was one of my bigger ones. Not only had I been a shitty boyfriend to Elle, but I'd been a shitty friend to someone who had only tried to help me. "I wasn't thinking clearly. Then when I stopped drinking, every shitty fucking thing that I did while drunk came at me. The guilt was overwhelming. I just... I needed to get away for a bit."

Peter watched me warily, trying to decipher the honesty of

my words. After a moment, he sighed and ran his hand through his short light brown hair as he regarded me. "I get it. I'm still mad, but I'll get over it. For what it's worth...I'm glad you're home, and I'm glad you got the help you needed."

"Thanks," I responded, my shoulders dropping as the tension left them.

With the apologizes out of the way, we started talking about the last four years and what we'd gotten up to. Ezra told me he landed a union job as a welder. Peter worked on a road construction crew for the city.

"What are your plans? Are you sticking around?" Peter asked me. He was still a little guarded with me, but he'd softened a little.

"Maybe," I shrugged. "I'm working at the garage again for now. Chuck seems to really need my help."

"Are you sure it's not Melissa that needs your help?" Ezra prodded with a shit-eating grin on his face. "That chick's always had it bad for you. She's the one who told me you were back in town; she couldn't stop talking about how hot you were now."

"Oh she needs help, but she's not getting it from me." I rolled my eyes and shook my head. Melissa Groove was a couple of years older than me and had worked as Chuck's receptionist since she'd graduated high school. She was also his niece. I'd been back at the shop for less than a week, and she was already trying to sink her claws into me, chatting me up every chance she got.

Don't get me wrong, the attention was flattering, but Melissa just didn't get me going. She reminded me of Molly Ringwald, straight down to her curly strawberry blonde bob and the slight upturn of her nose. She was snobby, too, almost like Molly Ringwald's character in The Breakfast Club. Sure, she had a great rack and she was pretty in that girl next door way. She made it perfectly clear that she was willing, but I wouldn't touch her.

I wouldn't touch anyone who had a connection to Elle, no matter how small. Elle had always been uncomfortable with the attention Melissa gave me, and even though we weren't together anymore, I held out the hope that one day she'd forgive me and grant a second chance. I didn't want anything else weighing against me.

"Don't tell me you're still hung up on her?" Ezra said quietly, his eyes disbelieving.

Saying nothing, I looked away from Ezra's scrutinizing gaze.

"Have you even been with anybody since her?" Peter asked, equally shocked.

"Don't be fucking stupid, of course I have," I shot back aggravated.

At the beginning, I had been able to block it off and think with my other head, but I had conditions. I didn't do repeats, and I made damn sure the girls knew what to expect from me. I wasn't interested in learning names, it didn't matter anyway, because as soon as I closed my eyes I would imagine Elle. It was the only way I could get off, and maybe that was fucked up, but I'd always been a little messed.

My irritation faded when I saw the sympathetic looks on my friend's faces. "I haven't been with anybody like that though. Just one-night stands here and there." I added, not meeting their eyes.

Shame and regret churned around in my stomach like some kind of dire tango as I remembered how I felt afterwards. Unfulfilled, empty. The space in my chest where my heart should have been was void, and each one-night stand I had did little to fill it. If anything, it only deepened the hole. When the hole got bigger, so did my thirst for a drink.

I didn't think I could do it again even if I wanted to; have another one-night stand, especially after seeing Elle again. Elle was the only woman I had ever connected to on such a deep level, and I missed that. I missed making love to her. I missed seeing her.

"Are you planning on entering the smash up derby this year?" Ezra asked, sensing the need for a topic change. "Because if you are, I'm so going to kick your ass."

"Not a chance," I shot back, forcing a smile.

"BRADEN," I looked up at the sound of my name being said in a sultry purr, my brows furrowing as they landed on Chuck's niece.

"Melissa," I responded with a touch of irritation. "What can I do for you?"

"I brought you coffee!" she cooed, stepping towards me. "I remembered how you liked it," she added as she held out the tray to me.

"Thank you." I took the nearest paper cup out of the tray.

"My pleasure," she said breathily. She looked at me and bit her lip seductively.

"I've been meaning to ask you..." Melissa's face perked right up at my words. "How's Chuck been doing?"

"Not so well," she answered, sighing sadly. "It's his heart. His cholesterol is really high, and if he doesn't change his diet along with his work habits..." she trailed off and sighed. "Anyway, now that you're here he can relax a little bit."

"Yeah, well. Glad to be back." I replied, shifting on my feet. "Look, I've got to get to work on that Cruze. Thanks for the coffee, I'll catch you later." I added, wanting to be rid of her.

Melissa nodded and thankfully left me to do my job. While I worked, my thoughts drifted to Elle again.

Seeing her again at the announcement dinner had only solidified everything I already suspected; I was hopelessly entangled in her. I considered it my penance for the actions of my past. I didn't deserve to be unaffected by her presence. I didn't deserve a second chance, but I wanted it.

She'd left town again before I had a chance to talk to her, not that Tessa had wanted me to do that. "Give her time, Braden. She's not going to be receptive to what you're saying right now, she's still mad and hurt," she'd told me after I expressed my interest in driving out to Barrie to talk to her.

So, I'd stayed away from her. I buried myself in work and focused on fixing the things that I could.

Twenty-minutes later, I emerged from the garage. Chuck was in the office, ordering parts from the distributor. Melissa wasn't behind her desk, although a quick glance at the clock told me she was likely on her lunch break.

I nodded at my boss and disappeared into the staff bathroom to take a leak and wash my hands. By the time I came out of the bathroom, Chuck was finished on the phone. He leaned back in his chair, rubbing a hand against his whiskery gray beard.

"Everything alright?" I asked, arching a brow towards him. He looked up at me and grinned.

"Oh yeah, just catching up on some office work while you're here," he answered, stretching out the muscles in his thick neck.

"I thought that was Melissa's job?"

"She's a good receptionist, but the girl is clueless when it comes to placing part orders," Chuck shrugged with an indulgent smile.

I said nothing, merely choosing to nod in acknowledgement. "Melissa told me about your health issues."

"Did she now?" Chuck looked back up at me, his expression unreadable.

"I think you should hire another mechanic." I cleared my throat, shifting uncomfortably on my feet. In all my years working for Chuck, I'd never told him how to run his business. He raised his eyebrows at me.

"You planning on quitting again?"

I shook my head, frowning. "That's not it. You know that I love the garage, Chuck. You've given me a job twice now when I needed it the most. You're a great boss and friend, I just think it's time for you to slow down a little bit. Hire another mechanic. I'll show them the ropes and we'll cover the repairs while you relax."

Chuck let out a heavy sigh. His tired eyes assessed me before he nodded. "I'll give it some thought."

CHAPTER FIVE

*lle*

Ten Months Later...

I stared down at my suitcase, packed and ready to go for my 'vacation'. My stomach flipped and rolled with dread and nervousness.

I wasn't ready for this; ready to face the memories I'd long since struggled to keep away. Those memories, that person— they belonged in the past, but I knew that going home for the wedding would just drudge it all up again, exactly like the last time I saw him. Unlike the last time, I wasn't as strong. A lot had happened in the last ten months.

Strong arms wrapped around my waist, freeing me from my thoughts. I closed my eyes, leaning back into those arms. My head rested against the broad chest of Alex, my co-worker-turned-roommate-turned-boyfriend.

I lost Tessa as a roommate almost four months ago—in March—when she had received an offer to help out at the Parry

Sound veterinary clinic as a part-time technician, and she took it. She knew it would take years to start up her own clinic, but she wanted a foot in the door at a clinic closer to Brock's house.

Alex had moved in with me out of convenience—he'd been looking for a new place, and I'd been looking for a new room-mate. We worked together and we got along as friends, so it made sense. I thought I could keep things strictly platonic between us.

But I didn't count on Alex's little crush on me growing, or me giving in to too many lonely nights by hiding out in his arms, letting him shelter me from the ache in my chest. Some-where along the line, I found myself developing feelings for Alex, although those feelings constantly confused me.

I cared about him, but I also knew that his feelings for me ran deeper than my feelings for him did. It wasn't that I didn't *want* to fall in love with him—God, I did. I prayed every night that I'd fall in love with this man, but the truth was...I was holding myself back. I was afraid to fall in love, afraid to truly let myself go with him. I knew that Alex was good for me, and yet still...I hesitated.

I was irreparable. Shattered, destroyed. Changed by four not-so-little words: post-traumatic stress disorder.

I'd seen so much death, so much trauma. My doctors had a difficult time pinpointing *exactly* when it happened, when I mentally snapped. Maybe it started with the six vehicle acci-dent nine months ago. Maybe it started when I had to comfort a little boy and clean away his deceased mother's brain matter from his ghastly pale face after a drunk driver struck them head on. Maybe it started when we arrived on the scene of a woman who had been brutally raped and murdered in a hotel room.

Whenever it was, whatever straw broke this particular camel's back—I couldn't seem to escape. The smallest things during a shift would trigger my anxiety and panic attacks: the sound of the ambulance sirens, the smell of blood-tinged asphalt, even the dispatch radio.

Thus, I was about to start my not-so-temporary 'vacation', or rather—medical leave of absence. I suppose I had my boss and the assistance of my doctor to thank. I wasn't exactly stoked about it, but as pissed off as I was...they had a point. I was no good on the team right now. I wasn't helpful, and if anything, I put my teammate—*Alex*—in more danger.

"You need this break, Elle. It's going to be alright," he whispered against my ear. His lips brushed against my lobe. "I'm going to miss you."

"I'll miss you too," I said, turning into his embrace.

He smiled warmly, his large, capable hands running up and down my upper arms. His touch eased my frazzled nerves. It calmed me and centred me. It soothed me. I knew with him that I was safe, and sometimes—that drove me completely insane.

Everything about Alex was safe. He was gentle, dependable, kind, attentive, considerate, and hard working. He was empathetic and understanding. He always put his dirty clothes in the hamper and he was the tidiest person I knew.

I had been placed on Alex's paramedic team shortly after graduating my program at Georgian College two years ago. He'd been working for five years already, and knew the drill. We'd instantly connected—he was easy to get along with and easy to work with. He was steady in chaos and tragedy and I learned a lot from him.

Except—it would seem—how to not let the job destroy my mentality.

Still, Alex had been everything that I hadn't known I needed. We'd only lived together for two months and had been an item for even less time than that, but Alex never wavered from my side. He didn't run when the doctors told me my sleepless nights, uncontrollable anxiety and frequent panic attacks on the job were caused by post-traumatic stress disorder.

But even after all that time with him prior to becoming official, even after how incredible he'd been during my diagnosis...I still didn't feel it in my bones.

And if I was being perfectly honest...I still hadn't been able to free the chains around my heart, left there by someone I wished would stay in the past. *That* traumatic incident—having my heart ripped out and shredded to pieces—also played on a constant loop in my mind.

"Well, I better go," I sighed, leaning closer against his chest. I was reluctant to leave, reluctant to face the shadows of my heart once again. I was afraid to see Braden Miller in what I perceived was a weakened mental state. I was terrified that seeing him again would only solidify all the things I knew in my heart I was missing.

"I love you, Elle," Alex said, framing my face with his hands.

My words got caught in my throat, and I gaped at him, unable to utter the words back. This was the first time he'd said it, and it caught me completely off guard. It seemed too soon...too wrong. He didn't seem to mind my silence. He lowered his lips to mine and kissed me tenderly.

Alex knew that I was guarding my heart, he knew why, and he was patiently waiting for the day I'd let him in. But he never pushed; he never made demands of me. He never fought—not with me, not with the ghosts of my past. Sometimes, I hated that. I wanted him to fight.

I kissed him back, responding physically in the ways I couldn't emotionally. I arched my body against him, feeling his erection pressing against my pelvis. He groaned, pulling me closer to him. "Do you have to leave right now?" he murmured, his eyes roaming my face.

A soft sigh escaped my lips. Alex forever sought permission. He didn't let himself get possessed with desire. He didn't ever take me roughly, caught in the throes of passion. He was steady and calm, even with his love making. That wasn't to say he was a bad lover—he was very attentive, but if I wanted spontaneous, I had to take the lead.

"Mom's expecting me for lunch," I responded, turning away from him to finish zipping up my suitcase. I willed him to grab me, to press himself against me and make his desire for me known, but Alex was respectful. He would never want to make me late for an engagement. But maybe it was for the best, I was still reeling from his confession.

"Okay," he said, reaching around me to grab my suitcase and carry it out to my car. I popped the trunk open and he set it in before he walked back over to me. He kissed me briefly, giving me a slow smile. "Call me when you get there?"

"I will," I told him, my lips brushing against his one final time before I climbed in behind the wheel. The moment I pulled away, I felt relief wash over me—and that relief made me feel guilty.

The drive from Barrie to Parry Sound took the usual hour and twenty minutes. An hour and twenty minutes that I tried to fill with music and excitement for my best friend, Tessa's, upcoming wedding, and not the tormented thoughts of who would also be in attendance...

Braden Miller.

The truth was, ever since Tessa had announced her engagement to Braden's older brother, I'd been thinking a lot about him.

Braden was my first love. I'd fallen for him in high school, at the beginning of grade ten. He'd been just a little dangerous and reckless, that cocky, self-assured grin daring me to give him a chance. I'd given him every piece of myself so completely and so willingly.

Our chemistry had always been explosive; he had never been able to keep his hands off my body. When Braden wanted me, he found a way to have me. He was intense, passionate, and temperamental, but he also loved me so completely, in a way that made everything else pale in comparison.

It took a while for him to let me in, but once he did...I truly thought I'd found my forever. It was an incredible, all-encompassing thing to be loved by Braden.

Everything changed when his mom got sick. Something in him broke. I tried to be there for him, but he wouldn't let me. He pushed me away and he broke my heart in the process.

I'd spent years trying to understand, trying to forgive so that I could move on. I was almost there, too, but then Tessa announced her engagement and the dreams started. I would dream of Braden's touch and wake up craving his hands on my skin. Nothing satisfied this primal need, and these dreams left me in a perpetual state of wanton frustration. I tried so hard to forget the dreams, but they started leaking into my conscious thoughts too.

Sometimes, I wondered if I threw myself into a relationship with Alex to escape those visions. Actually, that was a lie. I knew I did—I dove in because I was afraid of being alone. I wanted a dependable, functional relationship. I wanted to feel like I had finally moved on.

And it worked, for a while at least. I enjoyed spending time with Alex, I loved that I had strong arms to hold me tight in the night...but then, my life changed and I became acutely aware that something was missing. Haunted with a perpetual loop of all of my life's worst moments, I started to compare every word, every touch, every action. And I would hate myself for it. Alex was a good man, he cared about me and he'd never hurt me, and yet I was aching for the man that had destroyed my tender heart, a man I hadn't seen in years—save for once at the announcement dinner.

All he did that night was stare at me. He gave no apologizes, no words were spoken.

I pushed Braden from my mind as I turned onto the old

dusty driveway that led up to the small farmhouse I'd grown up in.

It hadn't been a working farm in decades, not like the farm Tessa had grown up on down the lane. Like the Armstrong's farm, our farm had been in my mom's family for centuries. When my maternal grandparents passed away, they left the house and land to my mom. Mom knew her way around the farm and how to run it, but it was a lot of land to upkeep so she ended up renting out fields to Tessa's dad.

We'd never had animals, except for a couple of cats and a dog when I was little, but this house held a lot of happy memories for me. It sucked that a lot of them included Braden, but I was going to need to get over that...somehow.

Mom came down the front porch steps as I pulled up. I'd barely killed the ignition before she was opening my door and pulling me out for a huge hug. "Elle," she said into my hair. "Look at how skinny you are! Are you still eating that Mr. Noodles crap?"

"Not all the time," I laughed. "I've just got a job that constantly keeps me on my feet and running." As soon as the words fell out of my mouth, I regretted them. I still hadn't been able to tell her.

"That you do," Mom's eyes narrowed at the reminder of my job.

She constantly worried about me and my chosen profession, even if she never verbalized her worries. Her method of coping was to redirect conversation away from it. It was exactly why I hadn't been able to tell her about the struggles I'd faced lately. I didn't want to justify her worries. I didn't want her thinking any less of me for not being able to handle it.

"Well, come on in. I've got lunch set out. I take it that Tessa will be commandeering your attentions soon?"

"I'm surprised she isn't here already," I remarked, following Mom up the worn wooden steps. I purposely avoided looking at the old porch swing. Braden and I had spent many nights curled up on it, star gazing and kissing and talking about the future. "She's been calling me every day in a panic."

"Planning a wedding isn't fun," Mom chuckled, shaking her head.

My mother had been married once, a long time ago. Twenty-two years ago, to be exact, to the man who had fathered me. He'd left shortly after I was born, after realizing that the domestic family life just wasn't his cup of tea. I hadn't heard from him since, and neither had Mom. I really don't know if she searched for him, after he left. We never spoke about it.

My mom was strong, vibrant, and independent...but I couldn't help but wonder how deep her scars were, even if she insisted she was happy.

I bit my lip, holding back the questions I had. Now wasn't the time to get into such a heavy discussion. Instead, I pulled my hair away from the nape of my neck. My skin was already sticky with sweat from the late June heat.

"I know. I have to help her meet with the florist and the baker to make sure that everything is the way Tessa wants it to be," I said.

She'd narrowed down her selections a lot during the last several months, but was still incredibly indecisive. Tessa was pretty lax, but this wedding stuff was driving her crazy and she couldn't wait for it to be over. In hindsight, I couldn't either... although I worried what would be next for me. Helping Tessa was a welcome distraction from dealing with the mess I'd made of my work and personal life.

"Plus the Parry Sound Stampede is coming up," Mom reminded me with a wink.

"Oh shit," I frowned.

"Language," she warned me, arching a brow as she led the way into the kitchen.

"Sorry Mom," I sighed, my eyes taking in everything around

me. Nothing had changed. Everything was still in the same place it had always been. It was like stepping back in time.

I hoped that not everything in this town felt that way.

AFTER FINISHING LUNCH WITH MOM, I headed upstairs to my old bedroom to unpack. I wasn't expecting to be hit with such nostalgia. I'd been home since the break-up, of course. Mom and I still went to the Armstrongs' for Christmas dinner, as we had for years, and my bedroom always felt like a time capsule but this time…it felt different. More torturous and forlorn.

I sat down on the faded pink quilt on my bed, hugging a pillow to my chest, and inhaled deeply.

The sound of voices drifted up the stairwell, along with the hollow steps of someone climbing the old stairs. Tessa appeared in my doorway a moment later, peering in at me. Her long, honey blonde hair hung down her back in waves, and she was wearing her signature cowboy boots and a cute little sundress. She looked like warmth and light. She radiated it, in fact.

"Do you have some kind of tracking device installed in me that I should know about?" I joked, raising an eyebrow and suppressing a smile. Just being in her presence again had me feeling more at peace than I'd felt in months.

Tessa grinned, propelling her body forward and diving beside me on my bed. She threw her arms around me and squeezed me tightly. "I'm sorry; I couldn't wait to see you! I missed you!"

"I missed you too," I told her, laughing. It hadn't really been all that long since the last time Tessa and I had seen each other. Just two weeks ago, we'd gone shopping for bridesmaid dresses and had lunch. Before she moved away, we hadn't gone more than a day without seeing each other since we were very small. We liked to joke that we were sisters from another mister.

"I'm so glad you're here," she sighed, her blonde hair fanning out on my pillow as she leaned back. "There's so much to do still." She sounded almost hopeless, as if she thought she would never accomplish everything.

"Relax, we'll get it done," I assured her, stretching. I was suddenly overcome with exhaustion.

Tessa rolled over to face me, her amber eyes carefully assessing me. "How's Alex?"

"He's fine," I shrugged.

"He's not at all worried that you're in town for the next *month*?" she prodded, arching a brow, her eyes never leaving my face. "By the way, how'd you swing that?"

"Why would he be?" I shot back, giving her a hard look and avoiding her second question. I still hadn't told Tessa the real reason why I was back home on 'vacation', and frankly…I wasn't ready to talk about it.

"Because…Braden's back in town. You'll be spending a lot of time with him over the next few weeks. He *is* the best man—you guys will be walking down the aisle together and stuff." Tessa's eyes had a strange glint to them, and it made me nervous and more than a little cranky. The prospect of touching him again did strange things to me. I wasn't sure I'd be able to take his arm without popping him in the nose first.

"Alex has nothing to worry about. There's nothing between Braden and me, and there will continue to be nothing between us. I'm only tolerating his existence because of your wedding." I frowned.

"Well, hopefully you can tolerate his existence tonight. We're going out for some beers with the girls—and knowing the guys, they'll probably show up at some point."

"What, why?!" I demanded, trying to keep the panic out of my voice without much success.

"Why not?" Tessa inquired innocently. She bent her legs and crossed one over the other, her right foot bouncing up and down. "There's only a month until the wedding. I know you've been super busy with work and Alex but the bachelorette party…"

"Relax, Tessa," I rolled my eyes dramatically and sat up. "Do you think I haven't been planning for that? Because I have. It's planned."

"I know," Tessa said gently. "But you haven't really had a chance to talk to any of the other bridesmaids. The girls are kind of in the dark."

I felt a surge of guilt. She was right, I hadn't really been in contact with the others, not since we'd all gone dress shopping. I found it difficult to speak to Becky. When I was with Braden, I was a part of the Millers' lives, of Becky and Aiden's life. They'd welcomed me in with open arms and we'd became close. When Braden broke up with me, I felt like I had lost them too. I was no longer Braden's girlfriend, but Braden's *ex*-girlfriend. It made things incredibly awkward between Becky and me.

As for Krista, well. I hadn't really had much to say to her in the last several years either. I'd found out months afterwards that Joanna had been the backstabbing bitch to make out with *my* boyfriend, Braden, and Krista hadn't even had the decency to tell me and she had been there. No, I'd had to beg and plead with Tessa to tell me. I told her I needed to know, because I had needed to know. I had hoped that hearing the truth would finally break the hold that Braden had on me.

Instead, I'd lost two friends and became even more bitter and jaded.

But I was going to have to deal with all of that. I couldn't put it off any longer, Tessa was right—her wedding was approaching quickly and we still had a lot of planning to do. The bachelorette party was scheduled for a Saturday night. We were headed to Toronto to hit up three of the best clubs, capping the night off at a male strip club. I'd already booked the hotel room and the limo.

"Alright, where are we going?" I sighed, feeling guilty for having put this off for so long.

"Just to Flanigan's," Tessa responded. "But first, I need to go to Walmart and see if they have any mason jars. Want to come?"

"Why do you need mason jars?" I asked, confused.

"For the centerpieces, remember?" Tessa looked hurt. "I sent you the Pinterest board..."

"Crap, right sorry. I was half asleep when I looked at it," I apologized, feeling like the world's worst maid of honor. I'd really dropped the ball in recent months. I pasted a smile on my face, offering my hand out to her. "Well, what are we waiting for? Let's go!"

FOUR AND A HALF HOURS LATER, we were sitting at a booth in Flanigan's, sipping beer and sharing a plate of nachos while Tessa went over her ideas for the centerpieces. She had a mason jar in front of her and some pamphlets from the florist. Krista, Becky, and Katie sat across from us, pouring over the pamphlets and cooing over Tessa's choices.

"We'll get together the night before the wedding to set up the centerpieces," she was saying, looking at each of us in turn to make sure we were paying attention. "The guys will set up the linens and chairs."

Tessa had chosen to have an outdoor wedding at her family's farm. She'd rented a large tent for the dinner and reception, and the ceremony would take place in one of the fields near the woods. Tessa had stayed true to her word and had only invited fifty guests. She'd wanted to keep the details of her wedding hush-hush, because Travis Channing was a part of her wedding party. He was a headlining country star and he was going to sing the first dance song for Brock and Tessa. The last thing anybody wanted was that detail leaking.

"Your wedding is going to be so amazing, Tessa," Krista said, her eyes shining with approval. I exhaled, nodding in agreement. It was going to be beautiful, no doubt about that.

"Thanks!" Tessa grinned, her entire face shining with excitement. "I can't wait. I'm so thankful you guys are helping me. Balancing work stuff with wedding planning is insane...sometimes I think we should have just eloped."

"Your dad would have *never* gone for that," I scoffed. "You're the only daughter, he has to walk you down the aisle. Besides, at least you're getting it out of the way *before* vet school. Imagine trying to balance all that studying with wedding planning!"

"I know." Tessa exhaled with relief. She grabbed my hand and laced her fingers with mine. She squeezed gently and smiled at me. "But still, it's a headache and I'm glad you're here."

"Where are you and Brock going to live once you get hitched?" Krista asked before grabbing a nacho off the plate and dipping it in salsa.

"We'll spend the rest of the summer at the cabin, then we're moving into an apartment in Guelph," Tessa answered, turning her attention back to Krista. "Brock is still working in Alberta, so he's gone for a month at a time anyway."

"So glamorous," Krista's eyes were bright with longing. "I wish I could get out of this stinking town. Living in the city will be so fun! You'll have to invite us out for a monthly girls night!"

Tessa gave her a small smile, the discomfort evident on her face. I knew how much she was worried about this move. Country ran in Tessa's blood, and she'd had a difficult time adjusting to Barrie—and Barrie was a far stretch from living in Guelph. But it was one of the best vet schools in Ontario, and Tessa was determined to finish her schooling. I knew without a doubt that Tessa and Brock would return to Parry Sound and make it their home. "Well, I have to pee, I'll be right back!" she said. I stood up, standing aside so that she could slide out of the booth.

Katie, Becky, Krista and I watched as she disappeared. For a Monday night, Flanigan's was pretty jammed. But more people meant more voices and more privacy.

"So, what's happening with the bachelorette party?" Becky asked, looking at me with her Miller blue eyes. They were almost the same colour as Braden's.

I forced a smile as I leaned forward, filling the rest of the bridesmaids in on my plans. I watched as their faces went from skeptical to delighted.

"Oh my gosh! It sounds like so much fun!" Krista declared, clapping her hands with glee. "I can't wait to see Tessa's face when we get to the male strip club."

"Male strip club?" a deep voice rumbled, startling the four of us.

The hair on the nape of my neck stood up at attention at that husky tone. I turned my head, my eyes landing on dark scruff and thick lips, twisted upwards in a bemused smile. Just like ten months ago, when he walked into the restaurant, my heart immediately started to pound frantically in my chest.

"Planning the bachelorette party, are we?" he added. His deep blue eyes caught and held my gaze, and he ran his tongue across his thick lips.

"Yes, we are. Do you mind?" I said dismissively. Braden slid into Tessa's still vacant seat beside me. I stared at him with dismay, trying to ignore the sizzling heat of his thigh brushing against mine. I moved over, desperate to break the contact, although the heat remained.

"Don't mind at all," Braden replied, his voice heavy with implication as his eyes roamed across my face. He pulled his gaze away, looking across the table at Krista, Becky and Katie. "Hey."

"What are you doing here?" Becky smiled, her eyes drifting back and forth from him to me.

"Meeting the guys for a beer. Travis just got back into town,"

Braden answered, tilting his head and glancing around the bar. His eyes rested on a table across the room, where Brock, Grady and Gordon were sitting, splitting a pitcher of beer and wings. Brock caught sight of Braden and waved, calling him over. Braden nodded once, acknowledging he'd seen them.

"You're having a beer?" Becky asked, concern lacing her tone.

I couldn't help but notice the pinched look her expression took on. Braden turned his head back towards her, almost scowling.

"No, Becky. *I'm* not having a beer," he said darkly. A silent standoff happened between the two of them. Becky assessed him and Braden stared right back, his expression hard. The atmosphere was taut with tension, but before anybody could say anything else, Tessa came back.

"Scram, Braden," she smiled, nodding towards the opposite side of the bar. "Your table is over there. We'll rendezvous once we finish our plotting."

"Alright, Tessa," he drawled, standing up.

He paused before her and kissed her on the cheek before glancing back over his shoulder at me. He winked, a cocky grin on his kissable lips. His defined muscles, clearly visible through his white t-shirt, made me forget my train of thought and lose myself completely in the fantasy of those arms holding his body above mine. The view of him walking away was almost mouth-watering, I had to remind myself who I was staring at—the man who ripped my heart out of my chest and stomped on it.

"Okay, Tessa, we're going to need a list of people you want to invite to your bachelorette party." Katie's voice brought my attention back to the table. She slid a pen and a pad of paper across the table.

"Obviously you guys," Tessa said thoughtfully, chewing on the end of the pen as she thought. "What about Laura and Olivia?"

"From Barrie?" I made a face. I'd never liked Olivia Bryant. She had been in Tessa's program and had struck me as faker than her orange spray on tan (which she seemed quite fond of).

"Oh come on," Tessa joked, shoving me gently. "If we vetoed everyone you didn't like, we would have no one left to invite!"

"Ain't that the truth," I muttered, glaring across the room. My eyes landed on Braden, who was unapologetically staring at me. My scowl intensified and I jerked my chin away, not wanting to have a stare-off. I'd always been the best at staring contests and I knew this was one I couldn't win.

I was afraid Braden would be able to see through my mask, and recognize the broken parts I desperately tried to cover up with my resting bitch face and well delivered scowls.

CHAPTER SIX

raden

SMALL TOWN LIFE as a recovering alcoholic was challenging. Everyone seemed to know my business—but then again, everyone had always known my business. My family's too.

I had to stay away from a lot of my old friends, because they didn't seem to understand the slippery slope I was precariously balanced on. One drink could just as easily turn into twelve. I hadn't touched the stuff since leaving rehab, but that didn't mean I didn't ever get thirsty for it.

Sitting at Flanigan's with the guys should have been harder, especially with the pitcher of beer in front of me. Maybe it would have been, if Elle wasn't across the room. Her presence there was enough to override my thirst for alcohol, because I had a different kind of thirst...a thirst for her.

I had a feeling she'd be at Flanigan's, which is why I hadn't turned down Brock's invitation to go out, as I usually did. Sure, Travis was back in town too—but honestly, I didn't care. Travis and I were never super close, but it gave me a solid excuse to see her again.

Now that I'd seen her, I felt dehydrated. All I wanted to do was walk back over to where she was and kiss her until I could breathe her in through my lungs, until I could feel her beneath my skin.

I'd heard whispers over the last several months that Elle wasn't single anymore. She was seeing some guy. Living with him, in fact. It had to be serious if she was living with him. I didn't want to screw things up further for her, but in the same breath...I couldn't seem to shake the thought that things weren't over between the two of us. Then again, maybe that was my dear old friend denial coming out to play.

My fingers clenched tightly around my glass, as I brought it up to my lips. The cold cola did nothing to quench the thirst, and I slammed it down harder than I intended. I closed my eyes against the sound of conversation around me, allowing myself a few moments to just breathe and centre myself.

In the last several years, I'd learned a few coping methods to help keep my dependency for alcohol in check. Meditation and taking the time to breathe, along with being self-aware were key things I had to do. Denial is an alcoholic's best friend, and I refused to allow myself to live in denial.

I'd also developed a fine appreciation for tattoos and exercising. I got my first tattoo the first year of college, and I'd quickly realized it was the perfect way to inflict the right amount of pain for a therapeutic gain. I could leave marks that meant something to me on my skin, marks that would forever remind me of where I'd been and where I never wanted to go again.

The first tattoo, the one that started it all, was a massive chest piece that started just below my collarbone, creeping downward and swooping back up to touch my shoulders. Most people don't get massive tattoos the first time around, but I had a concept in mind that I couldn't shake, and I needed it to mean something. The Roman numeral clock hands pointed to the time of my mother's death—also the time of my own descent into a personal hell. On either side of the clock were two identical roses, and flanked behind it all were incredibly detailed angel wings. Weaving around the clock and around the skull just beneath it was a beautiful string of pearls, the same pearls my mother had worn on her wedding day.

They'd been important to my mother because they'd represented hope, a hope that she'd carried with her throughout the worst years of her life. Her marriage to my father may have been a joke, he may have been an abusive piece of shit, but she still loved those pearls, even after my father had sold them at the hock shop in order to get cash for booze and gambling.

We came home to find Mom sobbing over her empty box, the same box that had once held those pearls. Without saying a word, my siblings and I put everything we had into getting her those pearls back. We didn't understand at the time why they were so important to her, but they were, and so they were important to us as well. Brock paid the majority, from his job working on Bill Armstrong's farm. I contributed eleven dollars and thirty cents that I had earned doing yard work, and Becky tossed in the fifty bucks she made babysitting for the neighbour. By a stroke of pure luck, we were able to buy them back after Dad died.

I made sure that the pearls would be etched on my skin as a reminder for evermore.

Not only did this tattoo remind me of my late mother, but it reminded me of my dickbag father too...the man that had destroyed everything that should have been good and healthy in my life. The man that had created the darkness within me.

I guess tattoos were just a way I could unleash some of the ugliness in a beautiful, artistic way. The pain of the needle entering and exiting my flesh helped to curb my desire for self-destruction.

And currently, my desire for self-destruction after the way Elle had regarded me tonight was pretty damn high. I made a mental note to find a decent studio and artist closer to home, now that I was back again.

"Braden, you alright man?" My brother's voice roused me from the complicated direction my thoughts had taken. I looked up, catching the concern behind his gray-blue eyes.

"Yeah, I'm fine. Just tired," I told him, giving him a reassuring grin. My eyes wandered again, this time pausing across the room. Brock followed my gaze and nodded with understanding, as conversation amongst the others continued on.

Travis was late getting to the bar and when he finally showed up, he brought his own entourage. Two women that were scarcely wearing any clothes trailed in, each of them holding one of Travis's arms. They looked ready for a night out in LA, not a local dive bar in a small town in Ontario. Their faces were heavily painted with makeup, their blonde hair blown out and straight down their backs. They could have been twins, for all I knew, but I was pretty sure the one on Travis's left wasn't a true blonde. Her eyebrows were darker, as were her lashes. In any case, they'd spent a lot of time and money trying to *look* like twins. It was almost comical, seeing the looks on their faces as they stepped into the dimly lit bar and looked around. I guess whatever they'd been expecting, it wasn't this.

Two tough looking guys in their thirties all dressed in black wearing sunglasses at night and a microphone came in behind Travis and the women, eyeing the bar as if searching for potential threats.

Travis tugged his arms free of the girls as he came up to our table, slapping the one on the right's rear end. "Go get something to drink. Tell Mick to put it on my tab." He said as he winked at her and nodded in the direction of the bar.

"Come on Tasha," the one whose rear he'd smacked said, linking her arm with the other girl. Both of them looked as if they smelt something vile as they walked over to the bar in their five-inch heels.

Brock stood up, almost frowning as he embraced Travis in a quick bro-hug. "What the hell is this shit man?" he asked, gesturing to the massive guys standing behind Travis. Because of Travis, we were suddenly the focus of the entire bar. I could feel the scowls from the table across the room, the table I knew Elle was at, without even looking for confirmation.

"Oh, yeah. That's Rob and Paul. They're keeping me out of trouble—and trouble away from me too. Figured it'd be smart to bring them. They can help out with security detail at the wedding, so Tessa's brothers can enjoy the ceremony and what not."

"Great job not drawing attention to yourself," Brock responded dryly. He looked as if he was having second thoughts about including Travis in his wedding party.

"Attention follows me no matter what I do," Travis said, working to keep his carefree grin in place.

"And the Hollywood twins? Who are they?" Gordon piped up.

"Tasha and Sandra? They're best friends and *super* close, if you know what I mean." Travis responded, waggling his eyebrows. "Don't worry, they're not here for the wedding. There was an issue with their flight back home, and they had a one-night layover in Toronto. They wanted to check out the old home town that inspired so many songs before they left," he added, seeing Brock's angry expression.

Dark hair flitted by, and I wasn't overly surprised to see that Becky was leaving the bar. She didn't like staying out late, even when she hired a babysitter.

"You're such a dog," Gordon laughed, standing up to give Travis a hug of his own. He looked over his shoulder at the bar where the girls were still placing their drink orders. They seemed to be having a hard time with the specialty drink menu.

My guess was that they were trying to find a beverage that contained less hops and more fruit. "Damn, they're fine! Where do you pick up these chicks?"

"These ones are from Vegas," Travis replied with a smirk, pleased that someone was impressed with his find.

"Is the media going to be a problem for us?" Brock scowled, still unimpressed.

He was probably worrying about the wedding details getting leaked to the media. That would create quite the shit storm for him and Tessa. They wanted a small, intimate wedding, not a wedding paparazzi would crash just for pictures of one of the groomsmen.

"No, Brock, it's not going to be a problem. Everyone thinks I'm just here for the show at the stampede." Travis frowned. "Speaking of brides, where is that gorgeous Tessa?"

"Right here," Tessa sounded far from impressed as she approached, flanked by an irritable Elle and a starstruck Krista. Tessa came to a stop in front of our table and Travis. She crossed her arms and tapped her foot against the old hardwood floor, her eyes narrowed. "And just what in God's name do you think you're doing, Travis Channing? You're making a goddamn scene!"

"Oh come on Tess," Travis grinned playfully, looking past her to the bar. "Flanigan's is practically empty tonight." It wasn't exactly true—Monday nights were dart club night, which meant an abundance of middle aged folks sat around drinking beer and throwing darts at the only dart board. Right now, the majority of males from the dart club were admiring the fresh sight of Travis's friends—and they were loving every second of the attention.

Tessa arched a delicate brow. "And who are the Playboy bunnies?" she added, her frown intensifying. "If I recall, the invitations said *plus guest*, as in singular, not *plus double penetration twins*."

Travis threw back his head and howled with laughter until tears formed in his emerald eyes. He tossed his arm around Tessa's shoulders and pulled her to him. "This is why I love Tessa, because she's hilarious and witty."

"Unlike the two high-class call girls you brought home?" Elle challenged, rolling her eyes. "What Travis, you can't find girls with IQs in Hollywood? As if you had to bring more trash into this town."

I'd been smiling up until Elle finished speaking. I was pretty sure that was a personal dig at me. It stung, but I deserved it and I knew it.

"Easy Elle," Tessa said, sending her a warning look. "Play nice. We don't know what their IQs are."

"Where's Becky tonight?" Travis asked, ignoring Tessa and Elle's commentary and glancing around the bar.

"She just left," Elle said through narrowed eyes. "Unlike some people around here, she has responsibilities."

"Ouch," Travis drawled. "She's feisty tonight," he added, glancing at me—as if I could somehow put a muzzle on her. That was an interesting thought...one that made me ache with the need to see if all my previous methods of keeping her quiet and making her smile still worked.

"That she is," I added, my eyes sliding over to land on hers. Elle smirked, as if reading my mind and the dirty thoughts running through it. I licked my lips slowly, and her smirk fell away.

For a moment, and just a moment, her mask of cold indifference fell away too. Her brown eyes were heavy with hurt and something akin to longing, and the set of her plump lips called to me like a siren. Then, the fleeting moment was over and Elle's mask was back in place. She turned her head away from me, slicing our eye contact as effectively as if she'd used a knife.

"Let's go, I think we've done enough planning tonight," she said to Tessa, nodding to the door.

Tessa looked at her friend for a moment. Something passed between the two of them, an unspoken conversation that I had a feeling had a lot to do with me.

"Alright, later everyone," Tessa said. Brock stood up to hug and kiss his bride-to-be goodbye. She indulged him for a moment, kissing him back with just as much passion as they'd always had, her entire body leaning into him like they were one being. Then she pulled away and fixed those amber eyes on his. "Brock, get your groomsman in line," she warned.

"Yes ma'am," Brock grinned, kissing her again before they separated. I watched Elle and Tessa head back to their table to collect their things, my heart growing more hollow with every step Elle took as she walked away from me without so much as a backwards glance.

THROUGHOUT THE NEXT DAY, I couldn't get Elle out of my head. My thoughts were consumed with her lips, her smile, her eyes, and her body as I worked.

Originally when I came back to town, I'd thought my position at Chuck's Garage would be temporary, until I found a job in my field. But a little over a month after I returned, Chuck had a heart attack.

When he was recovering from triple bypass surgery, Chuck had no choice but to finally heed my advice to hire another part-time mechanic. He'd also bestowed more responsibility on me—and he'd given me a pretty good raise. "I don't trust anybody like I trust you, Miller," he'd told me when I tried to refuse the nearly ten dollar jump in my hourly rate. It was hard to deny him when he looked so frail in that hospital bed, and I found I didn't want to. I enjoyed my job, working on vehicles gave my hands something to do while my mind ran wild with possibilities.

Now I was acting as shop manager, overseeing the new mechanic, Miles, that he'd hired fresh out of college. I was still swamped with all the work coming in, but Miles was a fast learner.

I was under old Mrs. Winston's station wagon, replacing her break lines, when two heels appeared beside my legs. One foot nudged me, and I rolled out from underneath the car.

I sat up, and scowled at Melissa. Since my return, she had been pursuing me tirelessly. I was getting real sick of it. I'd tried everything from politely expressing my unavailability to flat out ignoring her. It wasn't my fault Melissa wouldn't take the hint. Hell, I was being a hell of a lot nicer than I would have been in high school, that's for damn sure.

Melissa let out a soft sigh and leaned against the truck in the next bay, her hungry eyes roaming my body like it was some kind of twenty-four hour buffet. I suppose, to her, it was. She was dressed in a pencil skirt and a button up top with far too many buttons undone, her amble cleavage practically spilled out of her top. I knew she'd done that intentionally.

"What is it Melissa? I've got stuff to do," I grumbled, irritated at the interruption.

"It's lunch time," she drawled flirtatiously, batting her lashes at me. "Figured you'd want to have a break, maybe grab a bite to eat with me?"

"I'm working," I reminded her, my brow creasing with annoyance. "Mrs. Winston is waiting on her vehicle. It needs to be finished before her hair appointment is over." I added, rolling back beneath the car. Melissa stood there for several long minutes, and then she thankfully walked back to the office.

"Sure you aren't hungry?" Miles snickered from the engine bay beside the one I was working on. He'd been with the shop for a few months now, and he was familiar with Melissa's blatant come-ons and loved to razz me about it. He thought it was the funniest fucking thing.

75

"Get back to work," I scowled.

An hour later, I passed the keys off to Melissa to hand to Mrs. Winston, along with the bill for the work I'd done. The tight lines around her lips and eyes showed me that she was offended that I had refused to take a break with her, but I couldn't care less about Melissa's feelings.

"We got a call for a tow," she said, handing me the information stiffly. I took it without another word, grabbing the keys to the tow truck off the hook behind the counter. There was no sense in apologizing to Melissa. She'd get over it and get right back to hitting on me again tomorrow.

I walked out of the garage and into the bright sunlight, wiping my grease covered hands on my work jeans as I pulled my pack of smokes out from my shirt pocket. I was itching for some nicotine in the worst way. The tow truck was parked out front, and I climbed in, grateful for the quick break away from the ever overbearing Melissa.

I drove to the location written on the paper, and found a red Camry pulled over to the side of the highway, the engine smoking. "Well I'll be damned," I muttered, shaking my head in wonderment.

Long, toned legs and a delectable ass cased in denim greeted me as I got out, slamming the door behind me. I approached slowly, my thirst acutely growing. I'd know that ass and those legs anywhere. I licked my lips, repressing a grin. *It must be my lucky day,* I thought.

"Oh thank God," Elle spun around, her long hair catching in the wind. The relief fell from her face as she stared at me. "Seriously? Could this day get any worse?" she added, a frown pulling those thick lips down.

"I don't know, I was going to ask if this day could get any better," I chuckled, crossing my arms and surveying the mess of her car. "What happened?"

"I don't know, that's why I called for a bloody tow and mechanic," Elle retorted, exasperated with me.

"You called the right guy," I smirked. I knew I was a sight for sore eyes, covered in grease and dirt. Mechanics don't exactly have the cleanest job out there, but I also knew how much Elle used to love the sight of me all dirty after a day of work. Sometimes, I could scarcely shower before she jumped my bones.

Elle bit her tongue, holding back the retort that I know was sitting on the very edge of it. Thinking about Elle's tongue made me feel a little hot under the collar, so I got to work hooking her car up to the tow truck.

I could feel her eyes on me as I worked. I knew she was checking me out. You don't spend every day with someone for over two years, having crazy wild sex with them, and not know when they're checking you out. I may have made a bit of a show for her too, flexing muscles and taking my time.

"Are you going to finish this up any time soon? I'm supposed to meet Tessa at the florist's," Elle snapped, her patience waning. I looked at her over my shoulder.

"Why don't you come and hurry me up, then?" I dared, smirking at her. She huffed at me and rolled her eyes, her arms folded protectively across her chest.

"I wouldn't touch you with a twelve-foot long pole, Braden Miller. But if you don't hurry up, Tessa will kick your ass from here to next week," she replied, the corner of her lip lifting in an adorable sneer.

She had a point. I stopped fucking around and got Elle's car safely secured. "Can I give you a lift?" I asked, nodding to the tow truck.

"Looks like you're going to have to, now, doesn't it? Had I known *you* were driving the tow truck I would have arranged another ride but I'm late enough already," she grumbled, sounding completely unhappy with the arrangement as she stomped over to the passenger door and yanked it open. "Hurry up," she added, annoyed that I was still standing there.

Running a hand through my messy hair, I shook my head with a rueful smile. Elle was just as feisty as she'd been the other night, and it was fucking turning me on in the worst way possible. The last thing I needed right now was to pop a boner.

I climbed in and Elle's familiar scent washed over me like a wave of nostalgia, making me smile and ache at the same time. She still smelt like the sweetest mixture of apple blossoms, jasmine and French vanilla. It was the same perfume she'd worn in high school, the very perfume I'd bought her for our six-month anniversary and every other important date after that.

"Still wearing that perfume, huh?" I asked her, trying to suppress a grin. It had to mean something, right? I was the one that bought it for her, and here she was...years later, still wearing it.

Elle froze, my words doing something to her...and I wasn't at all sure if it was a *good* something. "Just drive," she said through clenched teeth.

Instead, I regretted my poor choice of words. If only I could take them back. Hell, if only I could take back everything I'd done to hurt this beautiful girl.

I cleared my throat, pursing my lips. "Yes ma'am," I said before checking my blind spot to make sure I was safe to pull back out onto the highway.

Elle fiddled with the stereo, trying to fill the endless void of silence that stretched on between the two of us. I had a million things I wanted to say to her.

"The stereo system doesn't work," I said, my eyes sliding over to her face. She stiffened again, her hand frozen on the dial.

"Why in the hell does the tow truck of a *garage* have a busted stereo? Isn't that giving the wrong impression?" she asked haughtily, sitting back in her seat and folding her arms across her chest, as if she was suddenly cold. My eyes dropped down, and I swallowed hard. Her protective stance wasn't doing much protecting. In fact, her folded arms just made the tops of her breasts spill out from her little tank top even more.

I grinned and shrugged, forcing my eyes back to the road before I drove right off it. "Or maybe it shows that we're more concerned with keeping said tow truck available for people who need tows. We only have one, and most people don't care too much. *Most* people don't mind talking to me. Hell, I'd say a lot of them even like to talk to me."

"I bet they do," she said dryly, eyeing me with her lips pinched into a tight line.

I pulled up to the garage and parked the truck haphazardly in the lot. Tessa was driving Brock's truck, and already waiting out front. Elle went to unbuckle her seat belt, and I turned to her. "Let me take you out to dinner," I said, my voice sounding borderline desperate.

Elle stopped what she was doing and slowly raised her eyes to meet mine. Her brow furrowed slightly, the tiniest tell-tale sign of her confusion. "Why on earth would you want to do that?"

"I need to explain," I said quickly, sensing she was going to bolt at any minute. "I need to apologize."

"Maybe I don't want an explanation, or an apology," Elle's eyes narrowed with disdain. "Maybe I want you to stay exactly where you belong—in my past." She finished unbuckling her seat belt and went to open the truck door. My hand automatically shot out to wrap around her wrist gently. We both looked down at the contact.

"Maybe," I said, forcing the word out. It was sharp and unpleasant sounding, just as sharp and unpleasant as it had felt to say. The possibility that Elle wanted me to stay in the past was painful. "Or maybe you do need this, hell I know I do."

My words made Elle take pause. I could see the thoughts racing through her head.

"Besides," I added, releasing her wrist. "It'd be nice to get on a semi-good basis with one another...for Tessa. We'll be seeing a lot of each other over the next several weeks, and I don't want any animosity between the two of us at the wedding." I knew it was a cheap shot, but I also knew it would work. Elle looked over to where her best friend—my soon to be sister-in-law—was patiently waiting. Tessa looked as if she was hopped up on caffeine and sugar. She was all but bouncing on the heels of her feet.

"I'll think about it," Elle relented grouchily. She opened the door and slid out.

I watched as she walked towards Tessa, her hips swinging subtly with every step she took.

CHAPTER SEVEN

*lle*

"WHAT WAS *THAT* ALL ABOUT?" Tessa asked me, her eyes wide as she watched Braden back the tow truck up into the garage, my poor little car hooked up and looking quite helpless.

I scowled over my shoulder in his general direction, trying to ignore the tingles his touch had left upon my skin, trying to ignore the fact that I felt alive for the first time in forever. "What do you think it was all about? My stupid car broke down, I called for a tow from the only tow service in town which happens to be run by the only garage in town, which *he* happens to work at!"

"Ah, I thought you knew he was working here again."

"No, I don't seem to know a lot of things about him anymore, do I? But it doesn't matter. Again, it's the *only* garage and the *only* tow service in town." I reminded her bitterly as I climbed up into the cab of Brock's truck. "Sorry I'm late."

"These things happen," Tessa waved away my apology with

her hand. "I'm just glad you're okay."

I huffed in response. *Okay* wasn't a word I'd used to describe myself right about now. I was a jumbled mess of nerves and anxiety.

Ever since that moment at the bar the other night, when Braden's eyes slid over to mine and he'd gazed at me with unrepressed desire, I'd felt off-centre. Probably because for a fleeting moment, I'd wanted him too.

It was just like my dreams, only a thousand times worse because he was *here* and I was just as powerless to those deep blue eyes as I'd been in every dream I'd had for the last ten months. The only thing that had stopped me from acting like a fool and giving in to those feelings was the cracks in my heart. Braden had broken me once before, and I knew he'd do it again.

Plus, there was Alex. I didn't know what I felt for him anymore, but I knew with utmost sincerity that I didn't want to hurt him.

He called me every night, and I had long since run out of things to tell him. Planning a wedding was exhausting. I didn't have anything important to add to our conversations, so I let him rattle on and on about work and hemmed and hawed in all the right places, all the while falling deeper and deeper into a pit of self-loathing and despair.

Thinking about pits of despair and self-loathing had me remembering the other night, at the bar, and the odd stand-off between Becky and Braden.

All my thoughts circled back to him, and it was driving me crazy.

"Hello? Where did you go?" Tessa waved her hand in front of my face, trying to capture my attention.

"Sorry, I'm just worrying about the car," I sighed. "I really can't afford a huge mechanics bill right now." I really couldn't—the mere thought about how much this was going to run me had my stomach twisting with anxiety.

"I wouldn't worry about that," Tessa said with confidence. Before I could ask her what she meant, we had arrived at the florist shop. She parked out front and turned to face me. She saw the questions on my face and shook her head, her beautiful blonde mane dancing against her shoulders with the action. "You and me, we're going to need to talk about this later. Right now, we're an hour late for a very important florist appointment."

I nodded obediently, not wanting to irritate Bridezilla. If Tessa's wedding had taught me anything, it was that even the most laid back of brides can turn into total monsters if provoked during this stressful time.

It was nearly eight at night, and I had yet to hear back from the garage—ahem, *Braden*—about my car. I had spent the majority of the day stressing about it while trying to provide my best services as a maid of honor to Tessa. I *really* couldn't afford to get a new vehicle right now, hell I hadn't been able to afford that one when I bought it and I was still paying it off. I didn't know what I was going to do if it was beyond repair, or hell...if it ended up costing more than what was currently sitting in my savings account. Plus, there was the bachelorette party to think of, and the fact that I wouldn't be back at work for at *least* a month—my car issues couldn't have come at a worse time.

I was in the kitchen, making myself a cup of chamomile tea when the sound of knuckles tapping against the screen door startled me. I sloshed half of the tea on the white t-shirt I was wearing. Cursing, I set the mug down on the counter and crossly walked over to see who was calling at this hour. Mom hadn't been home when I got back from running errands with Tessa and still wasn't.

Walking into the foyer, I could see Braden's tall outline

through the screen door as he stood on the porch. He had his back to me and was looking out towards the driveway. He'd obviously changed his clothes since earlier that morning—he was wearing clean jeans and a gray t-shirt now. His hands were in his pockets, his forearm muscles taut.

I appreciated the view for a moment, feeling guilty for doing so—but Braden had filled out in the last several years. The ink on his arms just added to that bad boy feel he'd always had. It really wasn't fair. A part of me had hoped that he'd be miserable and unsuccessful, but from the little bits of information I'd managed to discreetly tug from Tessa—he'd graduated at the top of the mechanical engineering technology program he'd taken, and his attractiveness had only increased with age.

My heart started to thrum rapidly in my chest. I tugged at my white t-shirt, now stained and damp from the spilt tea, and became extremely self-conscious of my too-short sleep shorts. I definitely *wasn't* expecting company. In fact, I'd been expecting a quiet evening in where I could reflect upon how confused I was about everything in my life and how powerless I felt about fixing it all. The last thing I needed was one of my mental tormentors showing up at my doorstep, literally.

"What are you doing here?" I demanded, opening the screen door cautiously. Braden turned slowly, his eyes rising slowly from my bare feet up. It was as if he could physically touch me through his gaze, leaving goosebumps in its wake.

"Your radiator had a leak and your engine overheated, but I've replaced it and you're good to go."

"Oh, thank you," I managed, crossing my arms across my chest when his eyes lingered a little too long at my girls.

"I thought I'd bring you your keys and see if you wanted a lift," Braden added, his voice sounding strained as he finally pried his eyes up to my face. He swallowed hard, his Adams apple bobbing with the action.

"Thanks again," I told him, holding out one hand. He remained still, uncertain. I looked down at my clothes. "But...I'm not exactly dressed to go out right now, Braden...although I do appreciate the gesture. I'll just have my mom take me over in the morning."

"Right, yeah," he said quickly, fishing in his pocket for my keys. "Well, if it's any consolation—I think you look incredibly sexy," he told me with a smirk, finding the keys and pulling them out. He handed them to me, our fingers brushing for the briefest of moments. My skin sizzled where he'd made contact with it, just like this morning in the tow truck.

I know he felt it too, from the way he pulled back as if the contact had burned. He swallowed hard, his eyes lifting from our hands to my chest, then to my collarbone, and finally landing on my eyes. His gaze smoldered.

"Braden," I warned. My heart clenched in my chest, like a fist was squeezing it. His eyes hardened, and his hand dropped to his side.

"Okay, well. I'll catch you later then," he said, pursing his lips. He turned around, walking quickly down the front steps and back to his truck.

A heaviness settled into my chest, and I closed my eyes at the sound of his tires kicking up gravel as he sped down my driveway.

THE NEXT MORNING, I woke up early. I had a shower and took my time picking out an outfit for the day. I needed to pick up my car and find out how much the repair set me back before Mom, Tessa and I went out shopping for Mom's dress for the wedding.

Mom's usual outfit of choice was a pair of worn blue jeans and a t-shirt. In fact, I hadn't seen her in a dress in years—

discounting the box of photographs I'd found from her modelling days, of course.

These days, she didn't put much time or effort into her appearance at all. I used to think it was because she was a single mom and didn't have many opportunities to dress up. When I was sixteen, I'd stumbled across that box in the attic though, and I realized that maybe she'd distanced herself from that world because it was too painful.

My mom had met my dad through mutual friends. He was a solider in the Royal Canadian Army. They'd fallen in love and married quickly. He was charming and brave, and adventurous. Mom was instantly drawn to him. Shortly after I was born, he deployed to Afghanistan. In 2002, he died during a combat mission. Mom never really moved on from him—not that I blamed her. From what I remembered; he'd been amazing.

Current wardrobe aside, my mother was a stunning woman. I'd gotten my dark hair and thick lashes from her, and most of my features as well. The big difference was that she had green eyes, while I had my father's brown eyes.

After Dad died, Mom moved back to her family farm and stopped caring about clothes and makeup. She invested herself completely in me, Tessa's family, and the community. She filled the empty parts he'd left in her with meaningful relationships, but she'd never given her heart away again.

I exhaled, trying to force my thoughts away from my late father. Instead, I studied my reflection in the mirror. There was a very real possibility that I'd run into Braden again at the garage, and I *needed* to look hot. I wanted him to see what he was missing out on, and I wanted him to regret it. I wanted to punish him a little.

I had chosen a patterned sundress, my tight blue jean jacket and a pair of flip flops. I'd gone for a natural look in the makeup department and left my long hair down, letting it fall in soft waves down my back.

Once I was satisfied with my reflection, I walked down the stairs to the kitchen. Mom was sitting at the table, sipping a glass of orange juice and reading the paper. The front page of it boasted an article about Travis Channing being back in the Muskoka's.

"Oh God, seriously?" I grumbled, snagging the paper from her to read. My eyes scanned the article, searching for any details that might have leaked to the media. The article was mostly detailing how he'd be headlining at the Parry Sound Stampede, although it did mention he was also in town for a friend's wedding. Thankfully, it didn't reveal which friend or the date of the event.

"Don't worry, I already checked," Mom smiled, shaking her head. "Not sure what they expected from him. Travis has always been a bit of an attention seeker."

"An attention whore, more like," I grumbled, dropping the paper back down on the table as I thought about that night at the bar, when Travis had sauntered in with his entourage. The look on Becky's face when she saw him was like she'd seen a horrific accident occur. She was ghostly pale and had made an excuse to leave immediately. "You should have seen the women he brought to Flanigan's."

"With fame and money comes a lot of bad decisions," Mom smiled sadly. "He'll get tired of it. He may be restless now, but behind all that restlessness is a heart that needs a home."

"I think you've said that about every guy in this town," I arched a brow, remembering how she used to say the same thing about Braden. "Maybe you just mean to say they're all *bored* and can't keep their pricks in their pants."

Mom chuckled and shook her head. She stood up, bringing her dishes to the kitchen sink. "That may be true, but they eventually settle down. Most of them, anyway."

I was long since used to my mother's view on love. While she had never dated anyone after my dad to my knowledge, she still wanted to believe in love. She still wanted *me* to believe in it.

"Whatever you say Mom. Any chance you could take me to the garage to pick up my car?" I asked, changing the subject so she wouldn't feel the need to broach the B topic.

"Of course, are you ready to go now? I'll drop you off, then I need to swing by the Armstrong's." She turned back to the counter.

"Why?" I tilted my head, my brow furrowing slightly. Mom waited until she'd finished rinsing her dishes to reply. She turned around, leaning against the counter and gave me her best smile.

"I need to pester Bill. He's got to do his speech for the wedding, and Lord knows he'll put it off until the last minute and be woefully unprepared."

"Woefully unprepared?" I said with amusement. "He should just make you write it."

"I've got my own speech to write," Mom smiled, pushing off the counter. She grabbed her purse from the hook by the door and headed outside. I followed her, shaking my head.

When I was little, I used to wish that Mom and Bill would fall in love and get married. I loved going over to the Armstrong's house. I'd always felt like a part of the family and at one point, I got it into my head that it would be perfect if Bill and my mom tied the knot. Only I knew that it would never happen: Bill had been madly in love with Tessa's mom, and even though she'd been dead for a long time, he had never gotten over her. Plus, Tessa's mom had been my mom's best friend. I knew without a doubt I could never entertain the thought of falling for the love of Tessa's life. Bill and Mom were kindred spirits; both of them raising their kids alone despite heartbreak.

Once we got to the garage, I grabbed my purse and told my mom I'd meet her back home in a couple of hours to go shopping before I slid out. I watched her drive away before I started walking towards the office door. I passed Braden's old Chevy S10, the same one he had in high school. Remorse settled on my shoulders as the memories that accompanied that truck washed over me. I didn't know why I was feeling remorse...it wasn't like I'd ripped Braden's heart into pieces. Frowning, I opened up the office door and walked inside.

Chuck's Garage was tiny and cramped. It smelt like metal and grease and was completely empty save for the receptionist sitting behind the front desk. Like most people in town, she looked vaguely familiar but I couldn't recall her name—she hadn't been in the office when I'd left my contact information. She had curly strawberry blonde hair cut in a bob and freckles that dotted her nose.

She looked up when the door closed behind me. The easy smile she'd been wearing prior to looking up vanished. "Guess you're here for the Camry." She said, without a note of friendliness.

I arched a brow, wondering what I'd done to deserve this icy reception. As far as I'd known, I had never had a falling out with her before, although her voice seemed slightly familiar as well as her appearance. Suddenly, it dawned on me.

"Oh! You're Chuck's niece, aren't you? Michelle? You dated Gordon for a bit?" I exclaimed, picking up the receipt without looking at it right away.

"It's *Melissa*," she corrected hotly, her eyes narrowing at me. "And that was forever ago."

"Sorry, Melissa. How much do I owe?" I asked, stopping before the desk. I looked down, searching through my purse for my wallet.

"Nothing. You don't owe a thing," she responded coldly. I looked back up at her, blinking blankly.

"Pardon?" I asked. Melissa responded by rolling her eyes and gestured to the paper in my hand. I read the receipt. There was no price on the bill, just a summary of what work had been done and Braden's signature at the bottom right corner. "But... Braden said he had to replace the radiator?"

Melissa made a strange sound of exasperation and rolled her eyes again, as if I was the most obtuse person in the world and she didn't have any patience at all to deal with me. "Obviously, *someone* covered it for you. Although I have no idea why he'd do such a thing," she muttered, suddenly focusing all of her attention on her computer screen.

Realization struck me like a bus. "That goddamn bastard," I swore, seething with anger. "Where is he?"

The world's most unhelpful receptionist shrugged a shoulder, refusing to respond or look at me. I tore out of the office and into the parking lot. Braden's truck and the tow truck were parked out front, so it was obvious he was here somewhere. My best bet was inside the garage. That's where one would usually find a mechanic, anyway.

One of the garage doors was open, so I stomped inside. "Braden Miller! Get your ass out here right now!"

A young guy dressed in blue coveralls with the name *Miles* embroidered on the pocket looked up from the car he was working on. He spotted me, standing with my hand on my hip and fire in my eyes, and grinned.

"Jesus Braden, what'd you do now?" he asked with amusement, turning his head towards the right side of the garage. I followed his gaze to a sedan. Braden was leaning into the engine bay, some kind of wrench or socket in his hand. He didn't bother looking up from his task.

"Fuck off Miles. Take your break now," Braden responded without looking up from the car. Miles set his wrench down and chuckled, heading to the office to give us some privacy. I watched him leave, my foot tapping impatiently against the floor. "Most people would just say thank you and carry on with their day," he finally said, his muscles straining as he worked the wrench to get some part free.

It was a distracting sight, and I had to clamp my mouth shut for a moment to prevent myself from drooling.

"Why did you pay for it, Braden?" I demanded, my eyes narrowed with anger. I stalked closer to him, my eyes never leaving his face. "I never asked you to do that."

He looked up, his eyes instantly locking with mine. "I felt like being charitable," he shrugged, smirking.

"I don't need your goddamn charity! Go be charitable to someone else," I hissed.

"Where's the fun in that when you respond so graciously?" he laughed.

"Tell me how much it was and I will pay in the office," I ordered, my teeth practically grinding together in aggravation. I didn't want to feel indebted to him in any way.

Braden crossed his arms, his muscles flexing, distracting me from my anger for a moment. He leaned against the car he'd been working on, a devious glint to his deep blue eyes that immediately set me on edge and aroused me, despite my best efforts to remain angry and unresponsive. "If you want to thank me, let me take you out for dinner."

"Dinner?" I frowned, the confusion I felt apparent on my face.

"Yeah, you know...the final big meal of the day, usually the best. Happens anywhere from five until eight, depending on the people and the schedule," his smirk widened. It was obvious that Braden was having a blast toying with me.

"I know what dinner is, smart ass," I growled, my skin hot and my mood aggravated. "I just don't know why you're trying to blackmail me into going out for dinner with you."

His expression softened as a yearning replaced the deviousness in his eyes. His lips loosened from their taunting smile, easing into a gentle one. "I already told you, I want a chance to explain...and apologize."

We stood there, staring at each other for several long beats as I contemplated my options. On the one hand, it seemed that Braden *really* wanted a chance to explain himself. In all the years we'd been apart, I'd never heard a whisper of an explanation. On the other hand, I was with Alex, and the last thing I wanted to do was hurt him in a quest to find out why a relationship that had been over for years had ended. I should be over it. I told myself for years I was, hell...I was with someone else now.

I had a feeling I'd never be able to let Braden Miller go if I indulged him and let him explain his reasoning. I was afraid that I'd understand, and that I'd forgive him. I'd been down this road once before.

But something was pulling me to him. We were like two magnets, drawn to each other without rhyme or reason. It was the same pull that had attracted me to him in the first place. It hadn't lessened at all in the time we'd spent apart. If anything, it had grown stronger, and I was terrified to test that theory. It would only end in heartbreak and sorrow. Braden's, mine, or Alex's—it didn't matter. I didn't want anybody else getting hurt.

"Well? You gonna give me an answer so I can get back to work, or are you just going to stand there and look at me like that all day? Cause if it's the latter, I won't be able to stop myself from pressing you against that truck and kissing you until I make up your mind for you."

"You really expect me to say yes after that?" I frowned, my heart pounding in response to his threat.

Braden chuckled as he turned back to his project. He picked up the wrench, looking at me briefly before he looked back at the engine. "You're going to say yes and hear me out, because I know you want to. You're just hesitating because you can't trust yourself around me."

"I trust myself around you just fine," I retorted, scowling. *Lies, lies, lies.* "I just don't trust *your* intentions."

"Maybe you shouldn't," Braden looked up, that devious grin back in place. "But that's not going to stop you from saying yes

—because you're not a coward, Elle. You've never been afraid to face things before, so why would you start now?"

Goddamn him. "Fine. I'll go out for dinner with you. But you're wrong."

"We'll see. I'll pick you up at seven tonight," Braden grinned, not looking up again.

"I'll drive myself, thank you," I said, turning around and heading out of the garage.

"You don't know where we're going, and I'm not telling you. So, be ready at seven," he called after me, the amusement evident in his voice.

I knew arguing with Braden would just be a waste of my time—and his. Once he got an idea in his head, it was impossible trying to talk him out of it. Instead, I bit my tongue as I walked over to my Camry. I could see Melissa peeking her head out the office window, a scowl glued to her face.

I waved at her, giving a catty smile that matched her disdain towards me. I didn't know what I'd done to get her to act the way she did, but considering she was already pissed off at me, I might as well drop the nice act myself. I never really had the patience to fake relationships. People either loved me or they hated me, and vice versa. I wasn't outright rude to people intentionally, but I also didn't stand for passive aggressive bitchiness. I was more in-your-face bitchy, especially if someone was treating me or someone I loved poorly.

I slammed my car door, and shoved my key into the ignition. The car purred to life, sounding better than ever. My eyes darted to my rear view mirror, and I caught a glimpse of Braden, as he watched me peel out of the parking lot.

My mind refused to shut off the entire ride back to my house. Mom's truck was still gone, so I didn't bother pulling up the driveway. Instead, I headed to the Armstrong's farm. Maybe Tessa would have a few minutes to listen to me bitch and moan about Braden before we all went shopping.

Just as I was pulling up the Armstrong's driveway, my cell phone rang. I fished it out of my purse and answered it—a total no-no when driving, but I was on private property and the only danger I faced was running into the ditch or perhaps one of Bill's cows (which in hindsight, wouldn't be very good for the cow *or* for me).

"Hello?"

"Hey babe, it's me. Just checking in," Alex's voice rang through the speaker. His voice had a magical way of soothing and relaxing me. It was the chamomile tea of voices.

"Hey, how are you?" I bit my lip, thinking about the plans I'd made with my ex-boyfriend for dinner.

"I'm good, missing my girl. What are you up to today?" he asked. I knew he was smiling. Alex was always smiling and rarely ever moody. If Braden was a stormy sea, Alex was the calm lake.

"I'm just about to drag my mom away from Tessa's dad to go dress shopping, actually," I told him. I hesitated for a moment on telling him about meeting Braden for dinner.

"Oh yeah, dress shopping with your mom should be fun. Doesn't she hate that kind of thing?" Alex laughed. I could hear his affection for me in his voice, and it made me wistful.

"Yeah, she does. It should take all of five minutes if she has her way. Longer, if I have mine," I laughed uneasily. I had no idea how to interject with the ex-boyfriend bomb. How do you tell your current boyfriend that your ex-boyfriend, who you still have intense physical feelings for, wants to take you out for dinner to explain himself? Or that he paid a really hefty repair bill on your car? Alex wasn't exactly the jealous type, but that didn't mean he'd accept that news with a smile.

The choppy sound of the radio in the ambulance calling for a team to head to a local public school interrupted Alex before he could respond. "Sorry babe, I've got to go. I'll give you a call later tonight—hope you have fun with your mom and Tessa today!"

"Yeah, okay. Thanks…and be safe," I told him.

During our conversation, I'd finished driving up Tessa's driveway and had parked beside my mom's truck. Tessa was waiting for me on the front porch, grinning from ear to ear.

"You should see the two of them in there, bickering like an old married couple," she shook her head.

Normally, I'd joke along with her and laugh about how ridiculous our parents were. But today, I didn't feel like doing that. Instead, I walked up to the porch and sat down heavily on the front step.

"What's wrong?" Tessa asked, sliding down beside me.

"Braden paid my car repair bill so that I'd owe nothing when I picked it up today," I sighed.

"Gee, sounds terrible. What a jerk," she responded dryly. I nudged her shoulder with mine.

"Don't be a dick," I frowned. "You're my best friend, you have to side with me. We're angry about this because now I'm indebted to him."

"What, does he expect a blowjob as thanks or something?"

I almost laughed, because the old Braden totally *would* have expected a blowjob after doing something nice…although I wasn't going to completely rule that out, not after the hungry way he'd looked at me. "He wants me to go out for dinner with him tonight. He's not taking no for an answer."

Tessa didn't seem surprised at all by this news. I stared at her, my mouth agape with disbelief. "Please tell me you're not in on this."

"I'm not 'in' on anything," she argued, frowning. "But when has Braden *ever* taken no for an answer? I knew he couldn't keep his distance for long."

"What are you talking about?"

"Are you blind?" she demanded, giving me an incredulous

look. "Braden is still carrying a very heavy torch for you. Anybody could see it. Hell, I think Mr. Smith can see it and he actually *is* blind. Legally."

"Right so then dinner is a terrible idea, as I suspected," I groaned, thinking about how he challenged me into saying yes by pointing out that I had never let fear run my decisions before.

Lately, that's all I did. I let fear run my life. I let it chase me away from a job I had loved. I let it keep me silent. I let it build walls around my heart.

I wanted to be fearless Elle again.

"I don't know about that," Tessa shrugged. "I do think you need to sit down and hash out the past, especially if the two of you are ever going to move forward."

"I'm not sure I want to hear him out," I sighed again, feeling confused and conflicted.

Tessa's fingers tapped against the wood of the porch as she thought. After several long minutes, she finally turned to speak, her expression empathetic and compassionate. "I don't think you've put your relationship with Braden behind you. I think it still lives in your heart and your skin, and I think it's trying to claw its way out...so I do believe you need to hear him out, if only to get the closure you need to move on with Alex. You do want to move on with Alex, right?"

I hesitated long enough for Tessa's eyebrow to shoot up in a questioning look. "I'm not sure. I've been feeling kind of...stuck for a while. Even before I came back to town," I dropped my eyes to my lap. If I couldn't speak the whole truth, I could at least share a morsel of it. "I wanted to move forward with Alex...but I'm not sure. I have feelings for him, but they're..."

"Not poignant?" she supplied, a sad smile on her lips. I nodded. "Elle, you've always been the most fiery, passionate person I've known...and I've noticed that you don't burn for him the way you should when you're in love."

"That's because I'm not in love," I confessed. It hurt to admit such a thing out loud. I'd been denying it for so long, hoping my feelings would change and grow. So far, they hadn't. If anything, I'd become more and more numb, more and more detached. I didn't know if this was just another unfortunate side effect of PTSD, or if I was on the wrong path. I had loved my job *so much* when I first started working, now the mere thought of returning made me feel sick with dread.

Since arriving home, I'd still had episodes of panic—like when my car broke down on the side of the highway—but it was *nothing* like it was in Barrie. Here, I felt different. I felt like healing was a real possibility now, but I had no idea what that meant for me—or my future.

Sensing my heartache, Tessa threw her arms around my shoulders and pulled me to her. A single tear escaped, trailing down my chin like a silent punctuation mark on my revelation.

"Have you told Alex how you feel?"

"How can I tell him? We live together, we *work* together. Besides, maybe I'm just depressed. Maybe my feelings for Alex are being blocked out by that."

"If anything, I think you're unhappy in life. You need to make changes." Tessa said wisely. "You need to tell Alex how you truly feel, because I think the guilt of knowing and not telling him is weighing heavily on you and making everything a thousand times worse."

"Yeah, maybe," I sighed, mulling it over.

"Elle, I don't think this has anything to do with Braden. I mean, not like how you're thinking. I think you just don't feel that level of passion for Alex that you did for Braden, and it's making you take pause—which is a good thing. You want that, you need it. You function on 'crazy, can't get enough of you' passion. That doesn't mean you need to forgive Braden, that doesn't mean he's the only one you'll ever have that kind of love with—but maybe it just means that Alex *isn't* that person. There might be someone else out there who is, though," Tessa finished her grand speech by nudging her body into mine and softening her words with a gentle smile.

I exhaled, massaging my temple with my fingers. "I hear what you're saying. But Alex has been good to me...he's been good *for* me."

Tessa watched me cautiously. "This is about more than your love life, isn't it?" She was giving me an opening, all but pleading me with her eyes. She could see me warring with myself between telling her the truth about what was happening in my life and closing down. I desperately wanted to close down. I didn't want to burden my best friend with my drama—especially not with the wedding and all the stress she was facing. "Don't shut down, Elle. Tell me what's going on—I know something's happening. You're not acting like yourself. At first I thought it was the whole wedding thing and having to see Braden again...but I know that's not it. At least not completely." She paused again, the wheels turning quickly in her mind. "Oh my God, are you pregnant Elle?!"

"Hell no!" I hissed, looking behind us to the screen door to make sure Tessa's voice hadn't carried. "I am not pregnant," I told her, frowning.

"Then?" Tessa pressed, her amber eyes wide. She wasn't letting go and I knew she wouldn't until I fessed up.

I drew my legs up against my chest, making myself into a small little ball. I couldn't meet her eyes, so I spoke to my knees. "I have post-traumatic stress disorder." My voice was barely above a whisper. "My boss—and doctor—insisted that I take some time off to try and deal with my symptoms."

Tessa sighed and pulled me against her, wrapping her arms around my body. "I'm so sorry Elle. I had no idea, why didn't you tell me? And here I've been, adding a shit ton of stress on you and making you worry about my silly wedding when you should be focusing on yourself." Her voice was thick with emotion, as if she was struggling not to cry.

"No, it's fine. Really, the wedding is a good distraction for me. And honestly...I didn't know how to tell people. I still don't, my mom doesn't know yet. Only Alex knew."

"You're not ashamed, are you?" Tessa demanded, pulling away just enough to meet my gaze with a determined look in her eyes. "You have nothing to be ashamed of. Your job is high-stress, you've seen things most people couldn't handle. You've saved lives and you've put yourself in danger on a regular basis."

"And I can't handle it, any of it," I responded, my voice breaking a little. "I want to, so badly. I want to handle this job. I want to save lives...I just...I can't turn it off. Ever. I can't get the images out of my head. It got to the point where I couldn't even sit in the ambu-lance—let alone answer a call—without having a full blown panic attack. That's not fair to my partner...and even though it's Alex, even though he understands...I hated that I was putting him in danger by not being one hundred percent focused on the job. At first, I dreaded the idea of coming home...but now that I'm here, I'm not all that sure that I want to go back. I don't know what I'm supposed to do—I can't just give up on my job, on my career."

"Well, you don't have to decide today, do you?" Tessa asked, arching a brow. I shook my head, sighing. "Then let's just focus on the now. Take things one day at a time. Let yourself breathe and just be."

"Yeah," I said, sounding every bit as unconvinced as I felt. We sat in silence for a few moments, Tessa's arms still around me. We turned at the sound of the screen door clanging as Mom stepped out onto the porch followed by a sheepish looking Bill.

"What's going on?" Mom asked, looking between the two of us with suspicion.

"Nothing, just waiting on you," Tessa answered with a smile as she stood up. "Are you ready to find your dress?"

CHAPTER EIGHT

raden

FOR THE REST of the day, I kept watching the clock. The hands moved painfully slow and yet—at the same time—agonizingly fast. Asking Elle out for dinner was an impulsive move. Yeah, I wanted to take her out, and I definitely wanted to be in her company again. I had to apologize to her, I had to make her understand that I'm not the same guy I was—that I won't ever break her heart or take her for granted again.

I didn't exactly leave myself enough time to come up with the perfect speech. Hell, I didn't think I'd ever have enough time to come up with the right things to say to make everything better, to erase the hurt I'd obviously caused her. Words had never been my strong suit. Communication wasn't my forte. I spoke by actions and gestures. My family knew I cared about them because I'd do anything for them—even dig myself out of an empty pit of self-destruction with my bare hands.

As for Elle…well, I had always showed my affection by physical touch and wordless glances. I used to just look at her and be able to convey every thought I couldn't put out there. She'd always just...known. She'd known what I needed and exactly how to get me to open up.

But she wasn't mine anymore. I couldn't touch her to reassure her of how deeply and truly I felt for her. She belonged to someone else, and even though I could tell she would respond to my touch the way she always had—she wasn't ready to. She'd never forgive herself if she gave in that easily to me. To Elle, this was about her pride. I'd hurt her pride, and she wasn't going to make it easy for me to get close again.

And it shouldn't be easy for me. I should have to work damn hard to prove myself, because Elle deserved that, and I was willing to do that.

Even still, dinner this soon wasn't a good idea, but she'd said yes and I'd be damned if I would walk away from any second of time spent with her.

When five o'clock finally rolled around, I rushed home and practically flew down the basement stairs to my domain, barely saying a word to my sister and nephew in passing. I was in the shower within seconds, not even allowing the water to heat up before submerging myself under the icy droplets.

I was completely keyed up, my entire body pulsing with the knowledge that I would soon be in her company. My mind easily recalled the memory of Elle, leaning forward against the engine of her little car yesterday. The shorts that she was wearing had hardly covered the globes of her ass cheeks. And just like that, I was rock hard. The cold water pellets did nothing to ease the desire coursing through my body.

I knew I wasn't going to be able to focus on anything until I dealt with my sexual frustration. I placed one of my hands against the tile of the shower and fisted my cock with the other, slowly pumping as I pictured her. The way she'd bite her lower lip, her lashes fluttering against her cheeks and the quiet gasps she'd made whenever I pleasured her with my mouth.

I increased the tempo, moving my hand quicker in time to the memories that rushed through my mind. I could still remember *exactly* what it felt like to be inside Elle Thompson —like fucking Nirvana. My knees buckled as I came, shooting my load all over the shower floor. After taking a few minutes to collect myself, I set to the task of washing my hair and body.

Less than ten minutes later, I came out of the bathroom with a towel wrapped around my waist. I exhaled deeply and ran my hand through my damp locks, tugging at the roots as I considered my options. I almost laughed at the absurdity of it all. I'd never been the kind of guy to give a shit about what I wore. Most of my clothes were old jeans and plain t-shirts. I didn't want to wear something that looked worn; I wanted to look good.

I pulled out my newest pair of dark denim jeans, and the white Henley shirt my sister bought for me last Christmas. I tugged the shirt over my head and my eyes skimmed over to the mirror above my dresser. I ran a hand through my unruly hair again, trying to get some semblance of order to it.

Satisfied that I looked about as good as I could get, I grabbed my keys and wallet, my eyes automatically focussing on the photo booth pictures. What I wouldn't give to have Elle look at me like that again.

When I came back upstairs, Aiden and Becky were sitting at the kitchen table eating dinner. "There's a plate for you in the microwave," Becky told me, gesturing with her fork to the counter.

"Thanks but I'm going out for dinner tonight," I told her, pausing to ruffle Aiden's hair.

"Really?" Becky said, skeptically eyeing me. My heart ached a little, a dull ache that I shoved into the back corner of my mind.

I didn't need to get all worked up and depressed that my family didn't trust me yet.

"Yeah, really. I'm picking Elle up for seven," I answered, trying to keep my tone light. Five years ago, I would have lashed out at her, pissed off and angry at the world. Sometimes, it's hard to turn over a new leaf. Your old skin calls to you, because it's familiar and easy and it doesn't take work, but I was determined to leave that person behind forever.

Now concern truly did line Becky's face. She shook her head a little, biting down on her lip. "Do you honestly think that's a good idea?" she asked, working to keep her tone neutral.

"Why wouldn't it be?"

My sister sighed, glancing towards her son. It was evident this wasn't a conversation she wanted him to partake in, or to overhear. "Elle's with somebody else now, Braden."

"She still deserves an apology," I responded, already walking out the door. I closed it on her reply.

I wasn't entirely sure *who* Becky was trying to protect—me, or Elle, but I couldn't even be angry at her for it. She was the cautious one. She guarded her heart and the heart of her loved ones fiercely. I hadn't seen her date or show an interest in anyone since Aiden's father, and I knew she was messed up from that still. I knew he'd broken something in her, and when I got to thinking about it—I wanted him to pay more than he had. The beating provided by Brock that landed him in the hospital with his jaw wired shut didn't seem like much compared to the cautious, fearful way my sister now lived.

By the time I pulled up the Thompson driveway, I was completely keyed up. I jumped out of my truck, leaving it running, and walked up the wooden steps of the front porch. Just as I raised my hand to knock, Elle's mother walked into the foyer.

Sue Thompson had always scared me a little bit. You'd think it would have been easier to date a girl whose father wasn't

J.C. HANNIGAN

around. Elle's old man might not be sitting on the front porch shining his shotgun, but Sue sure would be. She was terrifying, and she once told me that if I ever hurt her daughter, she'd castrate me herself using the antique cattle bull castrating knife that had been in her family for centuries. Elle had certainly inherited her mother's brash, fierce personality.

"Sue," I said by way of greeting. She pursed her lips with displeasure, and my heart sank a little in my chest. Sure, Sue had been terrifying at first, but she'd quickly warmed up to me and made me feel like a part of the Thompson household. I always got the sense that she rooted for me. Right now, I definitely didn't have that sense.

"Braden," her tone was cold, almost calculating, and she made no move to open the door for me. I stood there awkwardly for what felt like hours but was really only less than a minute before Elle descended the stairs.

She hadn't changed from the outfit she had worn earlier. I knew this was Elle's way of reinforcing that *this was not a date,* but it was hard to be upset about that when the sundress she was wearing kissed her thighs and clung to her curvy body. My hands were already itching to touch her, to peel off that thin layer of material and—

"I'll be home shortly, Mom," Elle's words broke me from my overtly sexual thoughts, and I raised my eyes to watch as she grabbed her jean jacket from the coat rack. "The second dinner is done," she added, her eyes flitting to me to make sure I understood that this was *just dinner.*

"Sounds good honey," Sue said in response, her cold eyes still on me. A smirk danced across her lips, and she shook her head. "Try not to do anything I wouldn't do."

"Yeah, leave the castrating knife at home," I interjected with a cocky grin, knowing exactly what Sue had meant. Elle frowned, looking confused. I'd never filled her in on that little chat her mother had with me the first time Elle brought me home. Sue grinned, pleased that I remembered and delighted that I'd caught her veiled threat.

"Let's just get this over with," she sighed, resigned. I arched a brow, pushing open the screen door and holding it open for her.

"Try not to look too excited," I said dryly. "I wouldn't want my ego to burst."

Elle smirked and chose not to reply as she walked through the doorway. Her arm was inches away from brushing against my chest, and my body responded immediately. "Catch ya later, Sue," I added, letting the screen door close behind me as I followed Elle down her porch steps.

I appreciated the view of Elle's fine ass the entire time she walked towards my truck. She opened the door, climbing inside and practically slamming it my face when I attempted to do the gentlemanly thing and close it for her. Her devious smile grew, as if she was pleased by the dumbfounded look on my face.

I arched a brow and walked around the front of the truck, then climbed in behind the wheel. This truck was riddled with memories, and they deeply affected me even when Elle wasn't sitting in the passenger seat. Now all I could think of was all the times we'd hooked up in the cab.

Judging by the pink tint to Elle's cheeks, she was remembering those times too.

I closed the door and turned to face her, our eyes instantly locking. She drew in a shaky breath, and I knew that she was unnerved by the intensity of my desire. "You look incredible, Elle," I said, my voice catching a little on the lump in my throat.

"This isn't a date," she rolled her eyes, breaking the contact.

"I know." The smile I wore was genuine. Even if Elle spent the duration of this evening insulting me, I was happy enough to simply *be* in her company, to hear her voice again and have her attention directed on me—even if it wasn't positive attention.

I took her to the fanciest restaurant in town—the same one

we'd gone to when Brock and Tessa told us all they were engaged, The Dock. The waitress led us to a table for two in the corner. The lightening was soft and romantic, the gentle glow enhancing the beauty of Elle's skin.

She didn't wait for me to pull her chair out, she did it herself with a defiant look on her face. She was still fighting this— fighting us. I couldn't help but smile in response as I pulled out my own chair.

The waitress asked us for our drink orders. Elle ordered a glass of wine and I asked for a coke. Elle's brows furrowed as she assessed me. "What's up with that?" she asked pointedly, gesturing to the waitress as she walked away.

"With what?" I tried to play stupid. I didn't exactly want to dive into how messed up I'd been after my mom's death. I knew it was something she'd need to hear eventually, but I had hoped I could enjoy her company a little longer.

"For as long as I've known you, you've never passed up on the opportunity to have a beer. I've seen you do that twice now," she said, delicately arching her brow to drive her point home.

I sighed heavily and leaned back against my chair, running a hand through my hair. "I'm an alcoholic, Elle."

She blinked at me for several beats. "No, you're not."

"Yes, I am," I inhaled deeply, my eyes dropping down to the table for a beat before I forced myself to look at her. "I fell apart after my mom died. After I... screwed things up with you. I started drinking more, a hell of a lot more than I had before. Harder drinks too...anything to kill the guilt and the regret."

Elle opened her mouth, searching for something to say. She looked genuinely shocked by my revelation. "I... I'm sorry Braden," she finally said. I knew she meant it; I knew that she was blaming herself, even though it wasn't her fault.

"It's not your fault," I told her, needing her to believe me. "It was only a matter of time. Addiction runs in my family. Brock and Becky got sick of it and told me to either sober up or get out. They told me I was walking down the same path our father had."

Elle winced as if my words had physically slapped her. She knew how much I hated my father, how much I resented everything about him and how painful it must have been to be compared to him. Her hands reached across the table to grasp mine. She squeezed gently. "You're not him," she told me, as she'd told me so many times before. Her brown eyes were locked on mine—searching—and I knew without a doubt that she believed it.

She was the only person to ever see *me*. Everyone else saw a rebel, a trouble maker. The wayward son of the old town drunk; the product of a broken family. Elle saw more. She still did, even after everything I'd put her through.

I swallowed hard and forced a smile, squeezing her hands back. "I know. But it was the kick in the ass I needed to smarten up. I went to rehab, enrolled in college, and left town."

"I heard that," Elle cleared her throat, pulling her hands away as if my touch burned her. "Mechanical engineering, right?"

"Right," I responded, my lips lifting up in a grin. She'd done her homework. "I heard you're a paramedic now," I added.

"Yeah," she nodded, looking away abruptly. Something dark clouded her eyes, something she wasn't going to be forthcoming about. I got a sense that this subject was off limits to her.

The waitress approached with our drinks. "Are you guys ready to order yet?" she asked, setting our glasses down on the table.

"Not yet," I drawled, flashing the waitress a smile that made her blush. "Why don't you give us another five minutes to look over the menu, darling?" She nodded and turned around, heading to tend to her other tables. When I looked back at Elle, she was frowning. "What?" I asked.

"You're seriously hitting on the waitress?" she snorted, shaking her head. I could detect a note of jealousy in her voice.

"You said this wasn't a date," I reminded her. "Besides, I was just being nice. I wasn't hitting on her. I don't bother with pleasantries when I want something Elle, I *go* for it."

She swallowed, likely remembering that fact about me all too well. She suddenly took a keen interest to the menu in front of her.

I didn't bother glancing at mine. I'd been there enough times to know the menu like the back of my hand. Instead, I took the time to watch the girl that still had a hold on my heart.

I could feel the familiar tug between us; it had never faded during our time apart. I didn't even have to touch her to know that connection was as strong as it had always been. Her soul called to mine; and I still felt at home in her presence.

"What are you staring at?" Elle asked without looking up, her lips pulled into a slight smile that she was trying to suppress.

I could have told her I was looking at my future—and I almost did, but it was too soon. Elle wasn't willing to admit that she still felt even a fraction of what she once felt for me. I knew my stubborn girl almost as well as I knew myself—it was inevitable. Instead, I tossed her an innocent smile and shrugged, the words I wanted to say caught in my throat.

"Are you ready to order yet?" our waitress asked, saving me from having to reply as she reappeared at our table, her pen posed over the notebook she held.

"The lemon and herb roasted chicken sounds good. I'll have that please," Elle said, closing the menu and setting it down in front of her. She looked up at me, waiting.

"I'll have the Greek style pepper steak," I added, my eyes never leaving her face.

"Sounds great," the waitress offered. She turned around, sauntering over to the kitchen.

"Tell me something," I leaned forward, my eyes locking on hers before she had a chance to look away.

"What?" Elle's brow furrowed, as if she didn't trust where this conversation would end up going.

"Anything. Tell me what you've been up to the last few years. Tell me about your job. Tell me if...tell me if you're happy," I asked, swallowing hard.

Elle exhaled and brushed a strand of her long hair behind her ear. She looked away from me, nodding her head slowly. "Well...I haven't been up to much, to be honest. I went to school, then I got a job. I've just been working, really." She stopped talking, lost in thought.

"Do you like your job?" I pressed, needing her to keep talking. I needed to know what was going on behind those brown eyes. I need to know the words her heart was whispering, even if her mind was counteracting it all. I knew it would—I knew that she'd talk herself out of trusting my company. I couldn't blame her either...but I still had to try.

She looked at me again, her eyes still guarded. "Most of the time. It's fulfilling but...there are times when it's really hard too."

I nodded, accepting this answer. "Yeah, Becky's a nurse now and I know it gets hard for her."

"Becky's a nurse now?" Elle's face lit up. "That's great! I always knew she'd make a wonderful nurse."

"She does," I agreed, sitting back in my chair. "Are you going to finish answering my question?"

The happy expression fell away from her face, and she went back to being guarded. "Are you happy, Braden?"

"In this moment? Yes. I'm the happiest I've ever been."

"You have a lot to be happy for," Elle said in agreement, forcing herself to hold my gaze. "You're sober and you've got the degree you never believed you'd get."

Elle brought a rush of memories with each spoken word. Nights of us sitting on her front porch swing, wrapped in a blanket and talking about the future—nights of Elle talking about college and me evading the discussion.

I always knew Elle would go on to do incredible things—but I didn't have the same hope for myself. I thought I'd be stuck at Chuck's garage forever. I didn't believe that college was in my cards. I didn't have the money and I certainly didn't have the motivation. I already had a job that I didn't hate, I was content. I was afraid of failing.

But things change in an instant. I lost who I was, what I thought I wanted, and I was left staring at the pile of debris that was my life trying to make sense of it all. I failed, and I had to do something to make it right. I thought going to university would give me a sense of direction that I'd been lacking my whole life, but I ended up right back where I started.

"Not exactly, I'm still kicking around at the garage," I pointed out, smirking a little to cover up my unease.

"Why? Why don't you get a job in your field?" she questioned, her eyes searching mine for the answer.

"That's the plan—or it was. But Chuck had a heart attack a few months ago. He needs me. I've already bailed on him once..." I trailed off, frowning. I wasn't going to leave him hanging again.

I was tired of being the guy that bailed.

Elle's expression softened. She knew how much I respected the old man. "It's good that you're back, Braden." She said, her voice was barely above a whisper, but it was jammed pack with meaning and sincerity.

"Now back to my question," I said, leaning forward again. "Are you happy, Elle?"

"Most of the time," she retorted defensively. "When I'm not forced to do things I don't want to do."

"You didn't want to have dinner with me?" I arched a brow, not buying her sass for a second. While her words were meant to cut, her eyes told a very different story.

"There's no sense in revisiting old wounds," she answered, swallowing hard.

"Frankly, I'm a bit surprised by your outlook. As someone who works in the medical field, you should know it's dangerous not to revisit old wounds. How else can you keep them clean and heal them completely? If you ignore it, you'll just let that wound fester until you've gotta chop your whole damn leg off."

Elle blinked at me for several beats, then her lips perked up in the tiniest hint of a smile. "I honestly can't figure out what your end goal is."

"Maybe there is no end goal," I replied. I scratched the back of my neck, trying to knit the words on the tip of my tongue together in neat little patterns. "Maybe I'm just tired of that old wound festering. Maybe I want to clean it out, help it heal for good." She said nothing, absorbing my words with her eyes fixed on the wall behind me. "I'm not asking you to dump your boyfriend and come back to me, Elle. I just want to be friends again. I just want to make up for what I did."

"The thing is Braden, I don't know if you *can* make up for what you did. I don't know if I can forgive you, or if I want to for that matter. And I'll be honest, I'm really not sure how I can be friends with you again," her voice shook a little with emotion, but her eyes were cold and guarded, the finality in her tone slicing my heart.

We ate our dinner in a sad silence that suffocated me. Elle refused to meet my eyes for the rest of the evening. Any time I tried to pull a question from her, she'd respond with one or two worded replies.

But I knew Elle—I expected this. I expected her to fight me, to fight what was between us tooth and nail. I knew how she operated, and she'd never forgive herself if she opened up her arms to me without making me work my ass off first. I just had to show her I was willing to jump through any hoop she put before me. I would do whatever it took, whatever she needed me to do, to prove myself.

CHAPTER NINE

lle

Dinner with Braden was a mistake. I should have never put myself in a position to hear him out, and I didn't feel any better for having done it. Instead, I felt guilty and confused. I hadn't even known he'd gone to rehab, I had refused to let Tessa talk about him around me. It pained me to hear he had self-destructed to that point. I couldn't help but wonder what would have happened if I hadn't let him push me out.

In my heart of hearts, I wanted to give him another chance. I wanted to help him burn away the regret, and soothe both of our aching hearts. I wanted to surrender again, and that was stupid. That was dangerous.

Stupid heart.

Braden was just getting his life together again, and he had shattered me before. I wouldn't—couldn't—give him the opportunity to do it again. I would always care deeply for him, but once you broke a Thompson's trust, it was gone forever.

I couldn't help but analyze his every word. He wanted to heal just as badly as I wanted to heal; I could hear it in his voice, but even though he'd said himself that he just wanted to be friends, I didn't think I could give him that. I couldn't even give my boyfriend what he wanted. I couldn't tell him how I was feeling or what I was thinking, either.

Where was the girl who wore her emotions on her sleeve? Where was the girl who could express exactly how she felt and what she was thinking without batting a lash? Why did that part of me have to die when Braden broke my heart, along with what we had?

The guilt I felt over my stupid feelings was consuming me, and I didn't want to face them. Thankfully, there was enough going on to keep me distracted. I was spending a lot of time hanging out with Tessa, helping solidify her plans for the wedding. When I wasn't doing that, I was preparing for the bachelorette party next weekend.

"Elle, you've got a visitor!" Mom's voice called from downstairs. Curious, I came out of my bedroom and paused at the top of the stairs. Alex was standing in the front foyer with a bouquet of flowers in his hands and a smile on his lips.

"Hey...what are you doing here?" I tucked my hair behind my ear and started down the stairs.

"Well, I heard the Parry Sound Stampede was happening, and I didn't have to work...figured I could accompany you and see what all the hype's about," he answered. I came to a stop in front of him and let him wrap his arms around me. I hugged him back, breathing in his freshly showered scent.

"Oh, that's awesome," I said hesitantly, pulling away. He held out the bouquet for me and I took it, inhaling the smell of the pretty roses and lilacs. "I wasn't really planning on going though." It was true; my intention was to avoid the fairgrounds and all that came with it. I knew the entire gang—including Braden—would be there all weekend. They always were. There wasn't much to do in this town, and the Parry Sound Stampede was the biggest event of the year.

"What do you mean you weren't thinking about going?" Mom asked me, frowning. "Tessa's competing tomorrow, and I could use the extra hands Sunday morning."

"What's happening Sunday morning?" Alex asked, looking from my mom to me.

"The chili cook-off," Mom answered when I didn't. "I participate every year. Usually Elle helps me, but I've lost her hands in recent years."

"I have to head out in the afternoon but we'd be happy to help in the morning," Alex told her, his hands rubbing my shoulders. "Wouldn't we?" He arched a brow at me, encouraging me to speak.

I painted a smile on and nodded. "Sure, of course. It'll be... fun," I swallowed. I felt weird about it—helping Mom with the chili cook-off used to be my thing with Braden. Having Alex there would just feel...wrong.

"I was just about to head out to the tractor pull," Mom added, arching a brow at us. "Are you two going to come?"

I didn't really want to go to the fairgrounds, but I also knew that staying in with Alex was a bad idea. I hadn't counted on him showing up this weekend, and I was still trying to process my feelings. "Alright, just let me find a vase." I said, looking at Alex.

Fifteen minutes later, we'd found a parking spot and the three of us were making our way to the stadium. Dusk had fallen but the fairgrounds were brightly lit, illuminating the crowd that had gathered to watch the tractor pull. Mom stopped to talk to almost every single person we came across.

"Your mom's pretty popular," Alex remarked, his lips inches away from my ear.

"Yeah, she's lived here her entire life. She knows everyone and everyone loves her," I shrugged. She was nice to everybody, and was the first person to show up and help someone out when they needed it. The town adored her for it—and her award winning chili helped keep her in their good favour, too.

Alex took my hand while I glanced around the stands, looking for free seats. "Elle! Elle! Over here!" my eyes followed the sound of my name being shouted, and I saw Tessa jumping up and down in the middle upper section of the stands. She was sitting beside Brock, Becky, and Aiden. Thankfully, I saw no sign of Braden.

I led the way up the steps to where my best friend and her future family were sitting. Becky and Brock smiled at us in greeting, and Aiden stared at Alex with distaste. I almost chuckled—he looked so much like his uncle when he made that face. My laughter died in my throat at the mere thought of Braden; and the accompanying pesky, throbbing ache in my heart.

"Alex, this is Tessa's fiancé Brock, his sister Becky and her son Aiden. Everyone, this is Alex," I said, making the introductions as quickly as I could. I sat down beside Tessa and Alex sat beside me.

"I didn't know you were coming to town this weekend," Tessa said, leaning forward so she could address Alex.

"I wanted to surprise Elle," he answered, putting his arm around me. I smiled tightly and tried to relax.

"Elle prefers to do the surprising." My heart thudded loudly in my chest as we all turned to see Braden standing a few feet away, his hands full of popcorn and drinks. He was staring at Alex's arm around me, his expression unreadable. Alex tensed beside me.

"Uncle Braden!" Aiden exclaimed, grinning. "Did you get the cotton candy lemonade?"

Braden's eyes broke away from us and landed on his nephew. He grinned, a smile that sent me back four years and made me melt all over again. "Of course I did!" He made his way past us without a second glance, and everyone scooted over to make room for him beside Aiden. "I also got you a candy apple—but save it for later," I heard him add when Becky went to scold him.

I inhaled, breathing in the evening air. I gave Alex a small apologetic smile before leaning into him. He relaxed, his hold on me tightening slightly as he drew me closer.

We sat like that throughout the entire tractor pull. Sometimes, I could feel Braden's eyes on me, staring at us. I knew he was watching to see how I acted with Alex. I knew that he was reading every single gesture, every single movement I made and it pissed me off.

When the tractor pull ended, I grabbed Alex's hand after saying a quick general goodbye and led him down the stands, searching for my mom. "Don't you want to stay and go on some rides or something?" Alex asked once we'd stepped off the stands.

I turned and stepped into him, looking him in the eyes. "Rides aren't really my thing—at least not carnival rides. I figured we could go back to my mom's and hang out...maybe watch a movie, or something?"

The concern that showed in Alex's eyes ebbed and he smiled. "Sure, that sounds fun too." He angled his head down to kiss me, his lips brushing softly against mine. I stupidly chose that moment to look up, my eyes locking with Braden's.

At first, he looked hurt. But a moment after our eyes locked, when Alex kissed me, Braden broke into a knowing smile. It was as if he was saying *"gotcha"*.

THE NEXT MORNING, I awoke to the smell of bacon and eggs. Voices floated up the stairs and through my bedroom door, which I'd left open a crack last night when I went to bed. Part of me had hoped that Alex would break my mother's "no males upstairs" rule and sneak up to see me, but he didn't. Alex was forever respectful. He wasn't a risk taker.

Unlike Braden. When Braden had spent the night on the couch, he'd always snuck upstairs after my mom passed out—he had been very practiced in avoiding the creaky parts on the stairs.

Stop comparing, I scolded myself. I ran my hand through my tangled hair, kicked off my blankets and made my way downstairs.

Scrambled eggs, bacon, English muffins, and orange juice were all laid out on the table when I walked into the kitchen. "Good morning," Alex grinned, approaching me with a cup of coffee fixed just the way I liked it. I accepted it with a small smile, and he kissed me on the cheek before gesturing to the table. "Are you hungry?"

I nodded tiredly and sat down—after all, the call of bacon was too hard to resist. "How long have you guys been up for?"

"Two hours or so," Mom shrugged. She was always an early riser—me, not so much. I'd choose sleep over waking up early any day. I spooned some eggs onto my plate and loaded up on the bacon, reaching for a slice of buttered toast. Alex and Mom started eating too, the only sounds in the kitchen the occasional scraping of forks and knives against plates. Out of the corner of my eye, I could see Mom and Alex exchanging looks with one another.

"Okay seriously, what's going on?" I demanded, halfway through my breakfast and more than annoyed at the strange atmosphere. They looked at each other again, something passing between the two of them.

"I was just telling Alex about the events at the fairgrounds today," Mom finally answered, taking a sip of her coffee, meeting my eyes with a challenge. "Tessa's jumping competition, for one. It starts in a couple of hours and I know she'd love to see you both there. Plus, there's the concert tonight."

"I still can't believe that you know Travis Channing. And the smash-up derby, how come you didn't mention that earlier?" Alex added with a grin, shaking his head ruefully.

Because I didn't want you to go, the little voice in my head answered. I took a sip of my coffee, buying myself some time while my heart hammered loudly in my chest. I knew that Braden was going to be in it—he always was. "I don't know, it's kind of lame."

"Your mom said it was one of your favourite events," Alex remarked.

I sent a dirty look to my mom. She was traitor if I ever did see one. "Fine, we can go if you really want to. But honestly, it was more exciting when I was in high school."

"I'll be the judge of that," Alex said with a wicked grin.

"Go on and get ready Elle, I'll keep him company," Mom said.

With an exasperated huff, I padded upstairs to the bathroom and turned on the shower. As I washed my hair, I thought about the night before and Braden's face when he'd told Alex that I didn't like surprises. It was true; I didn't. At least not *that* kind of surprise.

I felt like I was two different people. The Elle that Braden knew—the Elle that I *was* underneath it all—and the Elle that Alex knew...the Elle that I thought I was supposed to be. They both understood me in different ways—Alex knew the demands of the job we both shared, and he knew how it affected me emotionally. He also understood my reservations about love and trust. But Braden...Braden knew how I ticked. He knew how I was built. He knew how I loved and how I fought and how I rebelled at the thought of what I was supposed to do. Even when I was angry with him, even when I was avoiding him…I felt more like myself when I was around Braden than I did when I was around Alex.

When the hot water disappeared, I finally turned off the shower and stepped out. I took a long time getting ready; mainly because I just wanted to be by myself for a while. I dressed in a pair of my favourite jean shorts, a white tank top, and a plaid blouse. I paired it with my cowboy boots and blew out my hair.

"Are you just about ready, Elle?" Mom hollered from the front foyer. "I swear, that girl takes forever to get ready for anything. She'd be late for her own funeral," I heard her add to Alex. He laughed in fond agreement, and I rolled my eyes. "This time, you two can drive yourselves," Mom told me when I finally walked down the stairs.

"Why?" I asked, crossing my arms in front of my chest defiantly. "Got a hot date after?" Mom blushed a little and my jaw dropped open. "Oh my God, you *do* have a hot date! Details, now."

"If by hot date you mean a trip to the grocery store and an afternoon of chili making, then yes Elle…I have a hot date," Mom replied.

"Are you going to want some help?" I asked, practically hopping at the change to avoid the smash-up derby.

"Don't think I've forgotten about your disastrous use of salt," Mom responded, shaking her head with a smile. "Cooking really isn't Elle's strong suit," she added to Alex. "Keep her distracted and out of the house for me, and that'll be more than enough help."

"Come on," Alex said to me, shaking his head with a smile.

"DOES SHE COMPETE EVERY YEAR?" Alex asked as we sat in the stands again, this time for the horse jumping competition—and this time without the Miller's.

"Yep," I answered, taking a bite of the pretzel he'd bought me. "She usually wins, too."

"Cool. Did you ever compete in any of these events?" Alex looked at me, a grin on his lips. His hazel eyes assessed me with reverence.

"Nope," I said, my lips popping to accent the word. "My mom wanted me to try out for Miss North."

"What's that?"

"It's a beauty pageant," Mom cut in, leaning forward to see Alex. She'd met up with us at the stadium to watch Tessa jump. "It's just a fun little thing we do around here."

"Unfortunately, I didn't fit the requirements. You must be 'of good moral character and personality'." I said dryly.

"And what, you don't have good moral character and personality?" Alex grinned, entertained.

"Elle was a trouble maker, and she was quite loud about it," Mom said. I shrugged my shoulders, not disputing the fact. "I was Miss North two years running—until Tessa's mom won it and broke my record." Mom added with a chuckle.

"So you and Tessa's mom were beauty pageant rivals then?" Alex asked, his eyebrows drawing together.

"No, the opposite. They were the best of friends. Inseparable," I explained patiently, a subtle smile on my lips. I still felt weird about having Alex in town, but I was content to fill the voids of silence with conversation—so long as that conversation wasn't pertaining to my complicated feelings that I'd yet to make sense of.

"Sounds a lot like you and Tessa," he remarked, pulling me closer to him.

"They are definitely inseparable," Mom laughed, shaking her

head. "When they were growing up, you'd rarely see one without the other."

"Let's give a warm welcome to contestant twenty-five; Tessa Armstrong!" the announcer's voice blasted over the speakers. Mom and I stood up to cheer for Tessa, our hoots and hollers loud and proud. I could see Tessa's dad standing by the entry gate, a proud grin on his face. Alex stood up too, clapping along with us.

Once she'd trotted into the ring on Spirit, we sat down and watched the show. Tessa eased through the jumps in record time. She placed second, bested only by a younger horse's two-second lead in speed.

After the show jumping competition ended, Alex and I went over the barns to see Tessa as she got Spirit prepped for the trailer while Mom took off to do her grocery shopping. "Hey," Tessa said, smiling when she caught sight of us. "Glad you guys came today!"

"Wouldn't have missed it," I responded, stepping up to the beautiful palomino. I stroked his velvety nose and he whinnied at me. "You did good, old boy," I told him. "And you were alright too, I guess." I added, grinning at Tessa.

"You were awesome," Alex said. "I wouldn't even know what to do on a horse," he chuckled. He was keeping his distance, standing several feet back.

"Thanks," Tessa smiled. "You can pet him if you want, just hold your hand out and let him sniff you first. It's the polite thing to do, after all."

Alex stepped forward, holding his hand out for Spirit to sniff. Then he gave the side of Spirit's face a tentative stroke. "He's soft," he remarked, as if surprised.

"Seriously, this is your first time around a horse?" I asked him, a small smile lifting the corners of my lips up.

"Yeah, well. Barrie's more city-like than Parry Sound, not

many people have horses. I played sports." He shrugged, almost embarrassed.

"It's alright," Tessa told him. "Elle only knows how to handle them because she practically grew up on the farm with me and I always made her help me with my chores." I stuck my tongue out at her jokingly and she gave me the finger. "Are you two going to actually stick around today, or will you be bailing again?"

"We're sticking around," Alex answered on behalf of the both of us. "I really want to see the smash-up derby and eat some disgusting carnival food."

TESSA AND BROCK were perfect buffers to have hanging around. They lightened the mood and distracted me from my heavy, complicated thoughts. We had a great time wandering the fair and checking out all the different craft booths. Tessa even got me to go on a few rides.

I used to love carnival rides. Braden and I would ride every single one of them over and over again until I was so dizzy and disoriented that I couldn't stand. There were so many memories with him and me at this fair that it hurt to be here with someone who wasn't him.

Then it was time for the smash-up derby and the four of us made our way to the stadium. Brock caught sight of Braden and called out to him. He was standing near the stadium entrance, waiting with the other drivers while the judges inspected the cars. He was dressed in his regular uniform of torn jeans and a black t-shirt that amplified his broader chest and the muscles in his arms. The scruff along his jaw was every bit as enticing as the call of his eyes as they landed on me. His gaze dropped to my hand in Alex's and his jaw clenched. He turned around to say something to Ezra Johnson.

"Oh my God, Ezra! I haven't seen you in forever!" I squealed, tugging my hand free and practically flying at him. He walked a few steps towards me before his arms wrapped around me in a hug. Picking me up, he spun around twice before releasing me. Ezra may have been Braden's best friend first, but he and I grew close when I started dating Braden. He was lovable and loyal, and for a while…I'd tried to push him towards Tessa.

"I know!" he exclaimed, grinning at me. "Maybe if you came home more often…" he was joking, but his words still made me feel guilty. He was right, after all.

"Yeah well, you know how it is. I got busy with college and then working," I shrugged, keeping my smile in place. "This is Alex, my boyfriend."

"Nice to meet you," Ezra said politely, shaking Alex's hand.

"What have you been up to lately?!" I added, trying to ignore the fact that Braden's eyes remained glued to me.

"Working as well. I scored a union job," Ezra answered proudly.

"So basically, he works twice a week," Braden joked from just behind us. His eyes landed on me again, and his amused smile faded slightly.

"You won't be cracking jokes when I kick your ass in the derby, Braden." Ezra arched a brow.

"You wish," Braden smirked, shaking his head.

The announcer's voice poured from the speakers, telling the crowd that the smash-up derby was about to begin and asking the drivers to enter the ring.

We wished them luck and made our way to the stands to find a seat. I tried to keep my eyes on Braden's Honda, but the sickening sound of metal crunching against metal had my heart pounding frantically in my chest. I inhaled sharply, trying to keep my breathing steady even though it felt as if my airway was closing.

I squeezed my eyelids shut, and all I could see was every car accident I'd been called out to as a paramedic—only in place of those victims, I saw Braden's face. Bloodied and bruised, his eyes lifeless as he looked up at me. Soon, I was gasping for air, my heart pounding frantically in my chest. Alex placed his hands on either side of my face and told me to breathe. "It's okay, Elle. Just breathe," he said. I opened my eyes, fixing them on his face, and tried to focus on his gentle touch. He brushed away the tears with his thumbs. My body was trembling out of control, and despite Alex's calm voice—I just couldn't get my breathing under control.

Tessa was suddenly kneeling before me, concern lining her features. "What can I do?" I heard her ask Alex, but she sounded far away to my ears. I could scarcely hear over the roar of my blood.

"I'm just going to get her out of here. I think the derby is triggering her panic attack," I heard Alex answer. He tugged me up and carefully led me away from the stands. My eyes were pulled over to the stadium again—the first round had ended and Braden was getting out of his car, his eyes locked on me.

CHAPTER TEN

raden

I'D MADE it through the first round, but struggled to keep my focus for the second round. I couldn't get Elle's tear streaked face out of my mind. I had no idea why she was crying, no idea where that Alex asshole had taken her, and I was desperate to find out.

Needless to say, I wasn't all that disappointed that I didn't make it through the second round. My thoughts were occupied with Elle, and I immediately started searching for Brock and Tessa. I found them waiting near the stadium entrance, as if they'd known I'd go looking for them and wanted to make it easy. "Where'd she go?" I demanded, my eyes narrowed with anger. "What happened?"

Tessa exchanged a look with Brock. "She had a panic attack," she finally answered, returning her gaze to me. Her eyes were sad and worried.

"A panic attack?" I repeated, the words sounding unfamiliar

in my mouth. I'd never known Elle to have a panic attack in all the years I'd known her. "Why?"

"It's not my place to tell you why," Tessa said, giving me a sharp look. "It's up to Elle if she wants to tell you why."

"Where is she?" I almost growled, aggravated. My fists clenched and unclenched, itching to punch her boyfriend in his overly squared jaw. Of course I blamed him—Elle had never had panic attacks when she was with me. He had to have done something to cause it.

Tessa looked hopelessly towards Brock for help. "Braden, relax," my brother said, stepping forward and placing his heavy hand on my shoulder, grounding me. "She's safe with Alex."

"The hell she is. She's safer with me," I blurted out, angry. I was pissed that I wasn't the one comforting her right now, pissed off that Alex was even in the goddamn picture. I knew I'd all but pushed her into his arms and only had myself to blame.

Without another word, I spun away and started off in the opposite direction, my eyes searching the crowd for Elle's dark hair. I found her over near the food trucks, sitting on one of the picnic table benches with her head buried in her hands. There was no sign of Alex—and thank God for that, I was so pissed off I'd likely throw fists first and ask questions later.

I sat down beside her. "What happened?" I asked, emotion clogging my words.

Elle stiffened upon hearing my voice. She lifted her head up, her eyes red-rimmed from crying and her brow furrowed with confusion. "What are you doing here?"

"I saw you leaving the stands," I answered. "Why were you crying?"

She was silent, her cheeks tinged pink with embarrassment. She opened and closed her mouth several times, searching for something to say. "I had a panic attack," she muttered, closing her eyes as if she was embarrassed to see my reaction.

"What brought it on?" I angled my body towards hers, letting our knees touch. I brought my hand up and brushed her dark hair out of her face. Her eyes flew open, locking with mine.

"Post-traumatic stress disorder," she whispered after a pause, biting her lip. "I guess I'm not cut out for the life of a paramedic after all." Her jaw trembled, and she shook her head slightly. "I haven't even been on the job for two years, Braden. I've only seen a handful of truly horrific accidents, and I'm already unravelling."

She sounded so broken, so lost, so not the girl I knew and it tore me up in the worst possible way. All I wanted was to take her in my arms and hold her, kiss her tears away and somehow make it better—make it right.

My hand moved from her face to the back of her head, as I guided her to me. She rested her head on my chest and my arms wrapped around her. I tried not to think about how incredible it felt to have her in my arms again but damn, it was amazing. It was the best thing I'd felt in a long time—since I'd last held her. This was where I was supposed to be.

"This doesn't make you weak, Elle," I said, because it was all I could say and it was true. She needed to hear it.

"I know it's crazy, I know it doesn't make any sense but watching you in the derby...I kept picturing you in place of the...of the people I'd lost on the job, and it was worse. So much worse," her shoulder shook as the tears poured down her face. "I've already lost you once, and I could barely handle it. I couldn't bear to lose you again."

"You're never going to lose me," I assured her, looking deep into her eyes. "I've always been yours...even when I wasn't." I added, swallowing hard.

"Elle?"

We both looked up at the same time to see Alex standing about three feet away, holding two bottles of water. Elle stood up, pulling out of my arms and wiping the tears from her eyes. She turned her head, catching my eye for a second; a pining expression on her face. Then she turned back to him and started walking—taking my heart along with her.

It had felt like the walls Elle threw up when around me had finally come down, that she'd finally let me in. It seemed she'd even started to trust me again, at least enough to reveal that difficult truth about herself. I don't know what I'd thought, maybe that she would let me comfort her and make it right somehow—but seeing her walk off to Alex, seeing them converse quietly—her hand on his arm—it cut. Real deep.

I watched them for a moment before I quietly slipped away, my hands in my pockets and my heart feeling like a transport truck had driven over it. I wandered the fair aimlessly, thinking about how broken she'd seemed in my arms.

Elle was one of the strongest, most willful women I'd ever known. It was part of the reason why I'd fallen in love with her. She'd always known exactly what she wanted and went for it. She'd never been afraid to dive in with eyes wide open. There was a spark about her, and even though Elle was scared and maybe a little broken now—I could still see the spark in her. I was still drawn to it...to her.

I didn't know why she was still with Alex. I knew she didn't love him—and maybe that was an arrogant assumption to make, but I figured out of everyone...I knew best. I knew what Elle looked like when she was in love—I knew how she smiled, how she laughed, how she looked at the world. I knew the language of her heart almost better than I knew the language of my own.

I also knew without a doubt that *I* was the reason Elle had a difficult time calling things off with Alex and coming back to me. I'd hurt her so profoundly when I broke things off, and she was afraid I'd do it again. Little did she know that I'd sooner cut off my own right arm than cause her anymore pain.

DUSK FELL over the fairgrounds as hundreds of people gathered near the makeshift stage to watch Travis Channing perform. Growing up, Travis had been a regular feature in my life as he had been one of Brock's best friends. It was surreal to think of all the success his music had brought him. The last person from Parry Sound to make it big had been Bobby Orr, our claim to hockey fame.

Travis was a startling contrast to the successful hockey player. For one, he loved to show off and he loved the attention his fame brought him.

But he was a fantastic performer, I'd give him that. It was impossible to not get caught up in the infectious energy he let off as he sauntered around the stage like he owned it. His music was decent; I used to rip on him for his corny *"My dog died and my wife left me"* vibe, but it was clearly working for him. Travis' net worth was approximately $220 million dollars, and mine was well under 40,000. The guy was practically wiping his ass with hundred dollar bills and he'd already been romantically linked to several celebrities and models.

He was at the height of his career, but the best thing about Travis was that he remembered his roots. After he became established in Nashville, popular enough to make his own schedule, he started flying back every summer just so he could perform at the Parry Sound Stampede. He traveled home to see his mother every chance he got. Travis was home grown and proud of it, his pride and love of Parry Sound drawing in a lot of extra tourism. People would rent cottages up here, hell bent on getting a chance to meet the famous country singer. And often, especially during the summer, they were rewarded. He could act like a self-centred asshole all he wanted, but deep down he was a good guy.

Every year after Travis performed at the fair, a huge after party was planned at the Clayton's property. The Clayton's were a rich family that had a massive barn they'd renovated into a beautiful bar and venue hall for events. It was featured in magazines all over the world and as a result, weddings, proms and other special occasions were booked there year-round.

The last time I'd gone to a party at the Clayton's barn, I'd been with Elle. The fact that I was there without her pissed me off, so I didn't particularly mind spending my night listening to Travis act like a redneck version of Justin Bieber. It was entertaining enough to keep the majority of my thoughts from drifting to her again, although any time she snuck through my barriers, my heart ached.

I felt her absence from my life so profoundly, that it was taking everything in me to not march over to the bar and fall into the comfortable, old habit of washing away my regrets.

Seeing her fall apart earlier today wasn't helping. I couldn't help but shoulder the blame. If I had never hurt her, if I had let things play out the way that they were supposed to instead of pushing us to our untimely end, maybe we'd still be together and it would be me helping her through the darkness.

I tried to focus on the conversations happening around me. It seemed like the entire gang was together again—Gordon, Tommy, Ezra, Grady, Peter, Krista, Brock and Tessa were all present. Even Becky was out for the evening, after recruiting a babysitter to watch Aiden. I couldn't be sure if she'd come out to let off some steam, or if she'd come out to keep a watchful eye on me.

Even though they didn't say it, my siblings were still worried about me. I felt their eyes on me every time I had my back turned. They were waiting for me to fall back into old habits, to grab a beer with the guys.

It was disheartening, to say the least. I didn't know if I would ever earn their trust back, and their apprehension and lack of faith in me made *me* waver.

I watched the dance floor from my spot leaning against the railing of the loft as Travis made his rounds, his easy, dimpled smile wooing the girls he hit on. Out of the corner of my eye, I could see my sister go rigid. Her spine stiffened and the smile on her face slid away.

"Becs, you alright?" I asked, arching a brow at her.

Becky shook her head, as if clearing her thoughts away. She pasted on a smile and shrugged, bringing her white wine spritzer to her lips. "Yeah, why wouldn't I be?" she asked before taking a delicate sip.

"Alrighty then," I shrugged, biting back a smile. My sister didn't want to talk, that was fine. I understood it. I didn't like talking about my emotions either. Emotions were complicated, feelings were confusing.

My eyes landed back on the dance floor, and I kept scanning the crowd, searching for her. I didn't know if she was still at the fair, or if she'd left after the smash-up derby, but I desperate to see her.

"Braden Miller, I heard you'd come back!" a voice said, drawing me out of my thoughts of Elle. I turned around, catching sight of Joanna Poole as she sauntered up to me, hips swaying. She was dressed in shorts that left little to the imagination, and a crop top that didn't even pass as a shirt. She came to a stop in front of me, placing a hand on my arm. "Oh my God, how is it possible that you're more delicious than you were in high school?" she giggled, squeezing the muscle on my arm with wide eyes.

I pulled my arm away from her grip and forced a smile in place. I couldn't really blame Joanna for what happened between Elle and me, but she was a painful reminder of my idiocy. "Yeah, well," I said, shrugging and averting my gaze.

Tessa's eyes were narrowed in on my face. I furrowed my brow, frustrated. There wasn't a way to untangle myself from Joanna's clutches without seeming like an asshole, and Tessa knew it. She smirked, as if she was enjoying my discomfort.

"Joanna!" Peter said, coming to the rescue and enveloping his arms around her in a huge hug. "Glad you could make it out!"

"I know, I haven't seen you in *forever*," Joanna said, flipping her hair over her shoulder as her eyes fixed on Peter. "Daddy told me you were working for him now!"

"I am," Peter said proudly. "It's a great job. Your dad's an awesome guy to work for."

"He sure is," Joanna pursed her lips in agreement, her eyes pausing on Tessa and Krista. "Hi Krista." The note of distain in her voice was clearly detectable to everyone around us.

"Hey Joanna, how's Waterloo?" Krista asked, forcing a polite smile.

"More entertaining than this town, that's for sure," Joanna replied haughtily. "The art scene is so advanced. Honestly, you'd love it—but you never take me up on my offers to come out for a visit," she added, tilting her head with a sickly sweet smile on her face.

"I've been really busy with university," Krista said apologetically. "I'm graduating next spring, so maybe after that I'll have time."

"Yeah, maybe," Joanna shrugged. She looked back to Tessa. "I heard congratulations are in order. Guess there's a reason why I didn't get an invitation?"

"We're keeping it small, basically family and *close* friends only," Tessa answered, her eyes never wavering from Joanna's face.

"I see," Joanna clearly didn't like Tessa's answer. "Well, if you need a date Braden…" she added, trailing off and giving me a wink.

"Nah, I'm good," I replied. All I could think about was how badly Elle would hurt if I even considered taking Joanna to Tessa's wedding as my date. That gutted me more than the possibility of offending or hurting Joanna's feelings.

Joanna's eyes narrowed into slits, and she tried to shrug her shoulder nonchalantly. "Your loss," she said. "I'm going to go grab a drink. Come with me, Peter."

I watched her and Peter go with a scowl on my face. The scowl faded when my eyes landed on Elle as she walked into the barn.

I was captivated as I watched her walk across the dance floor. She paused to speak to Travis, getting swept up into his arms and wearing a huge grin as she introduced her *boyfriend* to him. The guy looked like a star struck teenager at a Taylor Swift concert. I was almost expecting him to start fanning his face before he fainted.

What a douche.

My displeasure at his presence evaporated as Travis hugged her once more before they said their goodbyes. I watched her walk up the loft stairs. It was like everything around us ceased to exist, and it was just me and her. It didn't even matter that she was holding another guy's hand; all I saw was *her*.

Her brown eyes were locked on mine, and I could barely breathe. I couldn't break my gaze on her until Tessa flew past me and jumped into her arms.

My throat itched as I forced myself to turn and engage someone in conversation. I needed a distraction. My eyes immediately landed on Krista. I took two steps closer to her and nodded at her, grasping her attention as if I'd called out. "Krista, how's it going?"

"What?" she seemed confused, and rightfully so. I'd never really spoken more than four words to her directly. She'd been a part of our circle of friends for so long, and I didn't know a bloody thing about her.

I didn't need to tell her that the only reason why I was talking to her was to make Elle jealous. I smiled at Krista, trying to mimic the ways I'd smiled for Elle. It seemed to work because Krista's shoulders dropped as she relaxed, a small smile gracing the corners of her lips as she twirled her hair around her finger.

"Oh, it's going good," she answered, leaning back against the large log pole that was directly behind her. She gazed up at me with heavy lids, her lashes brushing against the top of her cheeks as she blinked slowly.

I leaned into her a little, putting my right hand beside her shoulder on the pole. I gave her an arrogant smile. "Are you single?"

"Yes," she breathed, blinking more rapidly. I could feel Elle's gaze hot upon my back, and I chanced a look over my shoulder. Her jaw was tense and her eyes were hard and dark. Elle's eyes always appeared darker when she was pissed off. Somehow, it made her look even more irresistible to me. I smirked and looked back at Krista, catching her looking over my shoulder at Elle. "Oh my God, Braden, you're such a dick," she said, shoving at my chest. I held my ground, moving in closer again and narrowing my gaze in on hers. She stilled, her breaths coming out in shallow puffs.

"I need a distraction right now," I said lowly, my eyes pleading with hers.

She said nothing. After a moment she nodded slowly, as if understanding all the things I hadn't said.

I smiled and brought my lips closer to her ear. "Thank you," I murmured loud enough for her to hear over the music.

"You know, this is just going to cause unjust tension," Krista sighed. "Elle is going to be a super bitch to me again, and I'm supposed to be spending a lot of time with her over the next few weeks. The bachelorette party is next weekend!"

"She won't be mad at you," I assured her, grinning my promise. "I plan on telling her exactly what this is. I just want her to be jealous for a while."

"This is not going to end well," Krista cautioned me, her eyes leveled with mine.

I ignored her, because I begged to differ. Elle was confident and secure, but she had always aired on the jealous side when it came to me talking to other women. I was a player before her, and she knew it.

I chanced another look over my shoulder. Elle was hanging off Alex's arm, focusing all of her attention on Tessa and Brock. His phone started to ring, and he grabbed it after excusing himself. He made his way back down the stairs and across the dance floor to the doors, disappearing into the night while Elle watched after him with a frown on her lips.

Tessa drew her back into the conversation, and a few minutes later Alex was rushing back up the stairs. He said something to Elle and they walked closer to the railing, away from everyone. I couldn't exactly hear what they were saying over the music blasting from the speakers, but Elle didn't look happy about it. His hands came up to hold her shoulders as he gazed down at her, his lips moving as he spoke to her. He kissed her softly on the forehead and pulled her into his chest for a hug. A moment later, he was weaving his way back down across the dance floor and out the door while Elle rejoined Tessa.

When *Keeper of the Stars* by Tracy Byrd came on, Brock grabbed Tessa's hand and started tugging her towards the dance floor. Becky had disappeared during my little display with Krista, which meant that Elle was left hanging around by herself. I could tell by the lines beside her lips that she was contemplating leaving.

"Why don't you go get yourself a drink, Krista?" I urged her, passing her some cash for the bar.

"Do you want anything?" she huffed, aggravated at the dismissal.

"A bottle of water would be good," I told her, flashing her a dimpled simple before I spanked her ass. I knew Elle caught the gesture, and I knew it pissed her off from the way her fists clenched at her sides.

When Krista disappeared down the stairs, I made my move. I approached Elle with ease, flashing that special smile I knew I could never replicate for anybody but her. It seemed so natural to walk towards her.

"Where'd you boyfriend run off to?" I asked, raising my brow in question.

"Not that it's any of your business, but he got called into work," she glowered at me. I couldn't even prevent my smile from slipping into a ridiculously huge grin. "What are you smiling for?"

"No reason," I shrugged, trying for indifference. "Dance with me."

"No," Elle crossed her arms, her eyes cold.

"Come on, for old times' sake," I challenged. "We're going to have to dance together at the wedding. Might as well practice a little—don't need you stepping all over my feet or stabbing me with one of those glass mason jar vases Tessa's been putting together."

"I would never stab you with a centerpiece," Elle smirked. "Now the bread knife..."

"So funny," I said dryly, extending my hand out to her. "Now let's dance."

Elle debated for a few long seconds, her eyes dropping down to my hand and back up to my face again. Uncertainly lined her eyes. We stared at each other for another beat, and she must have seen something in my gaze. Her expression softened, the walls coming down a little—or at least, a door opening somewhere for me.

"Ugh, fine. But so help me God Braden, if you try anything... I'll kick you in the gonads."

I led her out onto the dance floor, placing my hands on her hips and drawing her close to me. Her arms went around my neck and I was struck again by just how well we fit together. It was as if she was made for my arms and my arms alone. The way she worried her lips had me wondering if she was feeling the same thing.

"What's with you and Krista?" she finally said, unable to handle the silence I basked in.

"Nothing," I grinned. "Absolutely nothing."

"Didn't look like nothing."

"Are you jealous?" I asked her, loving that idea.

"Of course not," Elle huffed, rolling her eyes. The lie she spoke written clear as day across her face.

"There's only one girl for me," I told her, my lips dangerously close to her ear lobe. Elle used to love it when I kissed her neck and nibbled on her ear lobe. She shivered, erupting into tiny goosebumps as my breath cascaded across her skin.

Frozen in time, I allowed myself a moment to linger there, my lips hovering above the sensitive skin just below her ear. The desire I felt for her was evident, but I didn't push myself against her like I wanted to.

She abruptly pulled away from me, her eyes locking on mine, wild and wary. Her breath was coming out in quick bursts. "Don't," she told me, her lips tight as she walked away without another word. I followed her out of the barn, watching as she pulled her cell phone out and called someone.

"Come on Mom, pick up," she grumbled, hitting end and redialing when her call went unanswered.

"Do you need a lift home?" I offered, keeping my distance from her. I shoved my hands in my pockets so I wouldn't be tempted to touch her. She froze again, slowly turning to glare at me.

"No Braden, I'm fine," she practically hissed.

I pulled my hands out of my pockets and raised them in surrender. "Easy, I'm just saying. I'm heading home now, and I haven't been drinking obviously so I can drive you."

Elle debated, looking down at her phone and back up at me. She knew as well as I did that nobody else was leaving any time soon. "Fine," she sighed. "Where are you parked?"

I gestured with my head over to the field on our left. The

Clayton's had made a couple of parking lots in their old fields to the left of the barn. They'd left the right fields for their beautiful thoroughbred horses to roam. I led the way to my truck, Elle falling into step beside me.

"Is it hard?" she asked me, looking at me funny.

"Not right now, but I'm sure if you took your top off—"

"That's not what I meant, Braden," Elle scowled. "I meant…is it hard for you to be at things like this?"

I didn't answer for several long minutes. I didn't want to appear weak to her, and I didn't want to make her doubt me like my siblings did. "Sometimes," I said honestly. I left out the part where she offered the biggest, most effective distraction. With her around, my thirst for alcohol all but disappeared. "But I'd like to think I'm strong enough to handle it."

"You are," Elle nodded, sincerity in every word. Sometimes, I caught her looking at me the way she used to, when her faith in me was immeasurable. It was the way she looked at me before I broke her trust and her heart. I'd give anything to have her look at me that way all the time, not just when she forgot to put her guard up around me. But the fact that she *was* able to see me in that light—no matter how fleeting—was enough to keep the hope that bloomed in my chest alive.

We reached my truck and climbed into the cab. I shoved the key into the ignition and turned it, the engine roaring to life. Elle said nothing as I pulled out of my parking spot and drove out of the dirt lot to the driveway.

I could tell she was completely lost in her thoughts because she didn't say a single thing the entire ten minutes it took to drive to her house. I drove slowly up her long driveway, coming to a complete stop and putting the truck in park. Glancing over at her, I tried to ignore the intense longing I had to reach across the space and touch her.

"Thanks for the ride," Elle told me, biting on her bottom lip gently. One hand was gripping the door handle while the other fidgeted in her lap. I wondered if she was fighting the same desires I was. From the looks of her body language, she was. I could read Elle like a book—I knew when she wanted something and when she was fighting it. She used to act the same way whenever we had a spat.

"I'll give you a ride any time you need it," I smirked, chuckling at the innuendo. Elle's eyes narrowed at me, but her lips curved up in the smallest smile.

"Goodnight, Braden," she said on an exhale before climbing out.

CHAPTER ELEVEN

 *lle*

SUNDAY WAS the last day of the Stampede, and it was also one of the busiest days. The chili cook-off was one of the stampede's main events, and my mother *always* won it. Prior to moving away for college and starting my job, I'd helped her every single year. Not with the cooking of the chili—cooking was *not* my thing—but with the serving after the judges announced a winner. All of the chili cook-off participants were able to serve bowls of the remaining chili.

I used to volunteer Braden for dish duty, just so we could spend the afternoon together. He always did it without complaint—usually because I made it worth his while afterwards.

This year, Mom seemed determined to make up for all the years I'd missed out on helping her. Not only was I on serving duty, but I knew I'd be on clean-up too. She'd help me of course —but Mom always cooked a *ton* of chili.

Truthfully, I was thankful that Alex got called back into work the night before. I just didn't know what to say to him anymore and every second that passed in silence made my skin prickle.

The entire time he'd been here with me, I looked at him and willed myself to feel fireworks and electricity between us. I always came up short. Things with Alex were comfortable; the fireworks and electricity just weren't there, and every second I unwillingly spent in Braden's company reaffirmed that. Whether I liked it or not, we had the fireworks and electricity. He made me burn, he made me feel alive, and I was fighting it because that was what I did best.

The lineup seemed never ending, and I ladled scoop after scoop of chili alongside of my mom. I saw so many people that I knew from school and around town, and every single one of them wanted to catch up. I was so exhausted by the time the lineup started dying down that I didn't even notice Braden approach until he was standing right in front of me.

"Any chili left?" he asked, smirking at me in that way that made me want to both punch him and jump into his arms. I hated the way his hair curled around the black cap he was wearing. I hated the way I wanted to run my fingers through it.

"No," I said, even though I still had several servings left.

"Oh come on Elle," Braden pleaded, his hands coming up to clutch at his heart. "You wouldn't deny a man your mom's famous chili, would you?"

"I wouldn't deny *a man* my mom's famous chili, but I'd deny a man-child who couldn't handle the heat," I responded, my tongue sharper and quicker than my common sense.

"You wound me," Braden responded, but his eyes were light and the smile on his lips told me otherwise.

"Fine," I rolled my eyes dramatically. "If I give you the stupid chili, will you leave me alone?"

"Nope," Braden grinned. "I've been instructed to fetch you by Tessa. But I'll take that chili regardless."

"Fetch me? For what?"

"We're going mudding before the bonfire," Braden informed me, a sly grin on his face. My ears perked up. I hadn't been mudding in *such* a long time, since the summer before I started college—when Braden and I were still together.

"I can't come. I'm helping my mom with the stand," I said, surprised that I felt disappointed by this. I found that I actually *wanted* to go, even if Braden was going to be there. We all used to have so much fun together. Everything felt lighter and free back then, and I wanted a taste of that again.

I could feel her eyes on me, watching my reactions. My mother had always been a very intuitive person. Lying to her was virtually impossible. Had she ever outright *asked* me if Braden snuck into my room at night, she would have known the truth just by taking one look at me.

"Give him the chilli and go," she said, a bemused smile on her lips as she studied us both. I hadn't seen her eyes twinkle like that in a while. It felt like ever since Alex had arrived, Mom was paying extra close attention to me. Even though I still hadn't said anything to her, I could tell by the look in her eyes that she just *knew*.

"Are you sure, Mom?" I asked, frowning a little. I didn't want to leave her to handle the clean up by herself.

"I've done it myself the last three years and I've survived," Mom pointed out, raising her brows as she smiled at me. She gently squeezed my forearm. "It'll be fine, Elle. Go blow off some steam."

"Alright," I sighed, ladling a scoop of chili into a bowl and passing it to Braden.

Wiping my hands on a towel, I bent underneath the booth to grab my purse. *At least I don't have to change,* I thought as I peered down at my outfit and assessed it. I was wearing a pair of shorts and a black tank top that I wasn't overly attached to anyway. My hair was already pulled up in a messy ponytail and stuffed beneath a Cabela's baseball cap. It was hotter than hell out, and my skin was coated in a thin layer of moisture already. Besides, mud always washed off.

By the time I'd gathered my things, Braden had already finished and disposed of his chili and was waiting for me with that irresistible dimpled smile. Instantly, I regretted my decision. An entire afternoon hanging out with my ex-boyfriend, who would undoubtedly take his shirt off at some point because *why the hell not?* I would have to endure an afternoon of staring at his washboard abs, and that hardly seemed fair.

"Who's all going to be there?" I demanded, following Braden as he led the way. I could see his 2002 Yamaha Big Bear secured in the bed of his truck ahead.

"Tessa, Brock, Travis, Gordon, Tommy, Ezra, Peter, Grady, Krista, Becky, and Aiden," Braden replied, his eyes lingering on my lips for a moment.

"Aiden goes now?"

"Yup, he's seven," Braden said with a note of pride. "He has his own little ATV. You should see how he rips around on that thing. Brock bought it for him last summer."

My heart clenched at the picture Braden painted for me. Back when we were together, I spent *a lot* of time with little Aiden. He had only been four at the time, and he'd been the sweetest kid. He had a huge heart and listened better than most of the adults I'd encountered. It sucked to think about the fact that I had missed three years of his life.

"Are we going to the usual spot?" I asked, needing to fill the silence.

In high school, we would always go to the property that Braden's family owned. His grandfather had purchased 180 acres of land on a small lake in one of the little hamlets near Parry Sound, and he'd left sixty acres to each grandchild.

Braden hadn't officially owned his chunk of land until his twenty-first birthday, but nobody was going to stop us from mudding there, especially not when we were thirty-five acres away from the roads.

"Yeah," Braden responded, rolling down the windows as he pulled carefully out of his spot. There were still a lot of people around, so he drove extra cautiously, wary of kids darting out from around vehicles.

He sped up when we hit the highway, and the wind blew the loose strands of my hair around. I closed my eyes, enjoying the warm breeze. In that moment, I was almost at peace.

Twenty-minutes later, Braden was pulling into Brock's driveway. He backed it up slowly towards the garage, placing his right arm across the back of the seat—dangerously close to touching the nape of my neck.

Brock's driveway was already jammed with vehicles, and all of the guys were hanging out in front of the open garage, along with Brock's dog, Hunter. Once Braden put the truck in park, we hopped out. Braden, Brock, and Grady had ramps up and the ATV out within minutes, making the whole thing look more effortless than it actually was.

"Yay! I'm so glad you're here," Tessa squealed, jumping onto my back. We were practically the same size, but my knees still almost buckled as I hadn't been prepared to suddenly take on her weight. "I know it's completely last minute, but remember when we used to do things like this all the time? Throw a last-minute plan together and wing it? God I miss those days," she added with a laugh.

"I do too," I admitted, my voice almost too quiet. Tessa tilted her head, taking a moment to study me.

"I know," she said carefully, a mischievous glint to her eye. "So, here's the run down. Basically everyone has their own ATV but you. Grady and Gordon brought their girlfriends, and Tommy's got a friend here so you can't ride with any of them."

"I figured as much," I sighed, shaking my head at her. I could almost *see* how this was going to play out. She started leading me over to where all the ATV's were parked, on Brock's front lawn.

"You're welcome to share mine though!" She grinned at me. Although she hadn't even suggested riding with Braden, I knew that's where her thoughts had taken her. I used to ride with him all the time. I had never owned an ATV, but I knew how to operate one. Braden would let me drive it whenever I wanted to, so I hadn't felt the need to buy one for myself. "Here she is!" Tessa stopped and touched the handle of a sleek black 2016 Grizzly.

"When did you get *that?*" I asked, almost whistling while I checked it out.

"The old Grizzly finally died for good, so Brock bought me a new one as my engagement gift!" Tessa's dad had owned an old green 1999 Yamaha Grizzly that she borrowed all throughout high school. The thing was so old that it was constantly breaking down on the trails, and Braden was always trying to fix it for her.

"You get a *ring* and an ATV? Damn. I need to get married," I sighed, pouting at her. She laughed at me and rolled her eyes.

"You will, one day. And whoever the lucky guy is better spoil you like you deserve, or he'll be learning a hard lesson from your best friend," Tessa joked. "Let's go help Becky, she's in the kitchen trying to put coolers together."

I nodded in response and we walked over to the open screen door that led into Brock's kitchen. Becky had three coolers open on top of the large island counter and was hard at work making sandwiches. One of them was full of water and juice boxes, the second was full of beer and wine coolers, and the third one, Becky was filling with sandwiches and snacks.

"You're such a mom," I grinned at her, shaking my head. Becky froze for a fraction of a second, almost as if my words had wounded her. I had meant them as a joke, and immediately felt bad at the thought of having hurt her feelings. But before I could apologize, she was smiling and lifting her shoulder in a delicate shrug.

"You can't turn it off," she said, as if it couldn't be helped. Tessa and I joined her at the counter and helped make a few more sandwiches.

"That should be enough," Becky finally said, closing the lid on the food cooler. We each carried one outside and tied them to the storage racks on the back of Brock, Tessa, and Becky's ATVs.

My eyes searched around the group of people that had gathered. Brock, Braden, Grady, Gordon, Tommy, Peter, and Ezra were hanging out by the garage still, and Aiden was beside Braden, his spine straight as he tried to stand up as tall as he could. Hunter lumbered over to him and nudged his hand with his head, as if insisting the boy stop what he was doing and stroke his fur. Aiden's eyes lit up as he kneeled to pet the dog.

"He's really shot up," I remarked to Becky, smiling in his direction.

"He did," Becky agreed, nodding as she gazed at her son.

"I bet he doesn't even remember me," I sighed. "Three years is a long time…"

"He remembers you," Becky assured me, her voice sounding ominous. When I arched a brow in question, she shrugged. "There's pictures of you in Braden's room. He never packed anything away before he left, and I wasn't about to do it."

I wanted to ask her if he'd packed those pictures away *now*, now that he was home, but I didn't. I was afraid of the answer.

The girls that Gordon and Grady had brought were hanging out with my cousin, Samantha, and Krista by the ATVs. Tessa dragged me over to them for introductions. "This is Paige, Grady's girlfriend. Annaka is foolishly with Gordon, although hopefully she wises up soon—"

146

"Hey! I heard that!" Gordon yelled out, scowling at Tessa. She flipped him off and he grinned.

"Hey Elle," Sam, grinned, lifting her hand in greeting. Sam lived with her grandmother and mother at the Dabrowski farm, the old apple farm connected to the Armstrong's property. Our grandpas had been brothers, but I never knew mine. He died when my mom was little.

"Hey, Sam!" I grinned back, stepping toward her and giving her a hug. I hadn't seen her in far too long. "It's so good to see you again! You look amazing."

She blushed, almost wincing in my arms, and stepped back. "Hardly. I look exhausted; like I've just crushed two years of online courses in one."

"Probably because you *did*," I snickered. She smiled, tucking a flyaway hair behind her ear. Sam and I shared the dark Dabrowski hair, which she kept mostly hidden beneath an old Blue Jays baseball cap and a low ponytail.

Unlike me, Sam hated attention of any kind; whether it be attention paid to her incredible smarts, or her looks...it all made her uncomfortable. She had a chronic pain bone disorder called Multiple Exostoses, and she had had *many* surgeries to remove the painful bone growths. She had a lot of scars that she'd spent her life trying to hide beneath long-sleeved shirts and jeans. I'd spent mine trying to crack her out of that thought; but it was hard. Sam just wasn't interested in fashion and makeup like I'd been.

Sam was beautiful, but she preferred to fade in the background. I didn't think my cousin realized how hard it was for her to do that; she could dress as Tom-boyish as she wanted, but her unique eyes pulled people in and unveiled her beauty. They were so blue, they appeared almost violet, and framed by thick dark lashes. She was one of those girls that had an intense natural beauty that needed *no* extra help to enhance.

I'd watched Tommy trip over himself for years over her, and

it was entertaining as all hell. I shot him a wicked grin over her shoulder, which he studiously ignored, showing me his back as he turned his attention back to the guys. Those two were stuck on a friendship cycle, but it was obvious to everyone but the two of them that they needed to get off that bike and make it official.

"Ladies, this is Elle." Tessa introduced me to the other two women once I'd finished catching up with Sam.

"Hey," I said, assessing the newcomers with a warm smile. Paige had a friendly smile, golden hair and freckles lining her nose and cheeks. Gordon's girlfriend, Annaka, seemed out of place. She was quite pretty in an edgy way; and was unlike anyone he'd ever dated before in appearance alone. She had gages in her lobes, her labret and left nostril pierced, and ashy purple hair with 50's style pin-up girl bangs. She had ink on every free square inch of skin, and she wore winged eyeliner and dark red lipstick, which was an odd choice for an afternoon of mudding—then again, who's to say that Annaka wasn't hit with this plan at the last minute, just like I'd been? "I love your makeup," I said to her.

"Thanks," she grinned, her white teeth flashing. She even had a gem on her right canine tooth.

"Annaka is a tattoo artist," Tessa said. "She works in a shop in Sudbury."

"Impressive," I said, arching my brow. "How in the hell did Gordon find you?"

"It's a long story," Annaka laughed. She looked over her shoulder to see if Gordon was paying attention. When she confirmed that he wasn't, she leaned forward. "Two weeks ago, he came to the shop to get a tattoo but greened out on my table."

Tessa burst into laughter. "Oh, it never gets old," she told me, grinning. "Gordon's always been such a wuss when it comes to needles. I can't even believe he attempted to get a tattoo."

"So he didn't end up sticking it out?" I asked, bemused. I

looked over to where the guys were standing, and caught Braden staring at me. He smiled a secret smile, and I felt my body flush under his heady gaze.

"Not at all, he's got one random dot on his shoulder. It basically looks like a dark freckle," Annaka chuckled. "But while he was passed out, I thought...*huh, he's cute.* I've never dated a farm boy before, so when he asked me out...I said yes." She continued, casting a brief smitten look at him over her shoulder.

We ended up waiting another fifteen minutes for Travis to finally show up. Thankfully, he came solo—without his usual bodyguard or entourage. Once his ATV was unloaded off his massive Chevy Silverado, everyone got ready to hit the trails. Becky fussed over Aiden a little, making sure that he'd strapped on his helmet securely.

I didn't even glance over in Braden's direction. I knew he'd invite me to ride with him, and I knew that I would have trouble telling him no. Instead, I climbed on to the back of Tessa's ATV. I held the passenger hand grips as she pulled out behind Brock, who led the way with Hunter ambling alongside. Braden travelled behind us, and then everyone else followed with Becky and Aiden taking up the rear.

Becky wanted Aiden to go slower than everyone else. I could tell that she was a little nervous letting him ride in such a big group, but everyone was cautious of the seven-year old. We didn't ride as hard or as fast as we usually did.

It was about a ten-minute ride to our regular mudding spot in the clearing. We had to go through the swampy area, so by the time we actually made it to the clearing, the majority of our legs were covered in mud. Especially mine—Tessa liked to hit every puddle that she could, laughing with delight every time she showered us. Her mood was infectious, and I laughed along with my best friend.

Years ago, Brock, Gordon, Grady and another one of their high school friends had created a large track in the clearing with miniature jumps for the ATVs, nothing too drastic or dangerous. The clearing had a couple of springs underneath running through it, but the ground wasn't as muddy as it usually was due to the lack of rain we'd gotten that month.

We all took turns running the track and eating the sandwiches Becky had made. Aiden hooted and hollered when the guys decided to race. Tessa and I, never refusing a challenge, demanded to be included. Tessa was as fast as they were, and she won the race by half an inch. I came in just behind her on Becky's ATV, beating out Braden and splashing him directly in the face when my rear tire squealed through the mud.

I smirked when I saw how muddy Braden's face was, but my laughter died on the tip of my tongue when he brought his shirt up to wipe away the guck from his eyes, exposing the taut muscles of his stomach. My heart sped up, my blood heated, and I ached for his touch again, the heat pooling between my thighs as if my body remembered in exact detail what it felt like to be beneath him.

Wrinkling my nose with disgust at my own traitorous body's response, I pressed my thumb hard on the gas and shot forward, driving back to where Becky and Aiden were waiting.

I turned off the machine and climbed off to the sound of Aiden begging to participate too. "Come on Mom! Just one race? PLEASE!?" he pleaded, his Miller blue eyes wide with hope.

I had no idea how Becky could refuse him. If I had a child half as cute as him, with eyes like that—so much like Braden's—I'd be powerless and give in to his every request.

"I don't know, Aiden," Becky said, her uncertainty ringing in her voice.

"But Mom!" he whined, pouting. "Even the *girls* got to race!"

"Hey now, that's not fair," I interjected, my hand on my hip. "Why are you using us girls as an example here, kid? Girls have every right to race. Hell, we're better than your uncle!"

"I know," Aiden replied sheepishly, his pout growing as he kicked at the dirt. "But I'm seven now! I can race too! I bet I'd beat Uncle Braden. It doesn't look hard at all!"

I couldn't help but laugh at his response.

"You can race me little man," Travis offered, grinning at Aiden. He ran a hand through his wavy, dark blond locks. Becky's eyes shot to his, and she frowned.

"Now I really don't know," she scowled.

"I promise, it'll be fine," Travis assured her, his eyes lingering longer than necessary on her face. I could have sworn I saw a look of longing pass across his features. Becky sighed heavily. Intrigued, I watched as her lips lifted in a reluctant smile.

"Fine, just one loop," she told Aiden.

We all watched while Travis and Aiden raced around the track. I thought that Aiden wouldn't do more than twenty-five miles per hour, but he surprised us all by going almost sixty. Becky practically bit her nails off watching. She didn't relax until Aiden had finished the loop first and was tossing his fists up in victory.

By the time we'd had enough, every last one of us was covered in mud.

"Let's go swimming," Braden suggested, and almost everyone agreed. We finished our snacks and loaded the coolers back up. Before I could climb onto the back of Tessa's ATV, she was taking off down the trail.

"Seriously?" I grumbled, glaring after her when she tossed a satisfied grin across her shoulder at me.

Braden revved his ATV from behind me. "Hop on," he instructed, the corner of his lip shooting up in a half-smile. Since most everyone else had left before Tessa, I had limited options. I climbed onto the back and tried to sit as far away from him as I could.

But Braden's ATV didn't have the same passenger grips that Tessa's ATV had. When he pressed down on the gas, we shot forward so fast and hard that my only option was to grab onto him for dear life. I heard his chuckle as I clung to his waist.

Holding him again like this did strange things to my heart. It thudded wildly in my chest. I could pretend it was the sudden jump forward, but the real reason my heart was hammering had less to do with the speeds Braden hit and *everything* to do with how close I was to him—and how hard and tight his abdomen was beneath my frantic grip.

We pulled up to the beach after everyone else had arrived. Tessa was waiting for me by her Grizzly, still wearing a smug smile. I hopped off the back of Braden's ATV the moment he stopped it, as if he was covered in thousands of tiny spiders.

I stalked over to my traitorous best friend. "How could you do that? Leave me with him like that?" I hissed.

Tessa winced apologetically, her amber eyes seeking my forgiveness. "I'm sorry, he paid me off."

"How much?" I sighed.

"A hundred bucks, actually," Tessa chuckled. "I figured we could split it."

"No, I'll be taking it all," I informed her.

Before Tessa could say another word, I was scooped up from behind. I knew from the feel of the calloused hands, strong arms and hard chest that it was Braden.

"Don't you dare!" I practically screeched, trying to wiggle my way out of his arms.

But naturally, Braden didn't listen, and Tessa's laughter followed me as he marched purposely down the dock. A moment later, I was submerged in the cool water of the lake, his arms still around me.

CHAPTER TWELVE

 *raden*

It was the best one hundred dollars I'd ever spent. Feeling her arms wrapped around me from behind, having her warm breath against the back of my neck and her scent enveloping me while we raced back down the trails was heaven.

But Elle hadn't been thrilled about the arrangement at all, and the moment we got back to the beach, she'd started hissing angrily at Tessa. I felt bad that my soon-to-be sister-in-law was getting the flack for my idea. I figured that Elle needed to cool off a little, so I picked her up and ran off the dock with her in my arms. I held her as long as I dared before releasing her.

"You're such a dick, Braden," she said, but her eyes were light and she was laughing.

"I know," I murmured, swimming closer to her. We stared at each other for several long moments, the air between us wrought with tension and longing. She had mud on her cheek, and I absently brought my hand up, using my thumb to gently wipe it away. Her eyes were fixated on mine, as if she was locked in a trance. In that moment, I almost kissed her. I wanted so badly to press my lips against hers, to feel her surrender in my arms.

Her hands came up to my chest, her fingers curling into fists, nails gently pulling against my soaked t-shirt. Goose-bumps erupted across my skin, and I moved my lips closer to hers, my hand still cupping her cheek. She inhaled when I exhaled, and we breathed each other in, our eyes locked on one another.

Her brow furrowed and she broke our gaze by looking away. Her chest heaved as she drew in another deep breath. Shaking her head slightly she pushed off me and swam away, back towards the beach.

I remained in the water for almost a minute longer, trying to figure out what the hell all of this meant and what I was going to do about it. I ran my hands through my hair, brushing it back from my eyes as I walked out of the lake.

"Could you try *any* harder?" Gordon ribbed, punching me in the shoulder when I came to a stop where he was standing by the picnic table with Ezra, Peter, and Tommy. I was dripping wet, my t-shirt clung to my skin.

"Fuck off," I told Gordon, pulling my shirt off over my head with one hand and twisting it to ring it out. I felt Elle's eyes on me, and out of the corner of my eye I saw her scowl. I smirked.

"I think it's kind of sweet," Ezra remarked. The sympathy I saw in his eyes pissed me off almost as much as Gordon's ribbing.

"Sorry man. I think you're kicking a dead horse. Elle's stubborn as shit, and she hates your guts." Tommy interjected, shaking his head ruefully.

"I know she's stubborn," I said carefully, working hard to keep my jaw from grinding. "But I'm more stubborn than she is, and she doesn't *hate* me."

I knew Elle better than anyone else, and I knew the only thing she hated was the fact that she still wanted me.

"Whatever helps you sleep at night," Gordon said, chuckling softly.

GORDON AND TOMMY'S words rumbled around inside my brain, echoing like a freight train in a tunnel for the rest of the afternoon. I couldn't help but watch her from afar as she splashed around with Aiden and Tessa, torturing myself with doubts and insecurities. I wanted to grab the beer bottle from Tommy's stupid hand and toss it back, put a stop to all the nonsense roaring around in my head, but I resisted.

When dusk fell, everyone started to get their stuff together to leave. It was almost time for the community bonfire, and nobody in town missed that event. By that point, my shorts and t-shirt had dried completely in the stifling summer heat. That's the benefit of wearing all black. The downfall is that the horse flies are drawn to the colour black. I grew up in the bush, and horse fly bites barely phased me anymore.

Elle's clothes were still damp, and I knew she'd get cold if she wore them to the bonfire. "Want a lift home?" I offered, gesturing to my truck.

She gnawed on her bottom lip for a moment, her teeth sinking in to the plump soft pink flesh, and all of my blood immediately started to travel south.

"I've got some spare clothes in the cabin if you want to borrow something?" Tessa suggested, probably to make up for having ditched her with me on the trail earlier. She shrugged at me apologetically when Elle wasn't looking.

"Thanks Tessa." She smiled with relief that cut into me more than I cared to admit. I watched her follow Tessa up to the house, the doubt consuming me. I knew Elle wanted me, I knew she was warring with herself about it, but for the first time…I couldn't help but wonder if that stubborn determination of hers would win out.

I stomped over to the cab of my truck, reaching through the open window to grab my pack of smokes from the cup holder. Smoking was a dirty habit, but it gave my hands and mouth something to do when the thirst got to be too much for me to handle.

In that moment, it was too much to handle. I turned around and leaned against the door, my gaze lifting towards the cabin.

I tapped the bottom of the pack against the palm of my hand and watched as Elle moved in front of the large master bedroom window. She paused in front of it and looked outside. It was almost like she was looking straight into my soul. I drew in a breath, pulling a cigarette out and holding it between my lips, my eyes still locked on her for several long moments.

The sound of boots on gravel had me turning my head to watch Ezra walk up, his hands in his pockets. He came to stand beside me, leaning up against the side of my truck. By the time I looked back up to the cabin, Elle had closed the curtains and moved away from the window.

"I hope you're not still pissed about what Gordon and Tommy said. Those two are clueless when it comes to women," he told me, puffing out a small laugh as he stared over at our friends. Gordon, Tommy, and the girls they brought were standing beside Gordon's truck. "Just look at them. Gordon can't make a relationship last past the three-month mark and Tommy doesn't even know what's in front of him."

"What do you mean?" I squinted, looking at the girl standing in front of Tommy. She had hair a few shades lighter than Elle's, all of it piled under a Blue Jays cap. Her face was makeup free and she gazed at him with hopeful eyes.

"She looks at him like he's a god. She's super sweet, too, she's just not his usual type, so all he sees is a friend."

"What's your point?" I grumbled, irritated.

"I already made it," Ezra said, flashing me a toothy smile. "Don't listen to Tommy or Gordon. I don't think for one minute that what you have with Elle is a lost cause. I see the way she looks at you. That girl is still in love with you, no matter what she's telling herself. She always has been."

Ezra had always been the smarter one. We spent every day together through middle school and high school. He always had my back and I always had his, without question. I knew he wouldn't give me anything but the truth.

Grunting, I nodded once. I tried to leave it at that, but Ezra looked like he was waiting for me to say something. I brought my hand up to scratch at the back of my head. "Well, what about you?"

"What about me?"

"Krista," I gestured over my shoulder. Ezra followed my gaze, and he smiled wistfully. He'd had a thing for Krista longer than I could remember, but he was too sweet and trigger shy to do anything about it.

"The girls who stay around here dream about guys who aren't from here," he shrugged. "She wants new and exciting, not an old friend."

I put my hand on his shoulder, squeezing it gently. "Sorry man," I told him, feeling bad. "She might change her mind one day."

"Maybe," he shrugged. I opened my mouth again, searching for something else to say, when my gaze was drawn back up to the cabin as the door opened. Tessa and Elle piled out, both dressed in tight jeans, tank tops, and plaid long sleeve shirts left unbuttoned. Tessa was in blue, and Elle was in red.

I had always loved it when Elle wore red. It made her cream-coloured skin all the creamier, and the dark brunette ringlets that hung down her back seemed richer. She was beautiful, the kind of beautiful that took your breath away and made you believe in something almighty.

"Let's try and take as few vehicles as we can since parking will be ridiculous as always," Tessa suggested as they came to a stop in front of us.

Tommy, Sam and Annaka ended up going with Gordon while Grady, Paige, and Peter rode in Grady's truck. Travis hopped into the front seat of Becky's car, and I ended up sitting in the backseat cab of Brock's truck with Elle and Krista wedged beside me and Ezra.

We pulled into the jammed parking lot of the fairgrounds. It took Brock nearly ten minutes to find a parking spot, and when he finally did, Elle cursed loudly.

"What?" Tessa peered over the headrest.

"I forgot my purse in Braden's truck," she sighed, running a hand through her long locks.

"It's okay, I've got you covered," I said quickly, the corner of my lip lifting.

"See? No worries," Tessa smiled. "Let's go have a good night!"

We piled out of the truck, and I grabbed the blankets that Tessa had carried out for us to sit on. We met up with everyone else and walked together, finding a spot on the grass big enough to house our large group.

Blankets were spread down and the majority of the group took off towards the beer tent or food trucks. "Can I get you anything?" I froze at the sound of her voice, closing my eyes for a moment to try and pull it together. Elle's hand brushed against mine gently.

"How about a second chance?" I mumbled, my eyes opening and landing on hers. Her hand was still inches away from mine.

"How about a bottle of water, or a pop?" she suggested instead, trying to repress the smile that threatened to grace her lips.

"That works, I guess. Water, please."

"I'll need your money," she reminded me, a smirk dancing across her mouth. Chuckling, I pulled out my wallet from my back pocket and handed her a couple of twenties. The tips of her fingers brushed against mine, and electricity pulsed between us. It was so much like it was before, back when she was mine. It was like the last few years had never even happened. She was smiling at me in that same challenging way, the way that always made me press my lips to hers and kiss her until she stopped smirking and gave into me.

I knew she was just as affected as I was from the way her long lashes fluttered against the top of her cheeks. She swallowed, pulling her hand holding the bills to her side. She tossed a look back over her shoulder at me as she walked towards the beer tent with Tessa.

I fell back onto the blanket, pulling my black cap down over my eyes.

Now that I was back, I had no idea how I survived being gone all those years, how I was able to justify being away from the ones who meant the most to me. I had no idea how I was able to let her stay gone.

I couldn't imagine not having her in my life, even if it wasn't the way I preferred. Ideally, I wanted her to be mine again. I wanted her to trust me and love me the way she did before. But even if I couldn't have that, I wanted her friendship. Her laughter, her smile.

CHAPTER THIRTEEN

*lle*

AFTER THE EMBARRASSING events of the previous weekend, and my confusing thoughts regarding Braden, I threw myself into being the best maid of honor I could possibly be. Every second of my time—every spare thought—went to planning the bachelorette party. The night was going to be perfect—I'd made sure of it. Becky, Katie, Krista and I took Tessa to her favourite restaurant in Toronto for dinner, then we headed back to the hotel room to wait for the rest of the bachelorette party guests to arrive.

Our hotel room was big enough for the seven of us to crash comfortably. There were two queen sized beds and a pull out couch. Tessa, her cousin Caroline and I snagged one bed, Becky, Krista, and Katie snagged the other bed while Tessa's friends from Barrie—Olivia and Laura, would share the pull-out couch.

I couldn't wait to see Tessa's face when she saw all the fun stuff we had planned. I had printed off ten dare cards to hand to our beautiful bride-to-be throughout the night. Most of the items on the list were sure to embarrass her, but I was sure my friend would be a good sport. I gave her three passes—she could pass off three of the dares to any member in the bridal party to complete without question. I had a feeling I knew which ones she'd pass up, and I couldn't wait to see if I was right. Dare card number one would undoubtedly embarrass the shit out of Tessa, and that made me positively gleeful.

Dare card number one is why I had spent the last twenty minutes hiding in the hotel bathroom, blowing up a massive inflatable penis that I was going to torture Tessa with—she'd have to carry it all night.

I stood back and stared at the flesh coloured monstrosity, a loud giggle exploding from my lips. Pete the Penis even had a face! My hands went up to cover my mouth, as I tried to cover the sound of my laughter without success.

"Elle! What the hell are you doing in there? The front desk just called up—the limo is here and waiting!" Tessa's impatient voice, muffled through the closed door, only made me laugh harder.

I threw open the bathroom door, and Tessa's eyes widened with shock at the sight of me holding the inflatable, smiling penis. "I'm sorry, I had to blow a dick okay!"

The room exploded into a fit of laughter and camera flashes at the sight of the penis and Tessa's horrified expression. While I'd been busy in the bathroom, blowing Pete the Penis up, Caroline, Olivia, and Laura had arrived.

"What in the *hell* are you doing with that?" Tessa asked, dumbfounded.

"This is Pete the Penis and he'll be your date tonight," I smirked, shoving the inflatable dick at her. "You have to carry it *all* night."

"Pete the Penis!" Krista repeated with a cackle, doubling over. "I'm *so* hashtagging this!"

"Elle!" Tessa whined, her face going beat red. "I'm not carrying that around all night!" She tried to shove it back at me, but I sidestepped her, dancing around her until I was free of the small hallway that led to the bathroom.

Becky walked up to join us, the neat pile of cards in her hand. "Sure you are! It's dare number one!" she grinned, handing Tessa the first pretty pink card that declared she needed to bring Pete the Penis clubbing with us.

"Dare number one?" Tessa questioned us, her brow furrowing as she accepted the card from Becky and read it.

"Yup." I clapped, elated. "There are ten of them! You only get three pass offs, so use them wisely."

"Can I use a pass off now?" Tessa pouted, staring at Pete the Penis.

"Are you sure you want to do that, Tessa?" I said seriously, raising my eyebrows. "Just think about it...if this is dare one...what else does your old bestie have in store for you?"

"It gets worse, doesn't it?" Tessa moaned.

"It sure does!" Krista snorted. "I would definitely save those passes if I were you! You know how Elle can be."

Tessa looked from me to Krista and Becky, to the inflatable penis, and then back to me, resigned. Her expression quickly changed to one of devious satisfaction. "Just wait Elle. One day, I'll be *your* maid of honor and I'll be in charge of *your* bachelorette party."

My best friend's words made the hollow ache in my chest more profound, but I knew she wasn't trying to hurt me. It wasn't *her* fault that the whole "marriage" thing was a sore subject for me, and had been since I'd had my heart broken in the wake of my first love's own self-destruction. It wasn't her fault that I couldn't fall in love with my boyfriend, or that I was still hung up on the past and conflicted over what to do about it.

I forced an easy smile to my lips and grabbed my clutch. "Well, let's get going—Pete *really* needs to blow off some

steam..." I joked, pushing the aching feelings deep down inside
to deal with later...maybe.

Thankfully, Tessa was too distracted by the inflatable penis
to pay attention to anything else. She held it as if it were conta-
minated while the seven of us headed down from our room to
the limo. Each time we happened to come across another hotel
guest or worker, Tessa would turn bright red with embarrassment, and the rest of us would explode into a fit of giggles.

I tossed my arm around her shoulders. "I promise, it will get
easier," I assured her with a wicked grin. "The limo has a mini-
refrigerator and it's full of enough booze to get this party
started!"

Everyone piled into the limo, and I immediately started
pouring glasses of champagne and passing them around. "Here's
to Tessa," I said once everyone held a glass. My eyes landed on
my best friend and I smiled slowly. "And to one last hurrah as a
single woman!"

Glasses tinked together and our night of fun officially
started.

ONE OF THE best things about a bachelorette party is that the
bride doesn't have to buy her own drinks. None of us really had
to buy our own drinks. Our tabs were picked up by single guys
and drunk girls more often than not. Everyone got a kick out of
Pete the Penis, too. He was pictured in so many selfies I was
almost certain that by the end of the night, he'd be an Instagram
sensation.

Tessa proved to be a good sport too. She was on a mission to
complete all of her dares. She found a man with a moustache
and kissed him on the cheek, asked a body builder if she could
see his abs and pretended to wash laundry on them, got a
younger guy to buy her a drink. She asked a bachelor to write

down why she should marry him instead of the groom, asked the DJ to play five Justin Bieber songs in a row, and danced on the bar to said Justin Bieber songs. All while carrying around Pete the Penis.

My feet were aching and I desperately wanted to kick off my heels by the time we hit our final stop of the night—the male strip club. Tessa's final dare was to accept a lap dance on stage. I was surprised that she hadn't passed up any of her other dares, and I sort of figured she'd pass up on this. To my absolute delight, she didn't. She allowed herself to be led up on the stage by the cowboy stripper. He sat her down in a chair and started dancing for her and practically *on* her to Save a Horse Ride a Cowboy by Big and Rich. Our group—positioned in the booth closest to the stage—was struggling to keep it together.

Needing an excuse to break away from the group for a bit, I moved closer to the stage to take some pictures and videos. I nearly peed my pants laughing at Tessa's pink face and the cowboy's Magic Mike inspired moves as he thrust his pelvis at her in time to the music.

Becky sauntered over, holding two drinks with a bemused grin on her face as she watched Tessa. "Elle, you are cunning," she laughed, holding one of the drinks out to me. I gratefully accepted it, taking a slow sip while she threw her now free arm around me. Normally, Becky wasn't the hugging type, but tonight…she was the drunkest I'd ever seen her, and seemed to have no qualms with hugging everyone around her. "This night has been incredible—Tessa hasn't stopped smiling once. You outdid yourself!"

"Yeah well, the company is good," I responded, trying to hold back a smile. I was glad my planning paid off, glad that Tessa seemed to be having the time of her life. Everyone she'd requested to be here was here and all were getting along perfectly. Hell, even Olivia seemed less annoying tonight, which was a bonus for me.

I could see Becky watching me carefully out of the corner of my eye. I tried to keep my smile in place and focused on taking some more pictures of Tessa on stage. Becky's eyes were very similar to Braden's—they were the same electric blue—and having them fixed on me made me feel uneasy.

"Are you okay though?" she asked me, her voice as low as she could get it over the sound of the club. "You've seemed a little distracted and distant...almost like something's bugging you."

"I'm fine," I said, working harder to keep my smile in place. "I'm just a little tired."

Becky snorted. "Dude, I'm a mom. You can't bullshit a mom. We read lies like printed words in a book."

"You're pretty deep for a drunk person," I laughed, hoping my unease wasn't showing.

Becky grinned and shrugged. "Is it Braden?" she pressed, her eyes widening slightly.

"No," I said on an exhale. It might have been a tiny lie, but there was also a lot of truth in my statement. None of this had anything to do with Braden—it was all *me*. It wasn't Braden's fault that I couldn't emotionally handle the difficult profession I'd chosen. It wasn't *Braden's* fault that I couldn't find that spark with Alex. I mean, lots of girls had their hearts broken and moved on. My inability to leave the past in the past was my problem, not Braden's. It didn't matter if he was the beacon, the focal point for my sadness a lot of the time—that's where *I* put him.

With a start, I shook my head, desperate to clear my thoughts and get back to the present. Becky was still staring at me expectantly, as if waiting for me to spill my secrets to her. Unfortunately for me...vodka made my lips loose.

"I'm just going through something," I finally admitted, averting my eyes. "With work, I mean. It's been...hard."

Becky nodded thoughtfully. "I figured."

"How so?"

"Most people don't take a whole month off work to come out for a wedding," she pointed out with a sad smile.

I took a shaky breath, trying to stop the drunk verbal diarrhea from happening all over my ex-boyfriend's sister. "Yeah, well. It was sort of at the assistance of my boss and doctor."

"Ouch," Becky whistled, compassion softening her features. She was quiet for a moment, watching the stage and Tessa. "I know how hard it can be…if you ever need to talk, you know—when we're both sober, I'm around. Seriously Elle."

"Thanks, I appreciate it," I told her, knowing I likely wouldn't take her up on that offer—at least not while I was stone cold sober. I hadn't even told my mom yet, although I knew I needed to soon…she was already suspicious that something deeper was going on than my evasive answers about my vacation time and life in Barrie. I turned to look at Becky again. "Same goes for you. If you ever want to talk about whatever happened at Flanigan's, I'm around."

"I don't know what you're talking about," Becky hiccupped, trying to rearrange her features. I gave her a small, knowing smile, recalling the heartbreak on her face that night when Travis sauntered into the bar with the porno twins, and the way she'd quickly disappeared.

"You and Travis. I saw how you guys looked at each other at your mom's wake. I figured something happened between you," I said, my voice as close to a whisper as I could get it in the loud club.

Becky crossed her arms, as if suddenly cold in the sticky, sweaty club. She opened and closed her mouth, as if catching herself. "Thanks, but nothing's up with us—or me. Same old single Becky, same old life."

There was something sad about her statement, but before I could call her out on it, the club exploded into applause. The cowboy was done stripping for Tessa and she started to make her way off the stage. I raised my phone again, snapping a few more pictures of her as her shoulders shook with laughter and embarrassment.

She came up to us and jumped on me, wrapping her arms around me. "Thank you, Elle," she said into my ear.

"Oh, did you like that cowboy? If you prefer him to the hick you have back home, then that's alright by me. He could be Channing Tatum's twin," I joked. Tessa laughed and shoved away from me, her amber eyes dancing with amusement.

"The hick back home is all I want," she assured me. "But thank you for an amazing night, Elle. Seriously, you've exceeded all my expectations and then some." She gave me a big, sloppy kiss on the lips, her eyes shining. "I have the bestest best friend ever!"

THE NEXT MORNING, I awoke with one hell of a hangover. Everyone in the hotel room felt the same.

"Ugh my head," Katie moaned from the bed beside us. "What did I drink last night?" she wondered aloud.

"Just your weight in alcohol," Becky answered, her voice equally pained. "Water and aspirin, followed by a greasy breakfast and coffee should cure it."

"I can't even think about food right now," Caroline whimpered from beside Tessa. "I think I'm going to be sick!" She tried to get up quickly, but she got tangled up in our blankets. She landed on the floor with a loud *thump* and an equally loud squeal. She hopped up a beat later, her hand over her mouth as she hurried to the bathroom.

"Pretty sure that was *the best* night ever," Krista remarked. "I met *the hottest* guy ever!"

"If by that you mean your tongue and his tonsils met, and if by "hottest", you mean your beer googles were in full affect than yes—you met the hottest guy ever," I said, smirking. I couldn't wait until Krista saw the pictures of her so called "hottest guy ever".

"You're just jealous," she huffed.

"Ladies, no arguing," Tessa yawned. "More sleep."

"No more sleep I'm afraid," Becky sighed, sitting up and checking the alarm clock. "We have twenty minutes to check out."

The room exploded into chaos as seven severely hungover girls attempted to get organized, packing up makeup, clothing, and hair supplies. We made it to the front desk to hand in our room key cards with minutes to spare.

After checking out, Olivia and Laura wanted to get an early start on their trip back to Barrie. The rest of us headed to a restaurant a few blocks away to grab breakfast and coffee. The grease and caffeine helped wake me up and ease the annoying hangover. It was a good thing too—since our day was far from over. Tessa wanted to do some shopping for her honeymoon at the Yorkdale mall.

"Oh my God," Krista said, her eyes wide with horror. "Who the hell is Ransom Cauz and why is he friending me on Facebook?"

"That's the "hottest guy ever" that you spent most of last night making out with," I smirked into my coffee mug.

"No fucking way," Krista shook her head. "Ransom *Cauz*? What the hell was I thinking? He's not even a solid three."

"Beer googles," I raised my mug in solidarity while everyone else chuckled. "I bet he's some wannabe rapper or something."

Krista shot me a dirty look and dropped her phone to the table as if it was poisonous. "Whatever, add him to the pile of horrible mistakes I've made."

"What happens in Toronto, stays in Toronto," Tessa amended, massaging her temples.

"Unless it's posted all over Instagram," Caroline laughed, her green eyes twinkling as she shoved her phone at Tessa. "Look! Pete the Penis is trending!"

"Oh God." Tessa's eyes went wide, she was mortified. I couldn't help but laugh at her reaction. "This is all your fault, Elle. Now my future employers will be able to find photos of me with a giant dick."

"I think it adds a little *spunk* to your resume," I grinned. "Besides, *I* didn't start the Instagram hashtag. That would be Krista."

"Just remove your tags and stuff," Krista shrugged. "That's what I'll be doing. Oh, and blocking anyone who tries to add me."

"Poor Ransom Cauz," I chortled.

"Okay, I'm done. I need to get home so I can sleep," Caroline said, stretching in her seat. She looked a lot like Tessa, all fair hair and delicate features, beautiful in that fresh-faced way with her green eyes and the freckles that dusted across her nose and cheek bones.

While Caroline was every bit as sweet as she looked, she was also mischievous and loved to have fun. Her mother—Tessa's dad's sister—busted out of Parry Sound the second she turned eighteen. She moved to Toronto, met some guy and got married. Caroline was used to city life; she knew all the best clubs in town and the quickest way to get anywhere. She was my go-to person during the location planning for the bachelorette party.

"I'll see you at the wedding, right?" Tessa asked, standing up when her cousin did.

"Of course," Caroline exclaimed as they embraced. "I wouldn't miss it. Mom and Dad will be there too. Can't wait to see Uncle Bill and the league of incredible douchebags," Caroline added mischievously.

"Hey now, Ben's not so bad," Katie argued in defense of her husband.

"Now," Tessa, Caroline, and I said in unison.

Shortly after Caroline left, Becky, Katie, and Krista followed. Becky and Katie had to get home to their kids and Krista supposedly had a hot date she had to get ready for. Tessa and I followed them out to the underground parking.

My phone kept buzzing as we said our goodbyes. Aggravated, I pulled it from my purse and sighed as I read Alex's name.

"What's wrong?" Tessa demanded, seeing me shove the phone back into my purse.

"Alex keeps calling," I muttered, irritated.

"How dare him," Tessa said dryly, arching her brow and repressing a smile. I didn't laugh. I just shrugged and climbed into my car.

"I'm still not sure what to tell him," I confessed. "I don't know what I'm feeling, what I'm thinking."

"You need to tell him that," Tessa insisted gently. "I know it's scary, and I know that you don't want to hurt him... But putting it off will only hurt him more when the truth finally does come out, because it will come out."

"I'm too hungover for this conversation," I sighed, my head throbbing. "Let's just go shopping and turn off our brains for a bit, shall we?"

"Sounds good to me," Tessa pursed her lips. "I'm all out of advice anyway. Those vodka shots really did a number on me."

CHAPTER FOURTEEN

raden

BROCK OFFERED to watch Aiden so that Becky could go to Toronto for the bachelorette party, and I hung out with them because I had nowhere else to be. My nephew had been a great distraction for me all day, taking up much of my attention while all three of us fished off the dock and went swimming. But when he finally crashed in Brock's spare room at the cabin, I had nothing to distract me from the call of social media.

Krista was posting pictures of their evening like clockwork. The first photo was of Elle holding a huge, inflatable penis out to a horrified looking Tessa. More photos of them in the limo and them ordering drinks at the bar, the inflatable penis in tow.

"Dude, you've got to stop looking at those," Brock grumbled, catching me on my phone again for the twelfth time in the past hour. I shoved it back into my pocket and picked up the Xbox remote.

"Yeah, well. Elle makes this party planning shit look effort-less," I muttered.

I was in charge of planning Brock's bachelor party, and it was proving to be an insanely complicated task for a recovering alcoholic. The cliché bachelor party typically happened to be a night at the rippers, and I was a little nervous about the tempta-tion I'd be in. Some days, I felt stronger than others. Other days, the thought of alcohol made me break into a cold sweat. Like right now, for instance. I wanted desperately to crack open a beer and play some Call of Duty with my brother, but I couldn't. One drink would lead to twelve drinks, and I'd be fucked again.

Still, I didn't want the other guys to feel obligated to have some kind of PG-13 evening just because I couldn't drink.

"I already told you I don't want a fuss," my brother said, taking a deep sip of the Pepsi he was drinking.

Ever since I went to rehab, my siblings were overly cautious about drinking in front of me. I was pretty sure Brock stopped keeping beer in his refrigerator *because* of me, and it irritated the hell out of me. I didn't want my siblings acting any differ-ently around me—but hell, I was an alcoholic. I couldn't really blame them for their behaviour.

"What if we went to Sudbury or Barrie or something and hit up the strip clubs?" I suggested, wondering if whatever store Elle bought the inflatable penis from carried inflatable vaginas.

"I don't want to do the strip club scene," he told me point blank. "I don't think it'd be good for you."

"This isn't about me," I argued. "It's your bachelor party, man! This is what's *expected* of you. Hell, even the girls went to a strip club!"

Brock simply smiled and shrugged, zero concern lining his face as his character took mine down again. There I was, over-whelmed with jealousy at the thought of Elle watching some dude flopping his sausage at her when she'd been strategically avoiding me ever since the day of the community bonfire, but my brother didn't seem worried at all.

"Tessa has never even been to a strip club," he'd pointed out. "I've been to several. It's a rite of passage that you should see what the hype's about. If Elle didn't take her, I would have. All I want is an evening of fishing with my buddies on the lake and maybe a keg of beer."

"That sounds lame," I frowned. "Who would you even want there?"

Brock was silent, thinking. "You, obviously. Gordon, Grady, Travis, Tommy, Steve, Grayson. Maybe Ben."

"So you literally just want to have a bush party with no chicks?" I furrowed my brow. "Where's the fun in that?"

"Plenty of fun in that," Brock shrugged. "Sounds awesome. A laid back night with the guys."

"Sounds *lame*," I repeated, scowling.

"Come on Braden, you know how I am. I would rather not do anything at all, but I don't think Tessa would let that fly. Just plan the stupid fishing thing for next Saturday. Hell, I'll plan it."

"No," I grumbled, dejected. "I'll message people on the meager list you gave me and sort everything out, not that there's much to do."

"Awesome, it's settled. Now get your head in the game before I kill you for the hundredth time tonight."

―――――――

MY HEART SPED up and my palms started to sweat as I listened to the phone ring, waiting for Elle to pick it up—or not. I wasn't holding my breath, but I was hopeful that she'd answer.

It had been over two and a half weeks since I took her out to dinner, two weeks since the Parry Sound Stampede (and our little mudding exertion), and nearly a week since the bachelorette party. I held off for as long as I possibly could, giving her the space and time I knew she needed. But this wasn't about us, at least—that's what I told myself. This was about Brock's bachelor party, and me being clueless about how to even throw one.

I'd invited the guys he'd mentioned, and they all gave their word that they'd be there. Then I left everything else to the last possible minute, and I was overwhelmed and had no idea where to begin. I had twelve hours to pull this off, and I wasn't even entirely sure *what* I needed to pull off.

"Hello?"

Her voice shot an electrical current through my body. "Elle, I need you. Badly."

She was silent for several long beats. "Is this a booty call, Braden?" she asked hotly.

I grinned. "No, but it could be."

"What do you want?" she sighed, already exasperated with me.

"I have no idea what I'm doing," I admitted, running my hand through my hair as I sat in my truck.

"With what?"

"This bachelor party. It was always you who sorted out the details and all that shit. I don't know what I'm doing."

"The bachelor party is *tonight* Braden," Elle exhaled, her temper spiking. "Please tell me you at least invited the guests."

"Obviously. I was always good at *that* part," I reminded her with a wry grin that she couldn't see.

Elle was quiet, I could practically hear the wheels turning in her mind. "Did you buy the food? The decorations and games? The booze?"

"I know what I'm getting food wise, I didn't realize we needed decorations and games for a fishing-slash-camping trip, and no to the booze." I took a shaky breath. I didn't want to admit it to her—or anybody else for that matter—but *that* was what really had me twisted up.

I was about to dedicate an entire night to hanging out with drunk people. Going mudding with the gang was a different environment than a bush party. For one, my nephew had been there, and nobody went hard on the drinking. Bush parties were a completely different scene, one that I'd avoided strategically because I worried I wouldn't be strong enough to stay away from the call of liquor when it was around me to that degree, especially when I knew that Elle wouldn't be there to distract me from my thirst.

"I'll grab the booze," Elle offered quickly, picking up on all of the things I didn't say. "For decorations and games, I have some ideas. I need you to handle the food and the ice. We need a shit ton of ice. Make sure you get that last though. I'll meet you at seven at the lake."

"Why don't I pick you up and go with you? The food and ice won't take long at all, and even though I don't know what I'm doing...I still want to do my part. I'll follow your every command," I suggested, my heart pounding in my chest.

She was silent again for several moments, moments that seemed to stretch on forever. "Alright, fine. Pick me up in forty-five minutes. I have to get ready."

"Deal," I said, ending the call feeling more gleeful than I should have felt. Truthfully...a small, rather conniving part of me had hoped to lure Elle into helping me, so that I could spend a little time with her, or in the very least hear her voice again while she gave me instructions. I was desperate for her attention.

Forty-five minutes later, I was pulling up the driveway to her house. She was waiting for me, sitting on the front porch steps. She stood up when I came to a stop and walked over, her hips swaying with each attitude-fueled step she took. Elle was dressed casually in shorts and a white t-shirt with a deer graphic on it that stretched across her breasts, and her hair wild and free, spilling over her shoulders and down her back like a dark mane. She wasn't trying to drive me wild with want, but she succeeded. My blood pumped south the moment she climbed into the cab, her scent enveloping me.

"Thanks for helping me today, Elle," I told her, my words sincere, as she pulled the seatbelt across her body.

"Don't mention it. I'm doing this for Brock and Tessa, anyway. I can't believe you left everything until the last minute," she grumbled, rolling her eyes. Elle was never really a morning person, and I knew she was pissed that I'd dragged her out of bed before noon.

"I didn't leave *everything* until the last minute," I pointed out, pulling away from her house. "I invited the guests. That's the most important part."

"Yeah, until the guests arrive and there's no plan and no food." Elle huffed at me, pushing her hair out of her face.

"I guess I've just been overthinking everything," I sighed. Honesty was my best policy with Elle. "I'm kind of pissed that Brock didn't want to do the whole strip club thing."

"Why?"

"Because, it would have been easier for me. This was our scene in high school. Bush parties, camp outs, bonfires and booze. I haven't done that shit since...well. Us. And I'm not counting that weekend we went mudding, there was barely any drinking and you were there."

I could feel her eyes on me, and I was afraid that I'd said too much too soon. The silence between us was thick and heavy. "I'm sorry, Braden," she said, her voice barely above a whisper. She swallowed hard, drawing her eyes away from me and out the window.

"Hey, you've got nothing to be sorry for," I told her, my eyes darting across the cab to look at her. "I was the one who turned to booze instead of dealing with my grief. I should have listened to you that day..." I added. The words were difficult to get out past the lump of pride and regret in my throat. I closed my eyes for a moment, remembering how Elle had cautioned me about drinking so much.

Even at the time, I'd known she was right. I just hadn't known how to stop. I was on a rampage, locked in battle with myself. I didn't think I deserved good things, and Elle was a good thing—a great thing. The best thing to have ever happened to me.

She was reflective, likely recalling the same day my thoughts were focused on. "I *am* sorry though. I'm sorry I blamed you when I should have fought harder to stay by your side. I knew how much you were hurting, and I let you push me away."

I tromped on the breaks and pulled over to the shoulder of the road, turning to face her. "Elle, I'm telling you right now— what happened between us was my fault and mine alone. You were perfect—you *are* perfect. You always had my back, you always believed in me. I was the one that broke your trust. I was the one that fucked it up and believe me when I tell you—I would do *anything* to go back in time and not screw it up for us."

Electricity zapped and sizzled, and the sexual tension between us could be cut with a knife, it was so abundant. Weeks of keeping our distance, weeks of circling around each other. Both of our eyes saying more than our mouths ever could.

I swallowed, my eyes drinking her in. It took all my restraint to stay on my side of the cab, to not reach out and let myself touch her in all the ways I wanted to.

She inhaled deeply, rolling her shoulders back. "Alright, well." She said, her voice shaky and her eyes wide and uncertain. "First stop is good old Walmart. I've been on Pinterest looking for inspiration and there's a couple of ideas I think you might like. We need to get cups and plates and all that stuff too."

I smiled sadly and nodded, going along with her topic change. She didn't know how to respond to what I'd said, and I didn't know if I wanted her too.

ELLE DUMPED the last remaining bag of ice into the old wheel barrow and tied the sign she'd made from an old piece of wood —the words "Beer Barrow" painted on it in white paint—to the wooden handles. I looked around the grassy waterfront, bewildered by Elle's ability to plan and execute a party.

We had picked up enough string lights from the party rental place to light the whole waterfront area up. Several chairs were arranged around the fire pit, the wood was already prepped and ready for a match to drop. The food was arranged on the picnic tables, lids all on to keep bugs and ants out until everyone arrived. A portable speaker system was set up, and all I had to do was plug my phone in and bring up my playlists.

Everything looked perfect, and as an added bonus...I'd gotten to spend the day with her. At first, she'd been tense and unmoving. But party planning put Elle in a glorious mood, and it wasn't long at all before she melted into the happy girl I remembered from high school, chatting my ears off about all the different ways we could do things.

And I lapped it all up eagerly. I was so relieved that she could let go of her contempt towards me, so relieved that she seemed to enjoy my company—even if it was for a little while. For the first time in a long while, I truly felt like this wasn't a lost cause, that *we* weren't a lost cause.

"You should be an event organizer," I told her while I checked everything out again.

She smiled, delighted at my praise. "Thanks, although we really have Pinterest to thank for all this." She looked around again, her hand on her hip and a satisfied look on her face. "Everything seems good to go. When are people supposed to arrive?"

"Within the next half hour or so," I replied as I moved closer to her.

I came to a stop in front of her, fighting the urge to put my hands on her hips and pull her to me and kiss her until we both couldn't breathe. She wasn't ready for that, and we'd had an awesome day together. I didn't want to do anything to ruin that.

She exhaled sharply, and I felt the warmth and sweetness of her breath on my chin. Her eyes were fixed on mine, bright and luminous. Time seemed to stand still as I raised my hand, gently cupping the side of her face. I swallowed hard.

"I can't thank you enough for this..."

"Don't mention it," Elle said, pulling her face away from my touch. Her eyes were burning—but I wasn't a hundred percent sure if she was pissed at me for touching her, or longing for something more.

"Let me give you a lift home," I offered, shoving my traitorous hands in the pockets of my jeans and stepping back, giving her some space. Giving me space.

"It's okay, I already texted Tessa. She'll be here any minute. We're supposed to start making the centerpieces tonight." Elle was avoiding my eyes, throwing up the walls I'd so carefully broken down.

I nodded, my hands still in my pockets, and dropped my gaze. I just so happened to end up staring at the barrow full of beer. I swallowed again, my mouth as dry as the desert sand.

"Braden...will you be okay tonight?" she added, her hand touching the skin on my forearm gently.

I looked up at her, shocked that she had initiated this touch. Her eyes were full of concern. "I'll be fine, don't worry about me," I told her as Brock's truck pulled up.

"Well, if you look inside the red cooler, I got you several alcohol free beers." Elle told me, gesturing with her head towards the red cooler.

"Alcohol free?" my eyebrows shot up.

"Tastes like real beer, looks like real beer, has zero alcohol to it. It will give your hands something to do, while everyone else is drinking," Elle swallowed, pasting a smile on. "And...I'll just be a phone call away...if you need an escape or something...okay?"

Elle's gesture made my heart swell to epic proportions. I honestly thought the damn thing was going to explode in my chest. She sent me a wistful look before she turned around and started walking to the truck. She paused when she reached it to say something to Brock. Turning her head to look at me once more, she gave me the smallest smile before climbing into the cab. Brock closed the door behind her and watched as Tessa waved and backed up, turning around and driving back up the private access road.

My brother started walking over to me, running a hand through his hair. "Looks great, Braden," he said, his eyes appraising the setup.

"Elle did most of it, I just followed instructions," I shrugged, grinning.

"Did you really con her into helping you today?" Brock's eyebrows lifted and he smirked, shaking his head at me.

"Not really," I replied. I felt at odds with myself—with everything. Normally, we'd be shooting the shit while drinking a cold beer. My fingers twitched in my pocket. I eased up when I remembered my own stockpile. "Ask and ye shall receive and all that."

The sound of tires crunching on the gravel had both Brock and me looking back towards the access road. Gordon's black F150 pulled into view. He parked haphazardly and driver's door opened. Gordon stood up, hanging on to the roof of the cab. "Hey fuckers!" he called out to us. "Ready for a night of boozing and fishing?"

The rest of Tessa's brothers—Tommy and Ben—climbed out of the cab, cases of beer in hand. "Just in case we run out," Tommy grinned, setting the cases down beside the beer barrow.

"Wow, this is fancy as fuck," Gordon added with a whistle as he checked out his surroundings and cracked open a beer. The other guys grabbed beers too, and I crossed over to the red cooler to grab one of my own—alcohol free.

Brock stormed over to me. "What the hell is that?" he demanded quietly, his eyes hard as he nodded his head towards the beer in my hand.

"Chill out," I frowned, irritated. "They're alcohol free. Elle grabbed them for me." Brock visibly relaxed as I took a tentative sip, expecting it to taste like absolute shit but it wasn't half bad.

"Sounds fruity," Tommy joked.

"Don't forget Tommy, I can still kick your ass," I told him through narrowed eyes.

He threw back his head and laughed. "I'm just playing, man. Seriously. I'm proud of you," he told me sincerely.

Grady and Steve showed up ten minutes later, and then a silver Lexus RX Hybrid pulled up. "Who's that?" I asked Brock.

"Must be Grayson," Brock shrugged. He started walking over to the Lexus to greet his friend while I hung back and worked on getting the fire started. Several minutes later, Brock returned with his friend in tow. "Guys, this is Grayson," he said. "Grayson, this is Tommy, Gordon, Ben, Grady, and my brother Braden."

"Hey," Grayson said, nodding at us. Brock grabbed a beer and handed it to him.

True to his nature, Travis was the last to arrive—about an hour into the party. He pulled up in a red Mercedes.

"Way to be inconspicuous," I shook my head.

"This *is* inconspicuous," Travis shrugged with a playful grin, unaffected by my razzing. "I could have driven the Porsche."

Gordon threw his arm across Travis's shoulders. "Where are your body guards tonight?" he asked, just to provoke him.

"Not here. I figured we were far enough out in the middle of nowhere that nobody would come across us."

"Fair enough, besides—they're *kind of* buzzkills," Gordon snorted, tossing back the rest of his beer.

"You're telling me," Travis said in agreement, glancing around. He nodded at Grady, Tommy, and Ben before settling on Brock. His face split into a grin and he started over. "Hey! Groom guy! What the fuck is with this backwoods sausage fest!? Aren't we supposed to celebrate your dwindling time as a free man by ogling strippers and shit?" He put the brown paper bag down on the table and embraced my brother in a one-armed hug.

"Guess I got enough of a stripper show when you brought the Vegas escorts by Flanigan's," Brock responded smoothly, the corners of his lips twitching. "Hey, Grayson—this is my buddy Travis."

Grayson and Travis appraised each other for a moment, flickering recognition passing in each of their eyes. "Hey, do I know you from somewhere?" Travis asked, tilting his head slightly.

"By proxy, yes," Grayson said, his voice low and almost threatening.

"Ah right, you're Everly's man right?" Travis asked. Grayson clenched his jaw and nodded once in response. "How the hell is she? Haven't seen her in a while! I think the last time I saw her was at the 2014 Music Awards."

"She's good," Grayson answered unwillingly. He seemed uncomfortable or pissed off—I couldn't tell which one.

"Everly Daniels was the lead singer of *Autumn Fields*," Travis explained to us, a huge grin on his face. "She left the music scene a year ago. I haven't seen her since!" He turned to look back at Grayson. ""Will she be at the wedding?"

Grayson remained silent for several beats before answering. "Yeah, she will."

"Fucking eh! It's a small world after all," Travis didn't seem the least bit concerned that he was seriously aggravating the fuck out of Brock's friend. He picked up the brown bag again and pulled a bottle of whiskey out. "Anybody want a shot?"

CHAPTER FIFTEEN

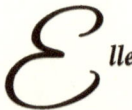*lle*

"Thanks for coming to the rescue today," Tessa smiled at me from across the wooden table in Brock's kitchen. We had spent the past three hours assembling centrepieces; tying twine and a piece of triangle material with the letter "m" to each Mason jar. On the day of the wedding, the jars would be full of water and wildflowers, placed on round disks of wood that Brock had cut specifically for this purpose with tea light candles to add a soft, romantic glow to each table. "I should have known that planning the bachelor party would be too much responsibility for Braden," she added, shaking her head.

"It was no problem," I shrugged, biting my lip. "Honestly, Braden pretty much had everything figured out except for the decorations and I'm pretty sure that's not a requirement. I mean, it's not like the guys would have shown up and said 'gee, there's no decorations. How lame!'"

"Was he on his best behaviour at least?" Tessa asked, arching a brow.

"Yeah, he was. It was...good. Hanging out with him I mean." And it had been—I had almost forgotten how it felt to spend time with Braden Miller. Being around him made me feel alive and carefree, but it also made me acutely aware of my feelings for him, which is why I couldn't be around him.

I wanted him. My body, my heart, it craved him in the worst way. The only thing holding me back was my mind—I *knew* going down that road again would lead to more heartache and pain. I wasn't sure if I could handle it, but I also wasn't sure if *he* could handle it. He was doing well right now, he wasn't drinking, he wasn't running from his problems. I didn't want to push him back when he fought so hard to be where he was.

I didn't voice any of it—but Tessa seemed to read between the lines. She smiled knowingly. "How's everything *else* going?" I knew she was referring to Alex.

"I cancelled on him today," I admitted. "He was supposed to come out but Braden called. I told him there was a wedding emergency I had to deal with."

"Elle!" Tessa frowned. "Why wouldn't you just tell him the truth?"

"Because I don't think the truth should be told over the phone," I shrugged. "Despite how I feel about...well, everything...Alex is still my boyfriend, and he's my friend. I still care about him, and I'm not going to break his heart over the phone."

"You had an opportunity to talk to him when he came down," she pointed out.

"Yeah, and I choked. I didn't want to hurt him. And how could I anyway? You saw how he was at the smash-up derby. It would have been a dick move to tell him 'hey gee thanks for talking me out of a panic attack, but I want to break up'."

"Oh, so just wait until the wedding. There's a plan," Tessa snorted. She leaned forward, her eyes zeroing in on me. "You realize that weddings bring...things...out in people, right? Like feelings? What if he proposes to you?"

"Alex wouldn't be that stupid," I said confidently. "I haven't even told him that I love him back yet."

"Because you don't," Tessa huffed, sitting back in her seat. "But you're kind of being a bitch about it. I mean, you *know* that you don't love him, and you're still stringing him along. Why?"

I fell silent, my heart squeezing painfully. She was right—I was being a bitch. I was stringing him along and I needed to stop it, but I was afraid of what stopping it would truly mean. I was afraid that if I broke up with Alex, I'd end up back in Braden's arms.

"I guess he's a safe guard," I admitted, my voice raw. "He is the logical choice. He doesn't have a history of hurting me. But I'm fighting with my heart, Tessa. I'm desperate to feel something other than the fondness I have for him. I keep telling myself I just need time, time to get used to the idea of falling in love...but seeing Braden again..." I trailed off, conflicted.

Seeing Braden again drudged up everything again—the way I felt when I was with him, and the girl I once was. Tessa's words kept washing over me though, planting seeds of doubt that grew into weeds. I knew Alex wasn't it for me. My heart wasn't in it; my heart longed for something dangerous. Something that would undoubtedly blow up in my face.

"Elle, you don't need a safe guard," Tessa said gently. I looked up at her. "Fate is going to do what fate does best—whatever is meant to be will just happen. There's no sense in fighting it or trying to put it off."

"You're right," I sighed, my eyes dropping to the table for a minute. I looked up again, catching her watching me. "I promise I'll talk to Alex, but Tessa—your wedding is in *seven days*, we've got enough on our plates without adding that conversation to the mix. It will have to wait until after, there just isn't enough time."

"Yeah," Tessa exhaled, looking at the ceiling. "This week is pretty busy, isn't it?" she asked with a small smile.

"Between the final dress fittings, the rehearsal dinner, and double checking that the caterer, the florist, and the limo company have everything ready -- I'd say so."

"I don't know what I'd do without you, Elle," Tessa said. "Seriously, I was floundering before you came back. Pinning things on Pinterest doesn't actually get anything accomplished on the wedding to-do list."

"Nope," I smiled. "It just adds a heap ton of stress. Stay off Pinterest, everything will be perfect. Now, could you give me a lift home please? I'm exhausted."

Half an hour later, I waved as Tessa drove back down my driveway. I turned around, about to open the door and go inside.

"Hey," Mom's voice startled me and I jumped a foot backwards, placing my hand over my heart. She was sitting on the porch swing, wrapped in a blanket, her face illuminated by the moonlight. "I wondered when you'd get home. I was hoping we could talk."

"About what?" I asked, my heart rate slowing. Mom patted the seat beside her and I walked over, plopping down.

"When Alex came out, he told me about your leave of absence from work," she said. I looked over at her, noticing the lines of worry and the hurt behind her soft green eyes. "Why didn't you tell me, Elle?" she asked, sounding every bit as hurt as she looked.

"I didn't want to worry you," I replied, my voice quivering slightly as I tried to hold the tears back. It had been an intense day, and I wasn't ready for this conversation.

She put her arm around me, pulling me close to her. I rested my head against her shoulder. "I'm going to worry regardless," she said. "That's what mothers do. We worry. I thought we'd always had the kind of relationship where we could talk to one another about anything."

"We can," I insisted. "I just...I didn't know how to say it. I'm still coming to terms with it myself."

"Hey," she said, using her hand to tip my chin up so I'd look at her. "You don't have to do this alone. I'm here."

"I know," I muttered.

She was silent for a few minutes, studying me. "Did your doctor prescribe any medication?" she finally asked.

"Just antidepressants," I replied on an exhale.

"And you're taking them, right?" Mom inquired with an arch of her brow.

"Yes, obviously," I rolled my eyes. "I also followed his advice for that leave of absence."

She was silent as she considered me. "Has it helped?"

"A little," I admitted. "But it brings its own bullshit along," I added, thinking of Braden and the day we'd spent together and how confused I was about everything.

"Have you thought about cutting the things that aren't so good for you out of your life?"

"I can't very well cut him out right now. Tessa's getting married soon and we have to walk down the aisle together," I answered, looking at her blankly. She smiled and shook her head.

"I wasn't referring to Braden," she told me. "I was talking about the job that brought it on. And, I guess I was also talking about Alex."

"Alex?" I frowned. "I thought you liked him?"

"I do," Mom sighed. "He's a sweet guy. He's nice and attentive and he cares about you a lot—but you don't seem to feel the same way about him that he feels for you."

"You sound like Tessa," I sighed, pushing my feet against the porch to get the swing moving.

"Well, Tessa is smart," Mom laughed. Her humour faded. "All

we're trying to say, Elle, is that you're hanging on to a job—and a relationship—that you don't really want when you should be trying to figure out what it is that you *do* want."

"So you're saying quit my job—the job that you took a second mortgage out on the house so *I* could get the education that would get me the job—and dump my boyfriend who stood by me when I was even more of a mess?"

Mom smiled. "I'm saying do what's going to make you happy. Hell honey, maybe just relocating somewhere closer to where you're happiest is the answer. This house will always be your home, and you're welcome to return to it and regroup if you need to."

"Thanks, Mom," I whispered, resting my head back onto her shoulder.

I KNEW my mom and Tessa were right, but I didn't have time to deal with my work and living situation. The week before the wedding really did prove to be busy. Between a mix up at the florist for the wedding arch flowers and the construction of the arch itself, I was too occupied running interference to even sit down and reflect upon anything. By the time Friday morning rolled around—and the rehearsal dinner—I'd sorted out all the mishaps and figured we were pretty much golden for the wedding the next day.

The chairs were already set up for the ceremony, and the wedding arbor was in place. It was a simple design—a rectangle arch made of thick birch branches and put together by Gordon and Tommy.

The reception tent was ready to go too. The illuminated bar was set up and stocked, save for the ice. The dance floor gleamed and the tables were set up with the seating chart right by the tent entrance. The linens were all in place—I'd made sure of it—and again, the only thing left to do was add the flowers to the centerpieces once the florist dropped the flowers off.

Even still, my mind raced with mental checklists. I wanted to make sure everything went off without a hitch so that Tessa could focus on enjoying her special day with Brock—I knew she'd do the same if the roles were reversed.

So occupied were my thoughts that I nearly jumped out of my skin when a hand pressed against the small of my back. "Are you ready?" Braden asked, arching a brow and gesturing to the wedding arbor. We were doing a trial run through the ceremony, and it was our turn to walk down the makeshift aisle. His hand fell away, taking all warmth with it, and he offered me his arm.

We walked at the proper pace, in time with the music. Once we'd reached the arch, we split off and Braden went to stand beside Brock while I stood beside Pastor Bruce—who was overseeing the rehearsal and giving instructions when needed.

Next came Becky and Travis. Neither of them looked very happy, and Pastor Bruce had to remind them to smile. Katie and Gordon came after them, and then Krista and Grady. Finally, Tessa made her descent with her father.

We ran through it once more before Pastor Bruce was satisfied. Then we all jumped into cars and drove to The Dock for dinner.

Ben, Tommy, my mom, Tessa's cousin Caroline and her aunt and uncle also joined the wedding party for the rehearsal dinner. Our table took up practically the entire back half of the restaurant. Alex hadn't been able to make it out to the dinner— he'd had to work, and would be coming out first thing in the morning.

I tried to focus on the fact that in a few short hours, my boyfriend would be back in town and my best friend would be getting married, but it was hard. So very hard. I couldn't focus throughout the entire dinner, not with the converted looks Braden would send me when nobody else was paying attention.

I had to get away. I needed air. I needed to breathe air that wasn't being breathed by *him*. I slipped outside the first chance I could after telling Tessa that I needed a moment.

I hurried outside, breathing in the fresh air like I was starved oxygen—and stomped over to the alley. I wanted to be left alone. I was pissed off that Braden was looking at me like he wanted me—like he couldn't wait to have me. I was pissed off that I was reacting, too. He was supposed to just want to be my friend, and I was supposed to accept that.

His intent was to toy with me. I was the mouse, and he was the cat. Braden didn't like losing, and he probably felt like he was losing. He was trying to stake a claim in me again, because he couldn't stand the fact that I was trying to move on.

Was I? I wondered to myself, closing my eyes against the gentle breeze. I'd barely given Alex a second thought since coming home—even when he was right next to me. My time was occupied with the wedding, and as much as I didn't want to admit it...with Braden.

"Thought I'd find you out here." I'd recognize his voice anywhere. I didn't even have to open my eyes to know it was him.

"You're something else, you know that?" I snapped, my anger swallowing me, driving me. I stared at him, anger seething from every pore. This was the man that had shattered me. Destroyed me, and here he was, back again and pushing all my buttons, driving me crazy and making me want him when I had someone else waiting for me.

"Oh, I know I'm something else," he said, that arrogant half-smile playing against those lips that had once kissed every inch of my body, those lips I still dreamed about in my weaker moments—which happened to be all the time, apparently.

"Where do you get off, looking at me like that?" I demanded, the raw pain and hurt pulsing in my chest. "Why can't you just leave me be, Braden?"

He edged closer towards me, backing me up against the brick wall of the restaurant. He put his hands on either side of me, caging me in. "I know it's not over, Elle."

"How do you know that?" I demanded haughtily, my eyes narrowing at his tragically handsome face and that chiselled jaw. *Focus, Elle!*

The heated look Braden gave me could melt panties, and to my dismay—I found my body was reacting to him. I pressed my thighs together, the throbbing heat building, and swallowed hard. I was hyper aware of every move he made. He slowly brought his hand up, catching a loose lock of my hair and toying with it. My skin burned at his nearness, remembering his touch and how it had once felt.

My chest rose and fell, my breathing becoming labored. My lids fluttered against my cheeks as he moved his lips closer to mine. I felt his warm breath against my mouth.

"That's your answer, Elle," he said, his voice deep with longing. "The way you react when you're near me. The look in your eyes...that's how I know it's not over." His eyes lingered on my lips for a moment, and then my hands went to his chest.

"Braden, please," I begged, not knowing what I was asking for—him to leave me alone, or him to kiss me and never stop.

His expression was almost tormented as his eyes bore into mine. "As much as I'd love to take you in this alley, right here, right now. I won't let you do this, Elle. I won't let you hate yourself in the morning. If I'm what you want, you need to tell *him* that. Then come find me."

My eyes snapped open, watching his face, intense with sincerity. My heart pounded in my chest as the gravity of the situation took over. Tears welled up in my eyes. I shoved him away from me. "You don't get to tell me what to do, Braden."

"Sure I do," he smiled tightly, his eyes remaining serious.

"This is about me just as much as it's about you. I don't want to fuck you once, Elle. I want to have you over and over again. I want to have you forever, and I don't want there to be a shadow of a doubt in your mind that you want the same thing."

I gaped at him, dumbfounded. My mouth opened and closed as I searched for something to say. I willed the words I knew I should say to come forth. I wanted to tell him it was over, that my reaction to him had everything to do with the champagne I'd had at dinner, but I couldn't speak, and I was beginning to realize it was a lie, anyway.

CHAPTER SIXTEEN

 raden

ELLE'S LIPS WERE PARTED, her breath coming out in short gasps and fanning my chin as I looked down at her. I stepped up to her again, leaving half an inch of space between us. My palms stung as I pressed them against the hard the brick wall. I could still feel the heat radiating off her body.

Her hands seemed to act on their own accord. They came up to press against my chest—but she didn't push me away again. I wondered if she could hear my heart pounding in my chest.

I knew I should walk away, give her time to think about the things that I'd said and meant with every fibre of my heart and soul. I knew I should step back and give her time to work out what she felt for me and what she wanted.

I swallowed hard, tilting my head. The corner of my mouth shot up in a smirk. I could practically hear her thoughts spinning. "Let me know when you figure it out," I told her as I brought my fingers up to sweep across her pouty lips.

"You're such an asshole," she seethed, finally using her palms to push me away. I watched as she walked back down the alley, her hands clenched into angry fists. Her dress was so short, it barely reached mid-thigh.

When she'd disappeared around the corner of the building, I let myself fall back against the wall, using it to support my weight. I was hard in the worst way. It had taken all of my restraint and control not to shove her back up against the wall and sink into her. I knew she wanted it just as much as I did— but I couldn't let her do that. I couldn't let her sleep with me when she was still tethered to someone else—even if her heart wasn't with him.

I pulled my pack of smokes out of my pocket and grabbed one with shaky fingers, lighting it. The nicotine did nothing to ease my taste for her, but I smoked it anyway, needing a moment to collect myself and my thoughts.

THAT NIGHT, the guys in the wedding party all crashed at Brock's cabin while the bridesmaids crashed at the Armstrong's farm. I had no idea what kind of shenanigans the girls were getting into, but the guys were drunk by nine. All of them—even Brock was a little tipsy. I'd practically poured the bottles down his throat myself, refusing to allow him another night of sacrificing fun to make me feel more comfortable.

Thanks to Elle, I was comfortable. Or at least, comfortable enough. I'd picked up more of the alcohol free beers she'd bought for me during the bachelor party and I found that by having them in my hands, the thirst didn't bother me as much.

When mostly everyone was sawing logs in the cabin, Brock walked up and threw his arm around my shoulders. "Let's go fishing," he said, his eyes sparkling.

"It's nearly one in the morning," I pointed out. "You're getting married today."

"I know," he grinned, jostling me a little. "I still want to go fishing," he added. Releasing me, Brock grabbed his fishing gear and I followed suit. We grabbed some bait and climbed into the boat. Brock waited for Hunter to jump in before he pushed away from the dock and started the engine.

We traveled out to one of the best fishing spots on the lake, guided by the light of the moon. We didn't talk as we baited our hooks. Brock's gaze remained fixated on the water after we'd cast our lines and got comfortable.

"Are you nervous?" I asked. He swallowed hard, taking several long minutes to respond.

"A little," he confessed, tossing a wry smile at me. I knew from the hard set of his jaw that Brock was thinking about the same thing I was thinking about—our parents.

"It's not going to be the same," I assured him, reeling my line in a little. "You're not him. If anybody's like him, it's me."

"That's not true," Brock argued, his eyebrows drawing in together as he scowled at me.

"You and I both know it's true. I'm the most like him. I'm an alcoholic and I hurt the people I love."

"You're a *recovering* alcoholic. You've been sober for three and a half years now, Braden. You have more strength than he ever had. And yeah, maybe you fucked things up with Elle all those years ago, but you never physically laid a hand on her. You never emotionally berated her. When she was yours, you loved her good. You still love her good. You were just immature and hurting. But you're man enough to know your mistakes and to try and make it right again, which is more than we can say he did."

I said nothing. I had no response. I was kind of speechless. I didn't think of myself as the strong one in the family. My siblings had been dealt the exact same cards I'd been dealt, and worse. Becky had ended up in an abusive relationship that had landed her in the hospital and Aiden had nearly lost his life because of it. Brock had gone to jail for beating the crap out of the guy that put our sister and nephew in the hospital.

Despite all they'd been through, they were doing amazing. Becky was loving her job as a nurse at the hospital, and she was raising a kick ass kid on her own. She never wavered. Even though I knew she got lonely sometimes, she never let it drag her down and she certainly never let Aiden in on it. The only reason I could recognize it in her was because it lived in me too.

Brock had made something of himself despite going to jail. He had a steady job, a great income, a beautiful home, and he'd fallen in love and was about to marry a stellar girl. One day, he'd have kids of his own too.

Becky and Brock had risen above their circumstances, and I was just...stuck. Stuck at my old job and stuck in my old life without the added benefit of having Elle in my arms.

"I mean it," Brock's hand squeezed my shoulder. He left his hand there for a moment, and patted me once before removing it.

"Thanks," I exhaled. We fell silent again, listening to the soft call of the loon. "I almost kissed her tonight."

"Braden," Brock sighed.

"I know," I interrupted him, almost glaring at him. "I didn't, I almost did...came bloody close to it...but she's with someone else. She wants me as much as I want her, but she's too scared to trust me. I did that."

"Yes you did," he agreed, his expression solemn. He ran a hand through his hair. It was long enough that the ends brushed against his shoulders. I'd been surprised that Tessa hadn't put pressure on him to trim it, but she liked it the length that it was. "I think you just need to back off. Give her time to decide what she wants."

"I know," I pursed my lips. "That's the plan. I've put the ball in her court, and it's up to her now. She knows where to find me, I'll be here." I sighed, reeling my line completely in and recasting further out.

BROCK and I fished on the lake for another forty-five minutes before heading back to the cabin and crashing. Six o'clock came with a vengeance, and the morning passed in a chaotic blur. Wedding photographers snapped photographs of us getting ready, and at one point, Brock nearly lost it when he couldn't find his tie.

Thankfully, Aiden found it in the bathroom and all was well. We piled into two separate trucks—Brock's and Travis'—and headed over to the Armstrong's farm with twenty-minutes to spare before the ceremony was supposed to start.

The girls were still up at the farmhouse, doing whatever it is the bride and bridesmaids do before the wedding. Brock went to stand beneath the birch arbor with Pastor Bruce while Travis, Gordon, Grady and I set to the task of ushering guests to their seats.

Elle's boyfriend showed up, scanning the wedding guests until his eyes fell on me. He nodded once, his jaw tense as Gordon led him to a spot near the front. He'd be sitting beside Sue Thompson.

My first reaction was to hate the guy, but I was surprised to find that I couldn't; not after the moment Elle and I had shared. Now I just felt bad for him. He seemed like a nice enough guy, and maybe if I weren't so selfish…I would have seen that sooner and I would have backed away.

It was too late now. I couldn't stop it even if I tried. I didn't have the strength to do the right thing, and I wasn't even entirely sure if giving up *was* the right thing. All I knew was that every time I was around her, I could breathe without pain. Everything was clearer. If Elle walked up to me and told me she wanted to be with me again, there would be absolutely *no* hesitation on my part, and I couldn't even feel guilty about it.

CHAPTER SEVENTEEN

 *lle*

TESSA, the other bridesmaids and I had slept over at the farm to make it easier to go about getting ready the next day. Caroline was a hairstylist and a makeup artist, and she'd offered to do everyone's hair and makeup but needed to get an early start. We awoke at the crack of dawn, ate a hearty breakfast that my mom had made in Bill's kitchen, and took turns sitting down in the designated chair. Caroline had done everyone's hair first, then set to doing makeup.

Thankfully, she had brought her airbrush kit and managed to hide the massive bags under my eyes. I hadn't slept at all the night before, my mind stuck on that almost-kiss in the alley and Braden's words—not to mention the guilt. I had no idea what I was going to say to Alex when he arrived. It was bad enough that I didn't feel for him in the same capacity that he felt for me, now I was going to have to tell him that I had almost cheated on him.

I closed my eyes, breathing deep and slow in an attempt to relax myself. Any minute, we'd get the signal to walk down the aisle together.

"God Elle...you're stunning," Braden whispered into my ear, his warm breath igniting the butterflies in my stomach.

I opened my eyes slowly, taking him in. I never thought I'd be attracted to a guy in a suit before. I preferred causal plaids and work boots, but Braden wore that wedding suit *so* well. My mouth was dry as my eyes finally made it to his face. He'd shaved the stubble, and the dimple on the right side of his cheek was visible again. His deep blue eyes were aglow with emotion, emotion that made my heart stutter.

"Yeah well, you clean up pretty well yourself," I finally managed, forcing a smile and tearing my gaze away from him. Braden's arm was linked through mine. I could feel him shaking a little as he chuckled.

The music cued, and we began our descent down the aisle to the beautiful piano and cello instrumental of *A Thousand Years* by Christina Perri. So many faces turned to stare at us. Braden was steady in leading, his body radiating warmth and strength. I glanced up, seeing Brock standing beneath the arbor with Pastor Bruce, a smile on his handsome face.

Alex was sitting beside my mom. He was dressed in a suit and holding an itinerary, a smile of adoration on his face. He mouthed that I looked gorgeous and I smiled, feeling transparent. The man I was with didn't ignite the same sensations in me as the man on my right, the man I'd tried unsuccessfully to move past.

Braden's hand gently squeezed my arm before we separated. I stood on the bride's side and Braden stood beside Brock underneath the birch arbor. The rest of the wedding party approached. Becky with Travis, Katie with Gordon, and Krista with Grady. After Krista and Grady came Tessa's beautiful niece, Alyssa, and Aiden. Alyssa tossed rose petals as she practically danced, and Aiden walked straight and tall with importance as he carried the rings.

Tears welled up in my eyes as my best friend started walking down the aisle with her father. She looked stunning. Her long, honey blonde hair was styled in a thick French braid, with flowers through it. The gown she wore was the same elegant lace gown her mother had worn on her wedding day, with a few alterations to make it more Tessa, such as the knee high slit that showcased the dressy cowgirl boots she wore.

"Who gives this woman to be married to this man?" Pastor Bruce asked, looking at Bill.

"I do," Bill answered, his voice thick with emotion. He looked at his daughter once more and kissed her on the cheek before releasing his grip on her. Brock held out his hand and Tessa accepted it. She held out her bouquet, and I quickly took it for her.

Tessa trembled throughout the ceremony. She and Brock had decided to write their own vows, and I was eternally grateful for waterproof makeup.

"Throughout this ceremony, Tessa and Brock have vowed, in our presence, to be loyal and loving towards each other. They have formalized the existence of the bond between them with words and with the giving and receiving of rings. It is my pleasure to now pronounce them husband and wife. You may now kiss your bride!" Pastor Bruce declared, a proud smile on his face.

The guests clapped as Brock stepped closer to Tessa, gently cupping her face and kissing her. The kiss with sweet, yet passionate...full of love and promise and happiness. I brushed away another tear, smiling widely as we all clapped and cheered.

DINNER WAS SERVED, and after that, it was time for the speeches. As the maid of honor, I went first, clenching my cue cards as I walked up to the podium. Tessa's older brother, Tommy, was the MC. He winked at me as he made introductions, then adjusted the microphone to my height.

I glanced around at the tables, recognizing all the faces there to celebrate Tessa and Brock's happiness, and my eyes settled on Alex. He nodded at me, offering a sweet smile. "Gosh, full house tonight, huh? Everybody here for the open bar?" I joked, taking a shaky breath. The guests chuckled as I adjusted my cards, my eyes barely seeing the words. I'd basically memorized everything I'd wanted to say. "Tessa and I have been best friends since the day I was born. I haven't known a life without her, nor would I want to. She's always been there for me, she's always been my best friend. Nobody gets me the way she does, and she'll be the first one to tell you that. We shared everything— our toys, our clothes, hell, even our parents. My dad died when I was six, and Tessa's mama died when she was two. Tessa's dad has always been like a father to me, and my mom has always treated Tessa like another daughter. So we really are sisters, more or less," I smiled, my eyes finding Bill and my mom. They were sitting side by side, and Bill reached over to hold her hand and smile at her.

"Growing up, I was the hopeless romantic and Tessa was the pessimistic one. I believed in happily ever afters, while she was cautious. Then she met Brock. I got to watch her protective walls fall away, I got to witness my best friend fall in love, and it was the coolest thing. I don't think anyone deserves this kind of love as much as she does."

I looked towards the head table, seeing Tessa sitting with Brock's arm around her, and smiled through the tears that had welled up in my eyes. "Tessa, I am so, *so* happy for you and Brock. I can't wait to be an aunt, so. Get on that, okay?" I laughed, brushing the tears from my cheeks. Tessa was laughing as she clapped her hands. "But finish school first," I added, mostly for Bill's benefit.

I stepped away from the podium, returning to the head table to take my place beside Tessa. I had to pass Braden as he made his way to the podium. Our bodies brushed against each other, and my eyes darted over to meet his. He had a look of regret on his face. I slid into my seat and hugged Tessa, kissing her on her cheek.

"Hey everyone," Braden said, flashing a charming smile at the crowd. "There's no way I can come close to topping Elle's speech...but I'm going to give this my best shot—because it's what Brock wants, and he's done so much for me. He's gone above and beyond just being a big brother. He's our defender, our protector. He's the head of the family and he's been so since a very young age. It's no secret, we didn't exactly have the best upbringing. But I am who I am today *because* of that, because of Brock and Becky and our mom. I've always looked up to my big brother, even if I've never really shown it. He's a hell of a guy, and I know he's going to treat Tessa like she's a queen. If anyone deserves a girl like Tessa, it's Brock. Congratulations, bro."

Braden left the podium to the sound of applause, and before he sat down, he looked at me. It was a fleeting glance, a glance that said a thousand unspoken words. A glance that undid all my resolve and made me want to know what truly put that hollow ache behind those blue eyes.

Next, Bill gave his speech. It was short and to the point, welcoming Brock into his family and giving some helpful tips on marriage (like the wife is always right. Even when she's wrong, she's right). My mom stepped up to share a story of when Tessa and I were little, and then it was finally time for the first dance.

"Tonight, our good friend Travis is going to sing the first dance song for the bride and groom...along with a special guest..." Tommy introduced as Brock and Tessa walked out to the middle of the dance floor. Tommy wore a wicked smile on his face as he motioned towards the stage where Travis was already situated. Every eye landed on the special guest. Her long caramel hair curled over her right shoulder, held in place with a sparkling silver clip. Her dress matched the clip, silver and sparkling, and she looked vaguely familiar. When she started to speak, I realized I'd heard her voice many times on the radio and TV before.

"Thank you so much for inviting me to sing, Travis." She said, speaking into the microphone as she grinned at him. She turned her attention back out to the audience, her eyes seeking out the bride and groom. "Congratulations Tessa and Brock— you guys truly are a stunning couple. I'm honored to be here tonight!"

"No way! That's Everly Daniels!" Krista squealed from beside me. "I wonder what kind of strings were pulled to get her here? I heard she stopped preforming!"

"She's here with Brock's friend, Grayson," Braden answered from beside Brock's vacant seat. He gestured to a table towards the back where a handsome guy I'd never seen before sat. His eyes were fixed on the stage, as if he was spellbound.

The band behind Travis and Everly started to play, while Travis began singing.

"Dancing in the dark, middle of the night.

Taking your heart, and holding it tight.

Emotional touch, touching my skin.

And asking you to do, what you've been doing all over again.

Oh it's a beautiful thing, don't think I can keep it all in.

I just gotta let you know, what it is that won't let me go..."

EVERLY JOINED IN, harmonizing Faith Hill's parts through the chorus as Brock and Tessa swayed on the dance floor.

Goosebumps raised on my flesh as I watched the scene

before me. It was like something out of a fairy-tale, and it made me acutely aware of everything that my relationship with Alex was severely lacking.

After the first dance, I watched as Tessa danced with her father to Heartland's *I Loved Her First*. When their song ended, they moved to stand just off to the side of the dance floor.

"Unfortunately, the groom lost his mother a few years back. But his sister, Becky, is going to dance with him during the mother son dance." Tommy announced, and Becky and Brock walked out onto the dance floor as Lynyrd Skynyrd's *Simple Man* began to play. Tears welled up in my eyes as I thought of Deanna Miller. It was heartbreaking that she wasn't there to watch her eldest son get married—that she wouldn't see any of her children get married.

"She's watching," Braden's voice startled me, and I almost spilled my champagne. I hadn't notice him take Tessa's seat. He was looking at me intently. "My mother wouldn't miss this—not even in death."

"I know," I took a shaky breath and forced a smile. I couldn't imagine how hard this was for the Miller siblings—and for Tessa, too. I couldn't imagine not having my mother around on such an important day.

"Beautiful wedding, huh?" he asked, his eyes still on his brother and new sister-in-law.

"Yes," I swallowed, nodding. My mouth suddenly felt dry, and I reached for the champagne flute before me. I took a heady sip, then realized who I was sitting beside. Guiltily, I placed my flute back down on the table.

Braden didn't even seem to notice—he was still watching his siblings, his expression unreadable. When *Simple Man*'s final chorus faded off, the dance portion of the evening began. People started standing up and making their way over to the dance floor and bar.

I should find Alex, I thought, standing up. I still hadn't had a chance to talk to him. He'd arrived this morning when Caroline was doing my hair, and my mother had immediately put him to work helping arrange the flowers in the reception tent.

I weaved my way around people and tables until Alex came into view. Most of the chairs were vacant, but I knew that Ezra, Peter, their dates and Krista's date were his table mates. After all, I'd spent hours with Tessa going over the seating chart.

I came to a halt when I saw none other than Joanna Poole sitting between Peter and Alex. My blood started to boil. I couldn't believe she had the audacity to show up. Tessa had purposely left her off the guest list, having lost touch with her shortly after she stuck her tongue down Braden's throat when we were still dating—and yet here she was, sitting beside my current boyfriend, her claws all but posed and ready to dig in.

Peter scowled off into the distance, clearly pissed that his date was ignoring him. She was too busy flirting with Alex, fluttering her fake lashes—fake lashes that I had a sudden strong desire to tear out—and leaning purposely towards him, her cleavage basically spilling out of her thigh length hooker dress. And yet...I was more pissed off about what she'd done with Braden.

My hands clenched into angry fists, and I resumed walking towards them, intent on giving Joanna a very overdue piece of my mind. Before I could reach them, someone grabbed my hand and tugged me back.

"Easy now," Braden said, dropping my hand and raising his in surrender when I whirled around with a venomous look on my face. "Where's the fire?"

"Don't," I warned, teetering on the edge of hysteria. Seeing Joanna again had brought back the wave of heartbreak and despair I'd felt when I found lipstick on Braden's lips. He sensed that I was going to implode, and he carefully led me away from the dance floor, outside of the reception tent. "Let go of me

Braden!" I demanded shrilly, trying to yank my hand from his grasp.

"Not until you tell me what's wrong," he insisted, his hold still firm as he led me around the side of the tent.

"You cheated on me!" I accused when he finally released me, tears burning in my eyes. Pain and anger dripped off each word. "With one of my best friends!"

Braden looked as if I'd slapped him. He swallowed hard, his eyes never leaving my face. His hands came up to cup my cheeks, forcing me to hold his gaze. "I'm not proud of that, Elle. It was a stupid decision, I was drunk and…there's really no excuse for it."

"How could I ever trust you again?" I fired out, seething. Braden was quiet for several long moments, then his face broke out into a smirk. "What? Why are you smirking?" I demanded hotly, slapping at his chest and trying to push him away.

"Because you're not even mad that she's hitting on your boyfriend, you're out here yelling at me for something that happened years ago," he answered, his smile growing. I opened and closed my mouth several times, searching for some kind of retort. I had none. "Face it Elle, you're in love with me still. And I'm in love with you." Hearing him say it out loud made my heart stutter in my chest. "And to answer your question—you can trust me, Elle. I'll never hurt you again. I'll spend forever proving it to you."

His hands were still framing my face, and his eyes were on my lips. I knew without a doubt that he wanted to kiss me, and I knew I wanted him to. I closed my eyes, feeling his breath hot on my lips. But instead of kissing me, he sighed. "I meant what I said the other night, Elle." He added, his voice hoarse. "You need to tell him it's over."

"Elle?" Alex's voice broke the spell we were under. I pulled away from Braden, my face paling with shock.

"Alex—" I started, but what I was going to say was written all over my face.

He looked up to the sky, running his hands through his hair, tugging at the roots. He shook his head, as if he was trying to make sense of it all. "I should have known," he said, dropping his eyes back to my face. The hurt I saw etched on him nearly knocked me over. "You might have denied it until you were blue in the face...but I should have known when I saw you with him at the fair."

He turned and started walking away, but I couldn't let him go. Not like this. I needed to explain myself, to apologize for hurting him because that was never my intention. "Alex wait," I called out, running towards him. He stopped walking but didn't turn. "I'm sorry. I didn't want to hurt you. It was never my intention, I—"

"You don't need to explain it, Elle," he said, cutting me off as he turned to face me. "It's pretty obvious what's happening here. I'm not an idiot." I was close enough to touch him. I stepped closer, my heart aching.

"I wanted to fall for you Alex," I told him, tears in my eyes. "I wanted it so badly. You're amazing—you're compassionate, self-less, dependable..." I trailed off. "But I gave my heart away years ago, and I never got it back. And I know I should have told you sooner...but I didn't know how. I keep telling myself if I had more time..."

Alex brought his hand up, stroking his fingers along the side of my jaw. His eyes were somber. "You should never have tried to convince yourself that you had to love me, Elle."

CHAPTER EIGHTEEN

*raden*

ELLE WATCHED Alex's headlights disappear down the Armstrong's driveway, her eyes wide with shock. "What have I done?" she murmured, shaking her head as if trying to wake up from a bad dream. She looked at me helplessly. "I just...I just..." she started to gasp, as if she couldn't draw in air quickly enough.

"Breathe, Elle," I instructed, positioning myself in front of her and cupping her face with my hands. I tilted her head so that her eyes had no choice but to focus on mine. "Just breathe."

She shook her head again, tears welling up in her eyes and trailing down her cheeks. "I just broke his heart, Braden. I just... God, I basically cheated on him!" Elle exclaimed, horrified.

I couldn't think of a single thing to say, so I pulled her into my arms and let her cry. I let her mourn the loss of a relationship that she wasn't truly ready to let go of—an ending prompted by my inability to stay away from her.

After ten minutes, Elle's sobs tampered off and she started to breathe a little more normally again. She took a step back, unable to meet my eyes. "I'm sorry, Elle," I said, my voice dripping with sincerity.

I hadn't liked Alex because he was—in my eyes—competition, and I knew that Elle wasn't in love with him...but I still hated seeing her in any kind of pain. She was hurting over the way Alex had found out about us, about her feelings for me, and I knew that she was thinking about how she'd felt when *I'd* broken her heart. It made me feel even worse than I already felt.

"There you guys are!" Becky's voice rang out through the crisp summer night as she approached us quickly. Her pace slowed when she caught sight of Elle's tear streaked face. "What did you do?" she accused, glaring at me.

"It's not his fault," Elle said, still trembling. "I—I think Alex and I just broke up."

"Oh Elle, I'm sorry," Becky responded, hugging Elle. She shot me another suspicious look, knowing that I was to blame for it.

"What's happening inside?" Elle asked, falling into her maid of honor mode as she stepped back from Becky—a tactic I knew she used when she wanted to avoid processing her emotions. She'd done it in high school too. Rough emotional time? Focus on that to-do list and get shit done. It used to drive me crazy. Still did, apparently.

"We're getting ready to do the garter and bouquet toss," Becky answered.

"Great," Elle exhaled. She went to walk inside, but I grabbed her hand and tugged her back. She brought her hands to my chest, stopping herself before she collided with me.

"We're not done talking about this," I told her, my tone serious and leaving no room for argument. Her eyes widened in response, and she drew in a shaky breath. I brought my hands up to her face and gently wiped away the slight black smear of eyeliner and tears that had pooled high on her cheeks, beneath her beautiful brown eyes.

I released her and the three of us walked back into the reception tent. Tessa's right eyebrow arched in question when she saw Elle and me trailing behind Becky. She approached us, warily looking back and forth from Elle to me. "Everything okay?"

"Yes," Elle answered, flashing a smile. Tessa went to ask another question—probably about where Alex was—but the sound of Tommy tapping the microphone to get everyone's attention stopped her.

"Calling all single ladies! Get your fine asses out on the dance floor for the bouquet toss! That includes you too, Mrs. Thompson!" Tommy's voice rang out from the speakers positioned all around, and a chorus of chuckles ensued after he had finished speaking. He gave Sue a wink and earned a smart smack on the back of the head from his father, prompting more laughter from the crowd. I laughed too, watching as Elle's mom made her way out to the dance floor, shaking her head the whole time.

The chorus of Little Big Town's *Little White Church* came on, and Becky took Elle's hand and joined the other single ladies. Tessa positioned herself in front of the crowd, bending her knees slightly as if she was about to bowl. "Three...two... one!" Tommy counted down and on one Tessa tossed the bouquet high over her head. It sailed through the air, and a wave of arms reached out to try and catch it. When the chaos cleared, I laughed when I saw that Sue Thompson held the bouquet.

"Who's the lucky guy, Sue?" Tommy joked, sending Sue another wink. Sue waved her hand, her face heating up with embarrassment. "Alright fellas, you're next. Anyone not hitched, step out to the dance floor!" As Tommy laid out the instructions, I rushed forward with a chair for Tessa to sit in. Once she was sitting, I joined the bachelors. "Go on Dad, that means you too," Tommy added.

Bill Armstrong shook his head, wearing what I thought was a bemused smile. I suppose it also could have been a murderous one—you never knew with Bill—but he joined the rest of us out on the dance floor.

The main chorus of Kenny Loggin's *Danger Zone* pumped out over the speakers. "Make sure you put your hands behind your back, Brock! And no helping him Tessa!" Tommy instructed, his voice rumbling over the speakers. Brock made a show of putting his hands behind his back and dropped to his knees in front of Tessa's legs. It took him almost a minute to get the garter off, while Tessa laughed and squirmed as if it tickled.

He finally removed the garter with his teeth and stood up, flinging it over his shoulder towards us. It landed right on Bill Armstrong's shoulder.

"Was that intentional?" Tommy wondered aloud, laughing like he found the whole thing hysterical. Bill's expression was bewildered, and then he buckled forward and laughed too. "Alright everyone—let's get this party going again. Drinks are on me!"

For the next couple of hours, Elle kept herself busy. She made the rounds, dancing with Bill and the majority of Tessa's brother's before Ezra took her for a spin on the dance floor. I narrowed my eyes as I watched them. I knew that Ezra wasn't a threat; he'd never go for her knowing how I felt about her.

Can't Take My Eyes Off You by Lady Antebellum song came on and everyone on the dance floor coupled up while memories washed over me with enough force to nearly knock me off my feet.

In high school, Elle had loved Lady Antebellum. There had been more than one occasion when her favourite song, *Just A Kiss* came on the radio when we were out together and I'd stop whatever it was we were doing just to hold her in my arms and dance with her. Even if we were on the highway, or in the mall. At first, it was just an excuse to get my hands on her body and my mouth on hers. Then it grew into something more when I saw how happy it made her. Making her smile like that became *my* addiction.

While it wasn't *Just A Kiss*, I could tell from the way Elle's eyes lifted to mine that the significance of this band wasn't lost on her. I walked across the dance floor and extended my hand out to her. "Can I have this dance?"

She looked down at my hand for a moment, then looked back up at me. The hurt still swirled around her irises. She drew in a shaky breath before placing her hand in mine. I pulled her towards me, not stopping until our bodies were flush together.

My right hand rested against her left hip, and I held her hand in mine, pressed against my heart. We swayed softly for several minutes, the woman singer's beautiful voice lifting lyrics about how she couldn't take her eyes off her love. The song fit our current predicament perfectly.

"Elle I—" I said, at the same time she said "I need to know something."

She paused, as if waiting for me to continue. Elle's brown eyes were locked on mine. Her eyebrows were drawn together and her lips rested in a small frown. "You first," I urged. I swallowed hard, my throat dry and scratchy.

"When I'm with you, he slips from my mind so easily," she said, her eyes misting. "Is that what happened with...with *her*? Did you completely forget I existed?"

"No," I assured her. I stopped dancing so I could cradle her face in my hands. I tipped her chin up to look even deeper into her eyes. All of the other couples on the dance floor faded away into the background as we stood there. "I never forgot you, not for a second. All I could see was your face, all I could hear in my head was your voice. But I had convinced myself that you'd leave eventually, everyone does."

"You threw us away because you were too scared to trust that I loved you?" she asked me, my words bringing her no comfort. "After everything we'd been through?"

My thumbs brushed the tears away from her cheeks. "I never said that it made sense," I paused. "I've regretted it ever since, but I wanted to be somebody before I came back into your life. I wanted to have something more than a job at the garage to offer you."

"Your love was the only thing I ever needed," she told me.

"You have always had my love," I promised her. The hurt in each word that she spoke carved places on the tender flesh of my heart as it throbbed painfully in my chest. "That's one thing that never changed, and never will."

She nodded, looking away from me. "I think the worst part is that I've already forgiven you," she said, shaking her head slowly as if she was repulsed with herself. My fingers dropped back down to press into her hip gently.

"You never could stay mad at me," I joked, smirking.

Elle gave me a small smile in response. It faded after a moment, and she sighed. "My life is a mess right now, Braden."

"I can handle a little mess," I raised my brow pointedly. "What I can't handle is not having you in my life. If all you can give me right now is your friendship, I'll take that. I just don't want to watch you walk away again."

I didn't tell her that I didn't think I was strong enough to withstand it this time; that wasn't her cross to bear. Whatever happened to me if she walked away was my problem, not hers.

Elle drew in a sharp breath, my words obviously affecting her. She pressed her body harder against mine, her hands coming up to wrap around the back of my neck.

CHAPTER NINETEEN

*lle*

I NUZZLED into Braden's neck, breathing in his clean masculine scent, our bodies swaying back and forth in perfect time to the song. I could feel his heart beating beneath my hand, the steady rhythmic thump calming me.

Lady Antebellum was one of my obsessions in high school—they still were, only I hadn't been able to listen to them since the whole *Braden breaking my heart* thing, because any time that I did, I'd think about all the times he had pulled me to him to dance with him. His hands on my hips, his lips softly exploring mine as we swayed together.

The first time it happened was on our first date. We were driving home from the movie theatre, and *Just A Kiss* came on through the speakers. I turned it up, because I always turned up their songs.

Then Braden pulled over to the shoulder of highway 559, hopped out of the cab of his truck. He walked around the front to open my door. "Dance with me," he said, holding out his hand for me to take. He led me to the front of his truck and stopped. He turned to face me, pausing for a moment to brush the hair out of my face and gaze into my eyes. His right hand landed on my hip, and he pulled me flush to his body, swaying in time to the music.

He'd taken me by complete surprise that night, moving against me in the dark, the truck's headlights illuminating the look on his face while his hands roamed my body and ignited me. Braden wasn't known as a romantic guy, in fact—he'd been known as a dirty player. I had never seen him dance at a single school dance, but I'd watch him make out with countless girls against his locker, which happened to be three down from mine.

He used to pull my hair and drive me crazy, then he started being nice to me and flirting with me. The make out sessions with girls against his locker stopped and he started asking me out. His persistence got me interested—I couldn't figure out why he wanted to take me out so badly. I'd always found him attractive, there wasn't a single girl in Parry Sound that didn't—except maybe Tessa, but it turned out she just had an eye for the other Miller brother. In the end, my curiosity got the best of me and I said yes.

We had our first kiss during that dance, and never in my whole life had I been kissed the way Braden Miller kissed me. His hands tangled in my hair and his lips softly pressed against mine. He barely put any tongue into it, but it was the most erotic kiss I'd ever had, only ever matched by future kisses from Braden. I felt that kiss in every fibre of my body, and I knew then and there that I wanted every single thing he had to offer me.

I started to fall in love with him that night, propelled by the way he looked into my eyes and the way he kissed me.

Being in his arms again like this had me remembering all of the good times we had, every little romantic thing he'd do for me to show me that he cared. We had a lot of wonderful moments, before we fell apart.

Was it fair to completely shut him out for the one mistake he'd made during our time together? A mistake that had been made when he'd just lost his mother and was beside himself with grief?

Granted, it was a big mistake. A *huge* mistake, and forgiving wouldn't come easily, but Braden had made it perfectly clear that he'd be patient.

And in that particular moment, with his hands still on my hips and our bodies flush together; all I could think about was how badly I wanted to lose myself completely in him.

I wanted to turn off all of my fears and insecurities and escape into the way he loved me; into the way I loved him.

The song ended and *For The Outlaws* by Moonshine Bandits kicked on, the bass vibrating the dance floor. Tessa screeched and ran at me, the grin on her face ecstatic. She dragged me to the centre of the oak floor, and we started rapping the verses back and forth. Braden watched us, an amused grin on his lips and his eyes lighting up.

Back in the day, this had been a regular occurrence, Tessa and I going nuts over songs we loved and singing like it was karaoke night at Flanigan's bar. Braden would watch our antics with a bemused smile.

Every single body was on the dance floor, which wasn't all that surprising considering the oldest guests invited were my mom and Tessa's dad—and both of them could out dance us all.

They reminded us of that fact when *Country Girl (Shake It)* by Luke Bryan pumped out of the speakers and they started to do the cowboy boogie together, practically burning up the dance floor with their moves.

"Oh snap! Look at Dad and Sue! I think they're challenging us to a dance off!" Tommy laughed into the microphone, the music fading as he spoke and returning as soon as he stopped.

Those of us brave enough to remain on the floor formed a line and joined in. I danced beside Tessa and Braden, with Brock on Tessa's other side and Krista on Braden's right. It was hard to keep up with Bill and Mom, but every single person on the dance floor was having a blast trying.

Mom's experience came from years of beauty pageant concerts and dance competitions, so her talent didn't surprise me. Luckily, she had passed on her love of dance—and her rhythm—to me. She'd enrolled me in dance classes as soon as I could walk, and I had no problem keeping up. Tessa struggled a little bit more, forever off rhythm by half a second, but she knew the routine like the back of her hand from years of dance parties in my living room whenever she slept over.

Bill though, Bill surprised me. "I didn't know Papa Armstrong could dance!" I exclaimed to Tessa, delighted with the whole thing. She seemed every bit as surprised as I was by this development.

When Everly Daniels joined us on the dance floor, Tessa made room for her between us. She fell into step effortlessly, her gaze focused on her fiancé as he stood just off to the side. She kept motioning for him to join her, but he shook his head, an indulgent smile on his face as he held his hands up. "I would do anything for love, but I won't do that," he joked, backing away to the sidelines.

We continued to dance, the songs rolling from one upbeat country tune to another. I only paused to down champagne when I got thirsty.

An hour, maybe even two hours, passed and Tessa's dad stepped up to the microphone. The DJ stopped the music, and everyone turned to see what the big deal was. "Alright, now I'm not sure how many of you are familiar with the *Dance of the Unwed Sibling*," he started, pausing to let the words sink into the crowd.

"Hell no, Dad!" Gordon and Tommy's protests came quickly, and Bill chuckled into the microphone, his eyes twinkling.

"This tradition was intended to embarrass the happy couple's older, unwed siblings by forcing them to wear ugly socks while dancing to raise money for the bride and groom. Gordon and Tommy, Tessa's older, unwed brothers, get your asses out on the dance floor. Sue's got your ugly socks, hand knitted by Lida Dabrowski herself!" Bill grinned wickedly, scratching at his auburn beard. I snorted with laughter—my aunt Lida was nearly ninety-six years old and still knitting up the storm. I think everybody in town had something hand knitted by Aunt Lida, myself included.

"Come on Dad!" Tommy grinned, shaking his head.

"Lord knows, you two knuckleheads have embarrassed Tessa enough, so it's time she got some revenge. Your dancing skills should suffice."

Gordon and Tommy tugged on the florescent coloured woollen socks while the opening rift for *Boot Scootin' Boogie* played. Sue tossed fuzzy blue cowboy hats at them, which they pulled onto their heads gleefully.

While they couldn't dance, Gordon and Tommy certainly knew how to entertain. Guests were throwing down crisp bills like crazy. I clapped along with everyone else, praying that Tessa's videographer was getting this all on film. At the very least, Sam was getting some good cell-phone shots that we could shame them with later.

When I looked back out to the dance floor, I saw Braden laying down with a twenty-dollar bill between his teeth. Tommy saw him and danced his way over. He dropped down over top of Braden and did some kind of horrifying stripper inspired dance move, shaking his chest in Braden's face before he leaned down and grabbed the bill with his own mouth.

I was doubled over, my stomach aching from laughing so hard.

"Was this your idea?" Tessa asked me, tears in her eyes, her cheeks flushed and glowing.

"Nope, I think it was all Bill," I answered, lifting my eyebrows, impressed. "Possibly with a little help from my mom."

Another two hours passed. The cake was cut, multiple bathroom trips with a drunk bride were made.

The champagne kept flowing, and I had gotten further and further away from the guilt I'd felt over Alex. It wasn't that I no longer felt bad, because I did...but the alcohol just made me focus on the *good* things, like how much fun I was having at Tessa's wedding, with Braden, with the way he was looking at me, and the feeling of his hands on my body as we twirled around the dance floor to Lee Brice's *I Don't Dance*.

Tessa hadn't been the only person forced to endure learning dance routines. Admittedly, I had spent one summer afternoon on the front porch, teaching Braden how to do the country swing. He had more rhythm than Tessa, and picked up the moves quickly, although swore me to secrecy and only danced like that with me around.

Except, Braden didn't seem to care that we weren't alone, that every eye in the large glittery tent was on us. His eyes remained on me, on my body, reading it and anticipating all of my moves.

It was getting closer to two o'clock in the morning, and my feet were beginning to ache. Only a handful of guests had disappeared, Brock and Tessa being part of that small group. They were supposed to be at the airport for four a.m. to catch their flight to the Dominican Republic to celebrate their honeymoon.

I wanted to leave too. I was having fun, but the alcohol and the desire in Braden's molten gaze had me practically withering with need. I wanted to kiss him, I wanted to rub my body against his arousal. I could feel his hard length pressed against my stomach.

"Let's get out of here," he murmured, his lips grazing against my earlobe. I shivered, goosebumps erupting and desire throbbing everywhere. I took his hand and weaved around the bodies on the floor, keeping my head low to avoid having to stop to talk to someone. We made it outside, the chill of the night doing nothing to cool off how much I burned for him.

We raced to his truck, both of us impatient to get back to his place. He held my hand the entire drive, his thumb tracing patterns against my palm. Every once in a while, he'd toss a look at me as if he couldn't believe this was happening.

My heart quickened as we pulled into the driveway of the Miller house. He was out of the cab quicker than I could blink. I unbuckled the seatbelt as he opened the door.

I slid out of the cab, my body against his. He took a step back, then pulled me back against him. Our mouths crashed together hungrily. His hands were everywhere; in my hair, on my breasts, my hips, my ass as he lifted me up and pulled me against his erection. He held me like that for several minutes, kissing me like he'd never stop. I didn't want him to stop, but I wanted him to hurry up and get me inside.

He regretfully put me down and we practically ran around the side of the house, to the door that led to the basement. He unlocked the door and led me down the stairs. He turned on the light on his bedside table while I looked around, my heart racing.

It was like stepping back in time. Everything was the same way it was in high school, right down to the photo booth pictures on the mirror above his dresser. I swallow hard, remembering the day they had been taken.

Back then, we couldn't get enough of each other. We didn't care about getting caught. We were locked in our own world together. I'd never wanted to leave that world, not even when he pushed me out of it.

He took a step towards me. The back of his hand ran up my shoulder, and I closed my eyes as he swept my hair aside and brought his lips to my neck. He kissed me, his mouth worshipping the soft skin there. His hand moved along the back of my neck, searching for the zipper to my dress.

The room was filled with the sound of our bated breath and my zipper dropping. He stopped kissing me for a moment and rested with his forehead pressed against mine. His eyes bore into me, searching. "Are you sure you want to do this, Elle?"

"I've never been more sure of anything in my entire life. I need you, Braden," I whispered honestly. All I could think about was him. Tomorrow, I'd deal with everything else. I just wanted to get lost and forget everything but him for a while.

My body trembled beneath his hesitant fingers. At my words, he pushed the dress over my shoulders and it fell to the ground. I was wearing nothing but a white lace thong. Braden drew in a shaky breath, his finger brushing the inside of the material against my taunt stomach.

His eyes drank me in, his lust filled gaze dragging across every inch of my exposed body. He brought his hands up to cup my breasts, rolling my nipples between his thumbs and forefingers. I moaned, leaning into his touch.

Braden brought his head down and took one of my nipples in his mouth, I arched my head back, my hands instinctively going to stroke the front of his pants, finding him hard and straining against the thin material. He involuntary jerked into my hand, his breath hissing out. Tipping my chin back up, he claimed my mouth possessively.

Desperate to have skin to skin contact, my fingers fumbled to free the buttons of his white dress shirt as he continued to kiss me, starved for my taste. I pushed the shirt off his shoulders, letting it drop wherever it fell, and raked my fingers against the hard muscles of his abdomen. I bit down firmly on his bottom lip, trapping his moan with another kiss.

I pushed his pants down over his hips. His dick sprang free, his hot erection falling straight into my waiting hands.

"Commando?" I asked, arching a brow.

"Why not?" he grinned wickedly. His amusement evaporated when I stroked his thick length slowly and brought my lips back up to his.

Suddenly, his hands were back on my hips and he was effortlessly spinning us around. The back of my knees hit the mattress, and I fell onto it, Braden falling with me. He kissed me for a few more minutes, his hand running up and down the length of my body as if he wanted to touch me everywhere and couldn't decide where he should start first.

His index finger and his thumb dropped to stroke against my damp panties. Every nerve was pulsing with need as he stroked me leisurely, still kissing me like he couldn't get enough of me.

He tugged aside the fabric and sank two fingers deep inside of me. I stopped kissing him, letting another moan escape my lips as I arched against the palm of his hand.

The look in Braden's eyes when I finally opened my heavy lids nearly sent me over the edge. He was so concentrated on pleasuring me that the sight of me arching against him made his eyes darken with need.

"You're so wet and tight," he said, his voice straining. "God, I want to bury myself in you."

"What's holding you back?" I challenged, needing to feel him inside of me.

"The fact that I need to taste you," he almost growled.

He crawled down and nestled between my legs, and I raised my hips so he could pull my panties off. He tossed them somewhere over his shoulder, his fingers sinking into the tender flesh on my thighs, forcing my legs apart. He ran his tongue tentatively against my opening and moaned. The vibration made me tremble. He worked me with his mouth, kissing and licking and sucking like he could do it forever. He slid two fingers in and out as he licked, and I felt my orgasm coming fast and hard. I arched up off the mattress, my entire body exploding in bursts of sensations.

"Braden, please," I pleaded, but even as I begged he was already lining himself up to my entrance. His tip brushed against my wetness, and he went rigid.

"Fuck," he growled, rolling over to reach into his night stand drawer. He was on his back, and I couldn't wait.

"Forget about the condom, Braden," I ordered. I didn't want that stupid barrier, I wanted to feel every inch of his thickness. Maybe it was stupid, maybe I was putting too much faith into him, but I was too drunk on him to care. Crawling on top of him, I slid straight down onto his long, hard cock.

"Elle," he half-exhaled, half-moaned, his eyes flying open as he looked at me. "Are you on the pill?" he managed, his eyes fluttering closed again as I slowly rolled my hips. His hands gripped against my skin, stilling me as he opened his eyes.

"I've got an IUD," I told him. I rolled my hips again, loving the way his brow furrowed together and how electric his eyes seemed as he watched me move against him. His hands gripped my hips and he started moving me faster and faster. I rode him as hard as I could, almost collapsing on him when the second orgasm hit me.

Braden lifted me off, and I let out a whimper of protest. He positioned himself behind me and grabbed my hips. I watched over my shoulder as he sank back into me, his eyes watching as he pulled out and buried himself inside me again and again, harder and harder until I couldn't breathe, until I was screaming his name and coming around his cock again.

He came soon after, driving into me. He let out a low moan, and I could feel him pulsing as he shot inside me.

We collapsed, barely tugging the sheets around us. Braden pulled me into his arms. I fell asleep with my head on his chest and his hand gently stroking my back.

THE NEXT MORNING, I awoke with a headache that almost rivaled the one I'd woken up with after Tessa's bridal shower. I was still naked, still in Braden's bed. Daylight filtered in through the small window, illuminating the room enough for me to see that Braden wasn't in the bed with me.

I could hear low voices murmuring and someone walking around upstairs, in the kitchen. I became acutely aware of the fact that Becky was probably home now too. She'd had a rare night free when one of Aiden's friend's mom's picked him up from the reception, and she hadn't come home. I tugged the blankets up over my chest, my mind racing with everything that had happened in the last twenty-four hours. I knew that Braden had meant every single word that he'd said, and I was tired of fighting my feelings for him. Our reunion was everything I knew it would be and more. I knew there wouldn't ever be another love like ours, and I didn't *want another one*. I wanted this one.

But the overwhelming weight of guilt pressed down on me, robbing me of my happiness. In the light of day, all I could think about was the broken heart I'd caused Alex, and how screwed up the rest of my life was. I still didn't know what I was supposed to do about work, and I knew I couldn't live with Alex anymore anyway.

I brushed away the few tears that managed to escape when I heard Braden coming down the stairs. He was dressed in a pair of Calvin Klein pyjama bottoms and carrying two steaming mugs of coffee. He sat down beside me on the edge of his mattress. "Morning," he said, his voice low and deep. I sat up, my hands wrapping around the hot mug that he held out to me. He kissed me softly, while I savoured the feel of his lips on mine.

"Morning," I practically croaked when he pulled back. I cleared my throat, my cheeks flushing. "Is Becky home?"

"Yeah, she just got in actually," Braden chuckled. "Looks like you weren't the only one doing the walk of shame this morning."

"Who says I'm ashamed?" I challenged, arching a brow at him. There was no way in hell I could be ashamed of what we shared last night. I could be ashamed about how quickly we shared it, and how I'd hurt Alex in the process—but I could never be ashamed of the actual act. He grinned and shrugged, but I could see the uncertainty that he tried to mask behind his dimpled smile. "Who did she go home with?"

"She wouldn't tell me," Braden scowled. "Besides, I didn't really want to hear it. I don't have time to kick someone's ass today. I'd rather spend the day with you, doing exactly what we did last night," he added, taking the mug from my hands and setting it down on the bedside table.

He kissed me again, his lips sliding against mine as he laid down beside me, almost leaning on me without putting any of his actual weight on me. His hand moved up to touch my face. He pulled away to look at me, his fingers stroked my jaw and brushed across my lips, already swollen from our activities the night before.

We made love again. Slowly, this time. Tenderly. Each time he pulled out and sank back into me, he did so at a leisurely, thorough pace, stroking spots that had me climbing higher towards an orgasm in no time at all.

When we'd finished, I curled up against his chest and let my hands trail down the hard muscles, my fingers tracing against his inked skin.

I'd been a part of Braden's life for a long time, and I knew the hands on the clock were pointed to the time of Deanna Miller's death. I'd also seen Deanna wear pearls similar to the ones in the design. I wasn't sure if the skull and the roses had special meanings too, or if Braden had just included them because they looked awesome.

"What are you thinking about?" he asked, his lips lifting in a small, affection smile.

"Just admiring your work," I told him, running my hands along his arms. They were also essentially covered with colourful designs. Some places had been outlined but not completed.

"You do that," he grinned cockily, his fingers running up along the side of my breast. "I'll keep admiring your work." My eyes fluttered as his lips traced soft kisses along my neck. Even though my body was aching from the strenuous workouts we'd already engaged in, Braden could still evoke pleasure and make me shiver with want.

"We really need to get to back to the farm though. We need to clean up before the party rental place shows up." I argued breathlessly.

My stomach flipped with nervousness at the prospect of showing up with Braden, having everyone see that we'd arrived together. I didn't want to have to defend what I was doing to everybody. I didn't want them to think I was some massive skank who couldn't even wait a full twenty-four hours after her relationship ended before screwing someone else. Technically, we still lived together, and I was going to have to deal with that fact sooner rather than later.

"Oh God," I buried my face in my hands, my heart rate thudding out of control.

"What is it?" Braden's playful expression faded away, concern lining the blue of his eyes.

I couldn't speak. I felt like something was squeezing me into a tight little ball, forcing the air out of my lungs.

"Breathe, Elle," he said, his voice strong and calm, his fingers pressing gently into the flesh of my wrist. The pressure grounded me, and I listened to him. I knew I had to. The only way to get past those panic attacks was to remind myself that they were fleeting, that if I just focused on breathing, I could escape the feeling of being suffocated. When my breathing slowed down, Braden released the gentle pressure and brushed my hair away from my wet cheeks. "Do you want to tell me what that was about?"

Swallowing, I adverted my eyes. "I just got to thinking about Alex."

He froze beside me, his expression unreadable. "Do you regret it?"

"No," I said forcefully, shaking my head animatedly. "I regret not telling him sooner. And I broke his heart, Braden. I broke his heart and I let him go home alone, to the place we share, and I didn't think about him again. I'm a horrible person!"

He was quiet, reflective. After a small stretch of silence, he sighed, rubbing his hand across his strong chin. "You're not a horrible person, Elle. What were you supposed to do? Leave your best friend's wedding to have a post breakup conversation?"

Braden had a point, but still. I knew I couldn't truly move forward until I dealt with the things I had run from, the things I'd left behind in Barrie.

"Now, stop worrying about it," he instructed gently, pulling me on top of him. I looked down at him, my hair spilling over the side of my shoulder. He gathered the thick tresses up and held it in place, using it to bring my lips down to his. His kisses brought me back to him, to our little world where only we mattered.

CHAPTER TWENTY

KIA'S WERE pieces of shit. There wasn't enough space in between the components in the engine block to work without practically scrapping all of the skin off your knuckles—which I'd already done twice. It took me twice as long to replace the power steering line as it usually did in a vehicle with a better engine design.

When I took the line off the pump, power steering fluid pissing everywhere. I wiped up the mess with the dirty rag I had wrapped around my bloody knuckles, swearing under my breath.

I couldn't wait to be finished work for the day. While Elle and I hadn't made any concrete plans to hang out, I still wanted to see her. I felt like the happiest man in the world when she came home from the wedding with me. Being with her again like that made me feel indestructible.

I'd offered to drive with her to the Armstrong's farm, since we were all supposed to meet up there and start cleaning-up, but she had insisted on driving over with Becky and made me promise to not touch her or look at her the way I'd been touching and looking at her.

"I just want to enjoy it for a while, before people start butting in," she'd told me before I even had time to get pissed at her for basically telling me to hide the fact we'd slept together.

Having finished putting on the new power steering line, I checked that everything was running smoothly in the KIA before I slammed the hood down. I crossed over to the metal basin sink to wash my hands. The orange soap burned, but I was used to it.

As I was finishing, I heard someone pull up. I grabbed a somewhat clean towel and walked over to meet them, intent on telling them we were closed and they'd have to come back in the morning.

The car door slammed and heels clicked along the pavement. I paused, watching as Elle approached me warily. Her long, wavy hair was pulled up in a messy ponytail, and she was dressed in shorts and a white tank top, wearing a pair of red kitten heels that instantly made me hard. I could picture her modelling them—and only them—so clearly.

I stepped towards her with a huge, stupid grin on my face, closing the distance between us with long purposeful strides. Then my hands were pulling her close and I was kissing her. Elle's hands were pressed against my chest, pulling herself against me, matching my hunger with her own. Then she pulled away abruptly.

"I have to go back to Barrie, Braden," she told me, keeping her distance.

"What do you mean? Go back?" I frowned.

"I have a meeting in the morning with my boss. I need to talk to Alex and I need to start packing my stuff..." she trailed off, biting her lip. I wondered if she regretted it, if she resented the fact that her life was in complete upheaval.

"When will you be back?" I asked, trying to hide my insecurities. I didn't want her to think that I didn't trust her alone with him—even if it was a little true. I knew she cared about him, but I also knew that she was feeling incredibly guilty over the way things went down. Who was to say that he wouldn't ride on that guilt and try something that made her doubt her feelings for me?

"A couple days?" she answered my question with a question.

"I can go with you," I offered, the words rushing out in my desperation. "I could help you pack and move."

She smiled sadly and stepped back towards me, her hands looping around the back of my neck. "I can't do that to him. I can't have you be there for this." Her eyes drank me in, the sadness that edged them foreshadowing pain.

I hesitated for a moment before returning her embrace. I breathed in her scent, pressing my lips to the top of her head. I understood, even though the disappointment stung. Elle wasn't the kind of person to intentionally hurt others. She was fierce when she needed to be, but always respectful. When she did cause someone unjust pain, she went out of her way to make it right again.

She didn't like loose ends. Maybe that was why she had a hard time letting me go; because I was a loose end. My actions four years ago went against everything she'd known about me, everything that was true.

I wondered if she'd have a hard time letting *him* go.

THIS TOWN WAS SUFFOCATING ME. Or maybe it was the fact that she'd left it again; returned to Barrie—to *him*. She'd left four days ago, and I hadn't heard from her once—not a single returned text or phone call. I couldn't help but wonder if she'd changed her mind about me.

I closed my eyes, remembering the way her body had felt beneath mine. The pain in my chest was acute and powerful. I'd truly thought that her coming to me like that had meant she wanted to press rewind on our time apart, but maybe it had just been her scratching an itch. A final hurrah before she went back to the good guy.

I was, after all, the asshole. I'd been the one to pursue her when I knew she was trying to move on. I had swayed her with pretty words—and no matter how truthful they were, I should have respected her enough to leave her alone. But I couldn't and I hadn't, and now she was gone—only this time...it was *her* choosing, not mine.

Which is why I found myself sitting at Flanigan's, a tumbler of whiskey in front of me. I hadn't touched it—not with my lips, not yet, anyway—and I'd been there for the past hour, trying to figure out what in the hell I was supposed to do now that I'd lost her.

I wanted to toss the entire glass back and feel the burn of the whiskey as it made its way down my throat and into my stomach. I knew it would erase the heartache and the pain. I knew that it would silence the thoughts that had raced through my head every minute—every second—since I'd watched her drive away.

I had thought I'd gotten the girl back. I thought our night of crazy, wild, passionate sex meant that she chose me.

I laughed, the sound bitter and poisonous to my own ears. Mick Flanigan—the bartender and owner of Flanigan's—shuffled slowly over to me. "Something wrong?" he asked in his gruff voice. I looked up at him blankly. "With your drink. You haven't touched it."

"That's probably a good thing," I replied. I sighed heavily, willing myself to find the strength to walk away from this bar—

from the enticing drink in front of me. I could practically taste it on my tongue.

"Do you need me to call someone, son?" Mick's gruff voice was as gentle as it could get, and his light eyes held concern I didn't want to see. I dropped my gaze back down to the glass of whiskey before me, holding it between my hands as if it could jump out at me.

"All those times my old man came in here," I said, focused on the drink. "Did you ever ask him if he needed you to call someone?"

Mick peered at me silently. He appeared locked in some kind of memory. "I didn't, no," he finally answered several long minutes later. I drew in a breath, finding the act of inhaling oxygen painful. "It was a different time back then. We didn't meddle, we just let people suffer in their brokenness, let them nurse their pain however they saw fit."

"So why are you asking now?" I demanded, my eyes flashing with contempt and anger.

"Let me tell you a story," Mick's voice was as tired as his wrinkled eyes. There was no humour in his gaze, no happiness or joy—just an old, exhausted sadness that seemed to pour straight out of his irises directly from his soul. "A few days before your old man died, he stopped in here. Same story as usual—wanted to drink until he was numb. I kept the whiskey coming, because that was my job. And then Brent Miller did something he'd never done in all his years sitting on that there stool," Mick said, gesturing with a subtle nod of his head to the very barstool I was sitting on. "He stared into his whiskey, and said 'what have I become'."

The silence between us was heavy and thick. I swallowed, my throat dryer than ever. "Then what happened?"

"He practically fell off the stool and stumbled outside," Mick answered. "But he left the whiskey. It didn't matter how drunk he got, he *always* finished any glass I put in front of him...except for that night."

As despicable as my old man was, and as much as I hated him and resented him for everything he put me and my siblings through—I knew the strength it took for him to walk away, to leave the glass untouched.

"Son, I can't pretend that I understand what you're dealing with. All I know is that there are going to be many things in this life that stress you out. Don't give in. Remember the days that are good and hang onto them with everything you have. Then it'll get easier to ignore the call." He nodded down at the glass in front of me pointedly.

"How do you know that?" I demanded, scowling.

"I've been bartending my whole life here, I've seen the drink destroy many men." Mick said warily. "You're doing good kid," he added. "Don't mess it up now."

I stood up and tossed down a couple of bills, avoiding Mick's gaze. I nodded once, saying nothing more as I turned around and walked out of the bar to my truck. I sat in the cab for several long minutes, staring at the clock. It was nearly one o'clock in the morning, and I'd been out all evening. I'd sat on that bloody barstool for five hours.

The drive home seemed to take forever. I slammed the truck door, about to walk down the pathway that led to the basement door. I came to a stop when I saw Becky sitting on the front steps of our porch, dressed in her pajamas and a bath robe, Hunter laying down beside her. We'd been tasked with the job of taking care of Brock's dog while they honeymooned. The poor mutt was sulking almost as much as I was.

"What are you doing up?" I asked, pausing.

"Krista texted me. Said she saw your truck parked outside of Flanigan's. Want to tell me what you were doing there?" she asked, fighting to keep the emotion out of her voice as she stood up. Disappointment had her lips pulled down in a frown.

I inhaled, my nostrils flaring as I drew in a breath. I didn't know how to answer; I didn't know how to tell my sister that I'd been inches away from throwing away the last several years of recovery.

"I swear to God Braden, if you started drinking again—that's it. You're gone. I can't have that around Aiden," Becky added, her eyes welling up with tears.

"I didn't," I assured her, my voice as raw as I felt on the inside. "I wanted to, Becky. God I wanted to, but I didn't."

Becky stared at me, as if trying to decipher whether or not I was telling the truth. I met and held her gaze, wondering if she could see the honesty in my eyes, or if she just saw the ghost of our father. "What stopped you?" she whispered.

"Mick, believe it or not," I replied. I dragged my hand through my hair, tugging at the roots. I opened my mouth, about to tell Becky the story the old bartender had told me—but it almost felt private, something that was meant for my ears only. "And the fact that I don't want to be like Dad. I just... sometimes the thirst overwhelms me."

"I think you need to stop this, Braden."

I lifted my eyes up, my brows knitting together with confusion. "Stop what?"

Becky was fidgeting, her fingers tapping against the table with her restlessness. She brought them down to her lap, then placed her palms against the table—almost as if she didn't quite know what to do with her hands. Her crystal clear blue eyes rose to meet mine. "I think you need to stop chasing Elle. It's upsetting you, it's making your recovery harder. You went to a bar tonight, alone for Christ's sake."

My eyes narrowed. The irritation I felt at Becky sticking her nose in my business yet again bubbled and boiled. "I'm not chasing her, and this isn't her fault." I replied, sternly. "She isn't the cause of this, *I* am." I added, turning my back to her.

"Besides, I haven't heard from her since Monday. For all I know, she's back with him, and maybe she belongs there."

I heard my sister exhale, before crossing over to me and putting her arms around me. "I'm sorry, Braden. But I think you're both hurting too much. You both need to focus on yourselves."

I pulled away from her embrace and stomped downstairs. There wasn't really anything I could say in response, anyway. Becky was right. Elle and I were both broken. If she had chosen to be with someone who wasn't broken, someone who could handle her issues and didn't bring more to the table, well I'd have to accept that somehow without self-destructing. If I had to lose Elle, I was just glad that she could be with someone like him.

I stared at my bed, my hands tugging at my hair. I couldn't stay in this room another night, not when my sheets still smelled faintly of her. I grabbed my duffle bag, tossing random articles of clothing into it.

CHAPTER TWENTY-ONE

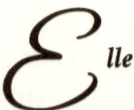

THE LAST FIVE days had been insane. On Monday, I'd officially handed in my resignation and was no longer a paramedic for the city of Barrie. The relief I felt was immense. I was no longer letting my coworkers down. I'd felt like a dead weight for so long, and I knew this was the best route for everyone.

I'd also had a meeting with the landlord to transfer the lease over to Alex. She had been sad to see me go, but was thankful my roommate would be able to continue renting.

Unfortunately, everything else didn't go as smoothly.

Alex hadn't shown up to the meeting with the landlord, but he'd called her beforehand to tell her that he would come sign the new lease agreement later. He hadn't been home, either. The first night, I waited for him. I wanted to tell him everything; lay it all bare.

The same thing happened the second night. I kept busy, packing up all of my things. I decided to leave the kitchen stuff

Tessa and I had purchased when we first moved in, so that Alex wouldn't have to replace everything. Besides, I was moving back in with Mom—I didn't need it anymore, and it seemed cruel to take it.

I mostly took my clothes, the quilted blanket my grandmother had made, and my photographs. I had no attachment to anything else in the apartment. The only thing I wanted to hang on to was my friendship with Alex, and from the way he was acting—I wasn't going to get to keep that. I knew it was unfair of me to even want to.

I'd stupidly forgotten my cell phone back home on my bed. I hadn't been able to call or text Braden all week, and while I had sent him several Facebook messages, I had an uneasy feeling that he hadn't got them. I was eager to get back to Parry Sound.

But I couldn't leave without talking to Alex. He'd finally shown up, about an hour into me loading up my little car with boxes.

He crammed the last box into the back seat and closed the door. His hand remained on the frame, the muscles in his forearm taut.

"Well, that's it," he said, drawing in a deep breath and turning his head to look back up at the apartment. He'd avoided my gaze all afternoon.

"That's not it," I protested, shaking my head. I keep my arms wrapped around my midsection, my eyes fixated on his face and the slight tick in the corner of his jaw. He was aggravated, and he wanted me to leave. "I'm sorry, Alex. I should have never started something with you. You deserve better—you deserve someone who can give her heart truly and completely to you. I never meant to hurt you, I never meant for it to happen. I wanted to love you like you deserved...but I've never gotten over him. I should have told you the moment I realized it, but I was afraid."

He chuckled without humour. His eyes locked on mine, full

of hurt and anger. "It would have hurt a hell of a lot less if you'd told me sooner, if I hadn't had to find you…with him…like that."

"I know," I stepped towards him, my hands reaching out. "And I'm sorry. I truly didn't want to hurt you. You are one of the most important people in my life."

"Just not important enough," he said, his tone defeated.

"Alex, you're an incredible human being and I wanted to be everything you needed, but *I wasn't. I* fell short, not you."

He nodded slowly and stepped away from my car.

I wasn't sure if Alex could forgive me and I didn't expect him to. Nevertheless, I wrapped my arms around him anyway. I wasn't sure when I'd see him again, or even if I'd ever see him again.

"Thank you, Alex. For everything you've done for me, for being an amazing friend and person. You truly are an incredible human being," I told him, my voice muffled by his shirt. My eyes felt heavy with tears, and a couple of them spilled over—his shirt absorbing them.

He said nothing, merely sighing. His arms came up to wrap around me for a second before he released me.

"See you around," he finally said.

I opened the door to my Camry, watching as he disappeared up the walkway to the apartment that I used to call mine—*ours.*

I climbed in, slamming the door shut. The gray sky opened up, raindrops splashing against my windshield. I started the engine, casting a final look up towards the building. I could see Alex in the kitchen window, watching as I pulled away.

I drove as quickly as the road conditions allowed me, which admittedly wasn't very fast. My fingers tapped harshly against the steering wheel. I closed my eyes, picturing Braden's face in my mind.

We were always inevitable, and I'd always known that—even in the deepest stages of my denial. I didn't know what I was going to do with my future; I didn't know what I would do for work now that I was no longer a paramedic. I didn't know if quitting the job that had me spiraling out of control was enough to make my post-traumatic stress disorder go away forever.

But the one thing that I did know was that I loved Braden Miller, and I wanted to be with him. I wanted to let go of the past and let myself be happy. I knew that I could find that with him; in fact, I'd already found it. Twice.

Bypassing the exit that would take me home, I took the one that would lead me to Braden.

His truck wasn't parked in the driveway, but I ran up and knocked on the door anyway, leaving my car running and the door open. The rain was picking up now, each droplet seeming bigger than the one before it.

Becky answered my knocks. She eyed me suspiciously, taking in the frantic look in my eyes and my heaving breaths. "Where is he?"

"He went to Brock's cabin—" she answered not quite finished speaking, but I'd already started running back to my car, my heart racing from the exertion and the desperation to reach him.

Ten agonizingly long minutes later, I pulled onto the access road that led to the cabin. The rain was really coming down, making the water level raise at the nearby creek, flooding the road ahead. My tires struggled to find purchase on the slick, muddy road. I should have replaced my tires, I should have bought a vehicle that could handle off-roading conditions. Impatient, I directed the stupid thing off to the side of the road, cutting the engine before I'd even put it in park. If Braden had caught that, he'd have lit into me about how I was damaging the motor. I grabbed my keys and took a deep breath.

The rain was cold, drenching me within seconds as I ran the rest of the way to the cabin. My breath shot out in puffs in front of me, and my skin was pebbled into goosebumps.

I pounded on the door, shivering before it. A moment

passed, then another, before Braden threw open the door. "I told you Becky, I'm fine!" he barked out before his eyes landed on me. "Elle," he said, almost in disbelief.

"I forgot my phone at home," I said, my teeth chattering. "I sent you Facebook messages, but I don't think you got them."

"No, I didn't get them. I've been here." The look in his eyes was still guarded, still wary.

"Why did you think I was Becky?" I asked, tilting my head. My brows furrowed as I studied him, noticing the way he winced slightly.

"She's just worried." He said, his tone booking no room for questioning. Naturally, being me—I didn't listen.

"Why?" my heart plummeted as I envisioned all of the terrible scenes that could have inspired worry in Becky.

"I went to the bar," he admitted, shame lacing his words. "I didn't drink, but I went. Alone. And I spent five hours there."

"But you didn't drink," I pointed out, stepping towards him. I ran my hands along his forearms, griping them gently.

"No, I didn't." At his words, I felt some of the tension roll away.

"Why did you go?" I questioned, knowing the answer before I asked it.

"Because I thought you were gone. You didn't text me or call me back." He didn't say it in an accusatory way, he was just explaining how he'd felt in the moment. I reached up to cup his cheek, the rough stubble rubbing against my palm.

"I told you I had a meeting with my boss. You knew I needed to get my stuff packed up too," I reminded him, not unkindly. I knew what insecurity could do. I knew how it could chip away at facts until it altered your perception of reality. He was already dealing with so much, my silence must have felt terrible to him.

"Yeah, I know," he said, scratching the back of his head sheepishly.

"I came here as soon as I got back."

"I see that," he smirked, peering around me. "Where's your car?"

"Down the road, I couldn't drive it in." I shrugged, shivering again. He pulled me inside to the warmth of the cabin. Hunter barely lifted his head from his spot on the floor. Brock and Tessa weren't expected back from the Dominican until Sunday night, and the fact that we were completely alone wasn't lost on either of us.

His eyes were feral, his tongue darting out across his lips, as if he wanted to bite into me. My skin was freezing, but the blood in my veins burned. He pulled me against him, not caring that I was drenched and soaking him in the process. His hands gripped my ass, the points of his fingers pressing hard enough to leave bruises.

I welcomed the roughness of it; welcomed the frantic frenzied way his mouth moved against mine. He lifted me up, carrying me backwards enough to slam the door behind me.

He spun around and held me against the front door, breaking away long enough to look at me like I was the most beautiful thing he'd ever laid eyes upon. He brushed away a few strands of wet hair that clung to my cheek, his eyes searching mine. His mouth slated against mine, claiming me once again. Hands fumbled on wet clothes, peeling and stripping.

He lifted me up when we were both naked, rubbing against my centre as he carried me into the spare bedroom. We fell into the bed together, his hands stroking and igniting.

He slid into me, stretching and filling me as he drove home. I gasped at the beautiful intrusion. He stilled, looking down at me with reverence. "Just so we're clear, you're mine now, like you should have always been." He said, his voice gruff.

I nodded, the smile on my face as bright as the lightness I felt in my heart. "I'm yours." I repeated, my legs falling open. I arched up, drawing him in more, loving the hiss of his breath.

WE SPENT the remainder of the weekend together at Brock's cabin. We talked for hours, filling each other in on everything that had happened during the last four years. We reconnected and spoke freely about the future while we sat on the front porch of the cabin, watching the sun rise with steaming cups of coffee in our hands and Hunter at our feet.

"I'm probably going to stay at Chuck's garage for a bit," he admitted to me, as if he thought this news would upset me. "Until he decides what he's going to do with the business. He might close it or he might sell it."

I smiled at him, lifting a shoulder up in a shrug. "I'll probably be jobless for a bit, until I figure out what it is I want to do with my life," I pointed out, pausing to take a sip from my mug. I closed my eyes for a moment, enjoying the fact that I wasn't panicked about the prospect of being jobless and without a career.

He was quiet for a few moments, lost in thought. "You should really be an event planner. Start up your own business," he said, his blue eyes twinkling.

"Don't be ridiculous," I laughed, rolling my eyes. "I'm pretty sure you need a diploma to do that, anyway."

"So go back to school," he smirked, his hand coming up to wrap around my shoulders.

"Maybe," I murmured on an exhale, leaning into him.

We were silent for a few moments, watching as the sun slowly set over the lake. "Move in with me, Elle."

I'd been taking another sip of coffee when he'd asked that, and I choked on it, coughing hard and sloshing the hot liquid over my hands. He took the mug from me, setting it down on the railing, and faced me with a vulnerable look in his eyes.

"I can't take things slow with you," he told me sincerely, his eyes locked on mine. "This—asking you to move in with me...it feels right. It's what would have happened if I didn't screw it up, right?"

"Yeah, but I can't Braden," I sighed, biting my lip. I wanted to —more than I'd ever wanted anything before, but so much was at stake. "Not yet, anyway. I need to get back on my feet, and I need to figure out what my next move is."

He pulled me closer and sighed. "I get it, I do, but I still want you to move in with me."

"Face it Braden, I'll be over more often than not," I joked, and he laughed. "But I won't officially move in until I figure everything out."

"You don't have to do it alone. I can help you figure things out Elle. We'll do it together," he told me. "You're my future."

His words made me swoon, and I smiled, the happiness I felt expanding in my chest until it felt as if my heart would burst. I thought it would be harder to believe him, to trust that he meant what he was saying, but it really wasn't. I still wanted to take my time, to not rush into things before I truly thought we were both ready, but hearing him say those words meant everything to me.

"You're my future too, Braden. You've always been my future," I whispered. I kissed him, pouring everything I felt in that moment into the kiss. He smiled against my lips, resting his forehead against mine when we finally came up for air.

PLAYLIST

1. You Don't Know Her Like I Do – Brantley Gilbert
2. The Trouble With A Heartbreak – Jason Aldean
3. Over And Over Again – James Barker Band
4. Stupid Boy – Keith Urban
5. Broken Window Serenade – Whiskey Myers
6. How To Talk To Girls – Brantley Gilbert
7. Craving You – Thomas Rhett, Maren Morris
8. Small Town Throwndown – Brantley Gilbert, Justin Moore, Thomas Rhett
9. Get Me Some Of That – Thomas Rhett
10. The Weekend – Brantley Gilbert
11. Stone Cold Sober – Brantley Gilbert
12. Hurricane – Luke Combs
13. My Kind Of Crazy – Brantley Gilbert
14. Beautiful Crazy – Luke Combs
15. Kick It In The Sticks – Brantley Gilbert
16. Slow Dance In A Parking Lot – Jordan Davis
17. Hell On Wheels – Brantley Gilbert
18. What Happens In A Small Town – Brantley Gilbert, Lindsay Ell

19. Make Me Wanna – Thomas Rhett
20. Knocking' Boots – Luke Bryan
21. Unforgettable – Thomas Rhett
22. Where We Started – Thomas Rhett, Katy Perry
23. Half Of Me – Thomas Rhett, Riley Green
24. Slow Down Summer – Thomas Rhett

ABOUT THE AUTHOR

J.C. Hannigan lives in Ontario, Canada with her husband, their
two sons, and their dogs.
She writes contemporary new adult romance and suspense. Her
novels focus on relationships, mental health, social issues, and
other life challenges.

Website: www.jchannigan.com
Goodreads: http://bit.ly/jchannigangr
BookBub: https://www.bookbub.com/authors/j-c-hannigan

If you enjoyed this story (or if you didn't), please take a moment to **post a review** on Goodreads, BookBub, your blog, or whichever platform you use.
Reviews help other readers find books, and I appreciate any and all reviews!

Sign up for my newsletter to receive exclusive stories, sneak peeks, and updates: https://jchannigan.myflodesk.com/g343nxhzay

And if you like shenanigans, join my readers group FANnigans! There's exclusive giveaways, monthly live video events, and tons of other perks of becoming a FANnigan!
https://www.facebook.com/groups/FANnigans/

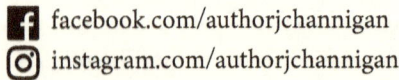

facebook.com/authorjchannigan
instagram.com/authorjchannigan

OTHER BOOKS BY J.C. HANNIGAN

Collide Series

Collide

Consumed

Collateral

Damaged Series

Damaged Goods

Reckless Abandon

Rebel Series

Rebel Soul

Rebel Heart

Rebel Song

Rebel Christmas

Hartwood Creek Romance Series

Wood You Knot

The Forgotten Flounders Series

Off Beat

Off Limit

Standalones

The Key to 19B

Coalescence: A Welder Romance

Riverside Reverie

www.ingramcontent.com/pod-product-compliance
Lightning Source LLC
Chambersburg PA
CBHW031057020726
47495CB00007B/1922